CARAVAN OF THE LOST AND LEFT BEHIND

by

Deirdre Shanahan

Bluemoose

Copyright © Deirdre Shanahan 2019

First published in 2019 by
Bluemoose Books Ltd
25 Sackville Street
Hebden Bridge
West Yorkshire
HX7 7DJ

www.bluemoosebooks.com

All rights reserved
Unauthorised duplication contravenes existing laws

British Library Cataloguing-in-Publication data
A catalogue record for this book is available from the British Library

Hardback ISBN 978-1-910422-47-2

Paperback 978-1-910422-48-9

Printed and bound in the UK by Short Run Press

CARAVAN OF THE LOST
AND LEFT BEHIND

for
Sadie and Con

Caulnamore
1

The bench was hard and a wind whistled through the bus station, sending sweet wrappers skittering across the concrete. He sneezed and wiped his nose with an old tissue. An empty chicken meal carton rolled to one side and rain clattered on the roof like bullets. The ticket office had not yet opened, but what could they expect at six in the morning? All the other passengers off the boat must have had places to go, people to meet or trains running on time. He and his mum had been travelling for over twelve hours, on the coach up the length of England and across the sea, and he was ragged with tiredness. The boat had lurched through the night, sending his senses into a spin, and he had been sick. He stretched out his legs while his mum dozed, leaning back to the support of the wall. She gasped a little intake of breath.

'You all right?' he asked.

'I am, Torin. I was only dreamin'. Any sign of the bus?'

'Not yet.'

'I can't sleep properly in this jakes of a place. I'm frozen.' She coughed and pulled her coat around her. 'Is it open?' She indicated with a nod to the tea kiosk. The hatch was mid-way down but a man stood behind the counter.

'Could be.'

'Take a look, will you lovey?' She tugged his arm.

'What d'you want?'

'Tea. Hot and sugary. And bring over a spoon so I can give it a good mix. Have you any money?'

He took a handful of foreign coins from his pocket. The money was running out, but according to her they'd be living free with his grandfather.

'I've got some of those euros we had on the boat.'

'Good. My mouth's dry as an old sack.'

He walked over to the kiosk. A spit of rain fell on his neck. He could do with more than a cup of tea: the sandwiches and biscuits she packed had been eaten hours ago. 'Two teas please.'

His mum had spread out on the seat when he returned, her handbag beside her.

'I've been doing nothing but I'm killed waiting. Travelling's tiring,' she said.

'Here. Try this.' He offered a cup.

'A dog of a journey.' She took a swig and wiped her lips, 'I'd forgotten how long it was, getting the boat. But I liked it, even if it was crowded. I love the wind on my face and to watch the trail of foam behind, as we speed forward. The first time, on my way to England, I was exhilarated. But I suppose I was excited by the great escape.' She laughed. 'I wonder have we anything to eat with it? Any biscuits left?' She searched her bag. 'Here we are.' Wrapping coiled off, revealing two custard creams. He took both and flipped them into his mouth.

'Ah, you greedy boy! I never taught you manners like that.'

'Haaaa,' he said, his mouth full. 'I'll see if I can get you a bar of chocolate.'

He pulled up his hood and crossed to the vending machine. A young couple sat on a bench, back-packs piled beside them, their heads leaning together. They were older than him but not much older. And free. The machine was broken. He kicked it, hoping a slab of chocolate might appear down the chute. His toe hurt as he walked back.

'Never mind,' she said. 'This is the last stretch. Let the last road be the hardest. We'll have a great feed when we arrive.'

'Will we?'

'I should hope Dad'll have something for us. A nice fry-up, or a piece of bacon at least. Dad always liked bacon and cabbage. And white sauce.'

His stomach turned. He would have to fit in with his grandad as well as her. The sign ahead said, 'Buses to Sligo, Galway and Belfast'. Under the cities in large letters ran a trickle of smaller towns he had never heard of. He wondered who would be going to them, as no one else was around. Too early for anyone with sense. He pulled up his collar. Splits between the panels of metal roofing let in the grey sky. His mum had never been to this town they were heading for. She probably did not know where it was.

'What time is it?' She fidgeted.

He checked his watch. 'Twenty past six.'

A siren streaked the air, hard and cold as an iron rod. His chest was tight. He shuddered and pulled his jacket close, as though it could shield him. Beyond the open doors of the garage a white police car flashed past.

'Not long, then. Soon be on our way. It'll be lovely. I'll be agog at the villages we pass, taking a good look.'

'Will your father meet us?'

She shook her head. 'Hardly. He's been only a couple of weeks on the site. The place around is strange to him. We'll have to seek him out. I reckon he'll have changed a wee bit. He'd a voice on him like the groan of wind up a chimney when I spoke to him on the telephone. All the years gone and me not laying an eye on him. The years crept up on me. And him travelling for a long time all over the place, Scotland and the north of Ireland. I barely knew where he'd landed.'

His phone said 'Thurs.' His mates would be down at the post office cashing their cheques. Off to the snooker hall. Or maybe not. Keeping low. The cement at his feet had a track of ridges. Rain pooled in little dips. Some sorry bugger laid it, he thought. Even if this was a crap place, it was better to be here than London. He was lucky to have cut out of it. Being questioned by the police was more than enough.

'I'd say we're in it together. Leaving that business behind,' she said.

'Yep. I know.'

She smiled, her lips moist and the skin around her eyes crinkly so she looked girlish. She hadn't a clue. At least they had got away. If he had stayed, even if they had been the other side of London, he might have been sniffed out, either by Big Ian or the police. Or both. There was nowhere decent they could have gone. An old geezer his mum knew might have given them a room, while Big Ian or one of his mates from that night loped around the estate, seeking him out, sneaking around the stairwells, cadging snippets of info from kids by the bins. Big Ian might have given them fags or spliffs and, eager to please, they might have told. It could have meant being dead meat. He hated having to agree with his mum, but she was right. Distance was best. Sunk into a place no one would think of. It was better to live.

'The one safe place I know,' she said.

Right. So safe there's no one around. But he couldn't complain.

'We'll be far from the police. We couldn't have made a stand against them in London. You might've ended up in one of those prisons.'

'Remand Centres.'

'Look at what happens to the young fellas in them. Dangerous places. They commit suicide.'

'They don't.' He leaned against the back of the shelter.

She had traced a whisper of his fear. He did not know where he might have ended up if he stayed. All he could do was wait. Marcus would let him know what was going on, and whatever it was would go on without him.

In the shadowy early light, a uniformed man appeared. A siren shrieked in the distance. Torin stiffened. They had caught up. Travelling had been no escape. He held his breath. His mum had not noticed but he would have to tell her. She had done her best but it was not enough. They would have him and soon he would have to 'fess up. The whole story would be out and beyond him.

'And don't breathe a word to the old man. There's no need to worry him.'

'I won't.'

He had carried phones and laptops across London for good money. He had lifted a crate of memory sticks and motherboards for a man who said he could put together a computer, but this weight was worse. He was stifled. Laden. Throttled by what he must say and what he must not. He was carrying a secret like a storm inside him.

The man in uniform headed for the wall opposite. It was a mistake. He should have stopped, nabbed him, got out the handcuffs. His mum's jaunt would be over. The man bent down. A clang and clatter. The wall was not a wall: metal panels slid up, revealing a wide sweep of road rolling past. Traffic swirled along, hugging the curve. New light blasted out. A morning opened. Gulls cried like kids from a playground. Torin was dizzy with relief. As the man returned and passed towards the kiosk, his badge was visible, with 'O'Regan's Security Service' picked out in green.

'Hello there, Pat. Have you a cup of tea?' the Security called. The kiosk man turned to his urn and blasted down a shot of boiling water.

'Waiting,' his mum said. 'Always waiting. For a decent flat. A job with a nice woman who wasn't asking too much from me in the way of cleaning her house. The right man to turn up... I reckon me father did all right and wasn't short of a bit of money. He made a pile of money out of the poor people in the Troubles. Burnt-out cars in the middle of the night. Having to leave their homes in a rush. So many perishing or shot.' She smoothed out her coat, its length flapping around her legs. 'It was a kind of death not seeing him for so long. I wouldn't want you to do that, and me not to see hide nor hair of you.' She elbowed his ribs.

'No, mum. Course not.'

A long white bus drove slowly into the garage and parked in a lane. The driver descended and lifted a cover at the back of the coach, revealing the engine, blackened with grease. Torin had not thought the engine for so large a vehicle was at the back. It was odd. Back to front.

'It's the one.' She pointed to a larger coach pulling into Bay 12. 'Ireland-wide' was written along the side.

A young couple came out of the ticket hall and in minutes a small queue formed. The driver nipped down from his seat and opened a compartment at the side of the coach.

'On time,' his mum said and rose, pulling a bag across her body, another dangling from her shoulder while she tugged a large suitcase. Torin was sure the tiny wheels would break under the weight. She walked ahead, stilettos clattering over the scrawl of the coach park until one caught in a gap of the paving. 'I shouldn't have worn these. I just wanted to look nice. I wonder should I change?'

'They're all right. You'll only be sitting. Come on.'

The driver took their bags, including the one of hers with rusty locks which she had insisted on using, claiming it had sentimental value as she had used it when she first came over. He slung them into the depths of the baggage area along the side, stood back and wiped his forehead.

'Ready for the off?'

'I am,' she said, checking her shoulder bag as though it might run away.

'A time since you were this way?'

'A big long while.'

'Where you heading to?'

'Caulnamore. My father's landed there.'

'Ah well, you've good cause to be travelling to it. We'll be off soon as I've this crowd seated.' He nodded towards the people gathering. She rummaged in her bag, producing the tickets with a flourish. 'Grand. Hop in. Have a good journey. And have you sandwiches packed?' he asked with a light laugh.

'I have,' she lied. 'Ready for anything, me.' She patted her shopping bag and climbed up the steps.

Torin followed along the aisle to a pair of free seats. She slipped in first. When everyone was settled the engine started. Beyond the bus station, car lanes were clogging. The morning was waking up. He leaned back. His mum dozed, her hands clasped in her lap like an obedient child.

2

A yellowed picture of the Sacred Heart looked down from the wall of the trailer. Another, made of shiny sweet wrappers, showed the Holy Family. Mary was in bright blue, Jesus in silver, but Joseph had the best of all, in tones of brown and gold. His grandad had put up a lot of pictures. Men with serious moustaches who were old politicians. The Pope and the young American president who got shot. Torin leaned against the wall opposite and used a pen-knife to flick out caked mud from the ridges in the sole of his trainer. He held onto the cooker and tried to stand without knocking up against the bags of dirty washing.

A whiff of boiled spuds and cabbage from last night hung in the air, along with the heavy, sweet smell of Guinness from used cans. The trailer had the smallest fridge he had ever seen, the size of a speaker, and his bed was the fold-out sofa running the length of the window. In the week since arriving, he had got used to the tricks which allowed one thing to become another. But he was caught, with little room to stand up.

'Shit.' Blood beaded over the pale skin of his finger. He fell to the sofa, licked his finger and ran it the length of his trousers, spreading a dark stain.

'Watch yourself,' his mum called. She leaned forward to view herself, smoothing on face cream.

'D'you see any one we used to know, when you were on the roads, Dad?' she asked. She splashed perfume behind her ears. A little bottle stood on the window sill, along with a broken mirror and packaging from hair dye with 'Honey Blonde' in gold letters.

'I did not. How would I? I was far away. After your mother died, I hadn't it in me to be amongst them and wanted to go my own way. I only understand the call of the road. The only thing I know like my own self.'

'I know how it is. I'm barely able to keep up with the living or the dead, myself. Did you see my lipstick, Torin?' She searched the cushions on the sofa bed.

'No,' he said. She had spent a good bit of the evening getting ready.

'Did you see it, Dad?' She turned to his grandad.

'I didn't notice a thing. Why d'you think I'd want it?'

'Where did I put it? "Fiesta" is me best.' She rose in a whirl, knocking against a pair of shoes sticking out from under the bed. 'There's not a bit of room in this damned trailer.' She gave them a good kick.

A hard object jabbed Torin. He pulled out the lipstick from under him. Her stuff was littered all over.

'How'd it get there?' She grabbed it, swiping a gash of red across her lips, as if she had kissed blood. 'I look better already. I may feel like a load of bones, but I look better.'

She moved her head from side to side in the mirror. He saw Harjit, his dirtied face in the shadows as he lay on the ground. A scuffle as the others shifted near and pushed away when they saw Harjit.

'Make yourself a sandwich, lad. Your mother and I'd a fry-up earlier,' his grandad said. He sat at the table flicking through the sports pages. 'We must feed you plenty, for you're a big fella, tall as a tree, the way my own father was. You put a strange name on the lad, whatever else you did, Eva.'

'But I gave him your name, Diarmid, for his middle, so he'll not forget who he is or the people he's come from.'

'Good girl. It's grand to have a strain of our people in him. But I reckon he'll know himself soon enough, whatever you called him. He'll make his own way, no doubt. The same as yourself. You did well to find me. I've been here barely a month.

I was days coming down from the north. I loved it there, the rich green fields. But cold sometimes, with a wind nipping off your nose.'

'I never went there.'

'You did not, for you were all the time in England. But you did right to come over and bring the young fella. Does he have any learning?' He shovelled four teaspoons of sugar into his mug.

'He has plenty. A real scholar, not like the riffraff you might see around, for I sent him to school over. I wasn't going to have any son of mine not able to read or write.'

'Of course. He needs them. Not to be like myself, leaning over a paper trying to make out the letters.'

Torin buttered a slice of bread, sinking a slab of cheese on top with ketchup. If they could only stop talking. They didn't know the half of it. Big Ian out to get him for weeks. It was all over his face. Big bastard had cussed his mum too many times. 'Slutty gypsy' cut. Most of what Big Ian had was only his own bulky self. Bulging eyes and fat lips. He was getting a double chin which stubble couldn't hide. In the alley, someone had pushed. Big Ian's knife slipped. The silver blade on the ground, a nice clean red and white handle. Torin had always wanted one. He leant forward, just to catch Big Ian. Scare him with a flick of the wrist. A graze or scratch. Or cut a sliver of skin to leave a tiny scar. A nice reminder. Nothing too dangerous. But Big Ian shifted and Harjit had got in the way.

Torin pushed back on the seat and tucked in his legs. His mum's blue dress shuddered on a metal hanger.

'I'd say he's like...' his grandad said.

'Myself?' his mum asked.

'How can I say, for I haven't seen the other side of him. But he's a light in his eye like yours.'

Torin could not recall his dad and whether he had straight or curly hair. He did not know if his eyes were brown, or blue like his grandad's. His mum had said he was tall and well built; a good size for a builder, with a strength bringing him to London from the west of Scotland.

She eased the dress side to side over her hips, sleeking it down, the newly-blonde hair about her shoulders. She was wide-eyed, with arching brows. The cheeks he'd kissed as a small boy used to be fresh and light with the faintest of powder, not caked with tan make-up smeared on every morning.

'You look...'

'What?'

'Nice.'

'Good. And this'll top me up for the night. I want to look my best for the party they're having out there.' She reached for the bottle of cherry brandy on the draining board, raised a glass to her lips and slumped into the seat between the cooker and the window, her legs stretched out. 'I don't want to overdo it. Only, being back I want to mark it.'

She put down the glass, her arms plumping out as she relaxed in the seat. Her dress with layers of blue and green sequins glistened like the scales of a fish. At least it would cover her knees. Her red shoes had scuffs. She did not dress as nice as she used to. She always said she had no time. It was true. She did not behave properly, the way mothers should. When he was twelve, she ran off to Liverpool with a man who had a Ford Transit, who said he was getting her a job, said he knew people, had contacts in catering. She had ended up crossing the Mersey and spending a few days in New Brighton. When she came home, she lay on her bed for hours, crying, unsettling him. It made him want to run out of the flat.

People were always moving. In the week since he'd arrived, three families had shifted off. No one knew where they had gone. He pushed the magazines to the back of the sofa and stood to search the cupboards above the beds for a clean tee-shirt. Beyond the window, towards the entrance, the site was muddier than anywhere he had seen in ages, worse than a football pitch. He didn't know how people could live there, or how he could, knocking his head against the ceiling, pressed in between walls. A framed photograph of a woman wobbled and slid down the wall.

'Here, lad, watch what you're knocking against,' his grandad shouted.

'Who's she?' Torin asked, peering at a dull black-and-white photograph.

'Kate. Your grandmother.'

He had not seen a photo so old and with no colour. It was watery, indistinct. It'd merge into the air if he touched it.

'She looks pretty.'

'She was more than pretty. D'you mind the fine meals we had, Eva, by the grass verges, when we'd the two horses? I've only Feather left from them days. Out in the field across, along with the horsebox. D'you mind how we'd the horse flying along the roads to Donegal?'

'I do,' his mum said.

'Be careful how you're putting it back and don't let it drop.'

Torin replaced the picture beside one of a young girl with a broad smile who stood awkwardly, one arm raised against the sun. By her side, the patient dark eyes of a sheep-dog looked out. 'Who's this?'

'Eva. Your mother,' his grandad said.

She could not have been so young. This girl could not have been his mum. Her dress floated out. Her face gazed ahead but her stance, the slight slope of her leaning against a wall, was like her.

'She looks different.'

'She does of course.'

'I'd no years on me then. And no cares. But aren't we all changing?' she said.

'Like myself. You'd never think I was a dapper fella once, in fine waistcoats.' His grandad's fingers, thin as flex, ran down the sides of his chest, preening himself.

'You're wearing an old fashioned dress.'

'It was the style. I think I look good all the same.' She peered into the picture.

'I often wish things stayed the same. But to want time to stand still'd be like trying to swim to Mongolia. You can keep the picture, for it's more use to you than to myself. Put it somewhere safe,' his grandad said.

'In here.' Torin opened the mouth of his grubby sports bag. Usually it held his good stuff: music and his new trainers. He sank the photograph to the bottom.

'I'll make the most of tonight, anyways. You never know who I might meet. Are you coming, Torin?'

He pulled on a jacket and followed her to the field beyond the trailers, where a crowd gathered. Two men circled each other. The taller was thin and wiry, and moved edgily about the shorter, bulky man, who was from the trailer with a sheet of plywood boarding up the window. A woman goaded them but a man stepped between them, telling them to calm down. A man next to Torin said there was a long-running quarrel between two families about a woman who had married into one of them but now wanted a separation. He moved to the back of a crowd of men. Big Ian stood in front of him. He could tell from the slope of his shoulders and the cut of his hair. Sussed. He had been found out. He edged back. Easy. Quiet and slow. The man turned. He had stark red hair and a paunch. Torin felt sick in his gut with relief and fear. He bought a bottle of beer from a man who had a crate at his feet while he sat on guard, moved away to the back of the field and slugged it down. He had to be calm. Had to be.

The atmosphere lightened when a lad handed around a few pounds of bananas he had lifted from a supermarket. An old man began to sing the low words of an Irish song and an older woman with a flourish of dark hair brought out an accordion. Notes throbbed through the light summer air. Two younger men started a fire. An older man threw on broken boxes, legs of a chair, parts of an old high chair and a small table. Flames jumped and spread, casting shadows. Men and women with children drew towards the heart of the flames. Night came down. Velvety and thick, it slammed fast against them. Torin was hemmed in by the crowd of people.

They had stood around and gaped as Harjit's face scrawled with pain, telling what Torin did not want to know. Harjit tried to catch breath. His jacket was messed with blood and his long lashes rested so he might have been sleeping.

Torin kicked a stone, hitting a can, sending it rolling. He sat on an upturned box and was warmed by the fire. His mum appeared on the other side of the circle. In the firelight, a slow smile spread on her as she moved between people, talking and laughing.

A thickset man with a frizz of black curly hair and a check shirt stood on a makeshift stage of planks and metal cases and called, 'Anyone have a song? Do I hear any takers?'

His mum walked from a clutch of women, towards the stage. He wished she would sit. The women clapped and cheered.

'Give us a one,' the man said.

'I will. I'll give it a whirl,' his mum replied.

'Mum, no.' Torin ran to the other side and pulled her back.

'I've a great voice.' She waddled off, the dress shiny across her hips and thighs.

He wished one of the men would get there before her, but the man with the curly hair greeted her with a kiss on the cheek.

'Tell us the name of the song, darlin'.'

'"She Moved Through The Fair".'

'A beauty. Let's have it, then.'

Torn between wanting to run back to the trailer or pretend she was no relation, Torin stayed in the crowd. She swayed, humming to herself while shimmers of light swam off her dress. She cleared her throat. A chord started but she was not ready, so the accordion player nodded and started again. The rhythm increased but no words came. Her mouth opened and closed like a fish.

'Sorry, I'll start again. *And my mother won't slight you till our wedding day...*'

Her voice was small. Even Torin could tell that the words were not right. They skittered out of control.

'A big clap for our singer.' The man moved back in an attempt to shepherd her offstage. 'Anyone else give us a song? We'll have a job finding someone to follow you.'

'Will I try another? I'd love if Dad could hear,' she said, approaching Torin.

'I haven't seen him.'

'Never mind. I'll start anyways.' She approached the stage, climbing up.

'As down the glen one Easter morning, to a city fair rode I...'

The words came sharp and clear. She was going to become a fixture, delighting in the new-found attention. He would be stuck, while Marcus and their mates would be out at the snooker hall or wandering the streets. They had probably bought cans and gone back to someone's flat, eating KFC or burgers and killing themselves over a film. If he could only run up and get her off... But when she finished, the man approached.

'Thanks. We'll be seeing you,' he said, leading her from the platform.

Lights from cars passed on the road and beyond.

'How did I do?' she asked, returning.

'Fine.'

'D'you think any one of them'd want my autograph?' Her eyes were strangely bright in the shadowy night.

She was crazy but she was his mum. When she was carried away with a man, admiring his clothes or his voice, Torin wanted to protect her, but sometimes she cracked him up and would not listen to him, like when he said there was no point in going to school. He was learning nothing, only got duffed up. She understood the day he came home with a black eye.

'If anyone does, they'll come up to you. Don't make a show of yourself.'

'Why shouldn't I enjoy the night, for what else is it we've come all the way over for, but to be with our own?'

The accordion player continued. Another song started from an old man, while his mum pushed out into the crowd before Torin could stop her. She glided off into a gang of people, chatting and cackling.

'Take a photograph of us,' she shouted over her shoulder. 'Get out the camera.'

He ran to the trailer and found the camera among trousers and shirts bunched in a cupboard. His grandad had rescued it from a skip but it still worked.

Torin ran back. Charged with energy, his mum danced towards the fire. She was taller, willowy, like a reed caught in the wind, yet she moved like a flame; her movements were dizzying. He looked through the viewfinder. She was within the tiny square of glass. He pressed down. Light flashed. Caught in shadows, as she skirmished near the fire, a spark leapt to her dress. Tigers of flame roared along the edge.

'Mum!' he called, dashing forward.

He threw handfuls of earth at her skirt. It scrawled a muddy trail, catching in the glittering sequins. The verve of her body scared him as it tilted away, just in time, from the fire.

3

His grandfather was propped against fat pillows on the pull-out bed, eating toast. The smell of burning from the toaster lingered as he balanced a plate. Chunks of strawberry jam slid down the side of the toast when he ate. He licked his lips like a child.

'This'll see me till dinner,' he announced from the mess of blankets. 'Eva? You there?' His face was washed with sleep, even though it was gone twelve. His growth of beard caught the light. 'Those thin sausages were good.' He pushed away his plate. 'And you don't mind the washroom, the way it's boarded up?'

The week-old paper fell apart as Torin turned a page. He could not concentrate, even on an article about the European Cup. If she didn't hush up, he might hit her. He wouldn't. But he might. If they didn't stop talking. He slid to the fridge and bread bin and made a sandwich.

'Course not, Dad. It's grand.' She balanced on the one foldaway stool, usually kept at the end of the bed.

'Did they unblock that pipe?' he asked.

'A man from the corporation is supposed to be coming to do it later.'

'I wouldn't've wanted you coming back to this. Makes us look like savages.'

'Don't be ridiculous.' She folded the clean washing and piled it into a cupboard un-ironed.

'It isn't healthy. Everyone needs clean water. We had it years ago, before ever there was a notion about sites. I do wonder if it isn't some blackguard from the town has done this on us? They set us out here, miles beyond, I suppose so we'd cause nobody any offence. Though we'd be able to do that anywhere,' he laughed.

'We've barely room for clothes.' She opened the door to a high cupboard and searched among the plates and cups, bottles of shampoo and soap.

'It's been good enough for me all the years. I thought you'd be grateful, saving you from having to look for a place. I don't know where you'd have gone,' his grandfather said.

'I am, but...'

'I've had it twenty years around the country with me, travelling wherever I wanted. It must've crossed the sea half a dozen times and only three others had it before me. Many's the long night I've spent in it since your mother died, with it too big. I suppose you've plenty of fancy ideas from over, but look at the material in them curtains.' He set his plate on the bedside table and leaned forward to grasp hold of the deep red fabric. 'Feel it.' She stroked down the textured material, its swirls and coils running riot.

'You look tired, Eva. Are you fit to go into the town?'

'Of course. I'm only pained at times with a kind of weight within. But I want to give a good look at the place.'

She rubbed her fingers. The joints were thick and stubbed from arthritis. She passed them through each other. She complained of pains on damp days in England when they were stuck in the flat, when she had no job to go to and persuaded him to stay off school to keep her company. She said she knew of the time for a change in the weather, for aches dulled the fingers and made her rub them. Coming over had not helped. Instead, she was more forgetful and tearful. When he was young, she said the rosary on long nights when they were stuck together in a tight room, twenty floors up. They floated in the sky, he used to think, as tightly packed streets with the run of cars drained into the night, in the distance.

'We'll have a good feed this evening, for I've a nice side of bacon,' his grandfather said.

'I can't abide meat very much.' She rubbed her stomach.

'A good cut never hurt anyone. Look what it did for me. How many more miles was I able to go with a plate of food inside me. You want to be looking after yourself. Have you your tablets?'

'I have. The two yellow, one green and three white ones.' She picked up three small brown bottles.

'We've nothing else, for there's no one with cures like your mother had.'

Torin rose and put his mug and plate in the sink. Water gushed from the tap. He shook off the drips.

'Are you ready to go to town, Dad?' she asked.

'Of course. Nothing's stopping me.' Crumbs flew off the bed as his grandad shifted the covers.

'The day's good, with the sky only scattered with clouds like the hide of a cow. Are you coming Torin?'

'Okay.'

Torin found his grandad's shirt in the mess of bed-clothes, the tail lopping out from under a blanket where it was kept to warm.

'I'll get my trousers on. But there's a bastard of a pain all the way from my knee up the top and the other one is going the same way, though I don't know why. My leg was never bad years ago, but on a cold day I can hardly move. I think the pain in my back has gone, only to be landed someplace else.' He struggled and fought the tails of his shirt. A pair of braces dangled. 'Help me on with these, will you?'

Torin stood behind and yanked up both straps.

'I used find a wee tot of whiskey was good for it but I don't drink like I used. I'm not fit for it any more. I'm not wanting to bring trouble on myself.'

If his grandfather knew what he had done, he might chuck them off. Tell him to go on his way and not bring trouble around. He'd keep it wrapped up. Dug down and hidden.

They passed caravans with awnings, with paving set in the front, others dry with rust on the corners, while in the neighbouring field horses roamed across scrubby grass. Feather nuzzled the grass, strode a few steps, paused and dropped dollops of shit. Torin leant on the gate; she raised her head, flicking her tail in wild confidence and drew close. Her eyes were large and very dark. He stared into their rich brown depths. Deep as Harjit's. She watched. She knew. Her neck strained up as she blinked, her lashes laying down. He stroked her forehead to the cool, dark cuffs of her nose and she pressed her head, warm, against his hand. When he gathered a fistful of grass, she took the bunch between her thick lips, into the pale skin of her mouth. She turned and pushed out into the deeper stretch of field through dandelions and pale daisies, her glossy coat catching the light, her hooves muddied. Life pulsed through Feather's sleek muscles.

'Let you not waste time staring. We've to be on our way. This creature's living like a princess all the years I've had her, while I've to make do with this.'

The car was rusted on the underside and the windows were smeary with grime. Torin ran a finger along a side window; a dark interior showed a pile of newspapers on the back seat along with a worn tweed jacket.

'Can you drive, grandad?'

'Drive? Didn't I work on tractors years back. It's near enough the same. I was riding the roads more than forty years. Poor Feather's travelled up and down the country for me. I'd to give up on the old caravan but I'd no desire to give her up. But what d'you reckon to this lady?' He slapped his palm on the side of a door. A shimmer of rust fell.

Even though it was old, maybe he could borrow it. If he got a car of his own, it would be decent: a low smooth racer, metallic silver or red, or black.

'You can't say I do nothing for you.'

'It looks worn.' Torin opened a door, settling in.

'There's nothing wrong but it's well used.'

So well used it's clapped out, Torin thought. 'The seat's low,' he said.

'D'you think this is a Rolls Royce? D'you want a ride into town or not?'

'What's this?' A piece of metal stuck out aggressively

'Only a spring gone. Take no notice. Push it back. You'll find they go right in,' his grandfather directed. 'It may look old but that doesn't mean it is. On the road for fifteen years and I never had much trouble out of it.' He started the engine and tugged at the gear stick. A small roar of thunder rose.

They moved off onto the main road to town. 'I could go far. Could go anywhere in this. God, the road is rough, all lumps, they never bother making them up. The corporation does nothing but make a fuss over the likes of us. This car gives us a great run.'

'This seat's wonky.'

'Never mind, so long as you can still sit. Is your mother all right in the back, there? The main thing is, it'll take us places.'

'I am. I'm grand. It's great to be getting a lift and not relying on the old buses,' his mum said.

'It is. And I'm looking forward to going out to this bit of the country I've not been in before.'

Held up behind tractors, slowing for bikes, his grandad hunched over the wheel, peering out the window. Reaching the town, he headed for the square and dropped them off.

'I'll see you here later,' his grandad said. 'I'll be taking a good look around myself.'

'We'll take a look this way,' his mum said, setting off.

Torin trailed after her. Shops spilt out bright yellow plastic pails and red spades, sticks of rock and sunhats: leftovers from the summer, remnants from other people's holidays. Her lavender blouse and red scarf were too obvious. He did not want to be seen with her, partly because of the smudges of mascara around her eyes but mostly because she was his mum. A policeman strolled ahead. They were out to get him.

Searching. Asking in all the shops. He had to steer out of their way.

'It's a fine day. A breath of the sea air in it. Are you pleased with them trainers? Though they don't look strong.' She glanced down. 'Useless and dainty, like a woman's shoe. They'll never last.'

He slowed, wanting to run back the way they had come.

'What's wrong with you, dawdling? Come on.'

The policeman had paused, talking to two old ladies weighed down by shopping. This was it. He could run for it or...or...What the hell could he do, only keep going and walk past? The policeman broke into a huge laugh with the two old ladies.

'If they're what you want for your birthday, fine by me. Seventeen. A lovely age. I remember the night you were born. Four in the morning in the Whittington.'

He hung behind while she walked on, full of the past. 'And I'd a party when you were three, at the back of a pub in Harland Street. It had a patch of a garden and the woman at the bar arranged balloons tied to the chairs. D'you remember?'

'No. I don't.' He checked over his shoulder. The policeman was still talking and one of the old ladies had grasped his arm and was laughing as well.

He recalled more clearly the year before, when he and his mates got out of their heads in the cemetery at the back of Kensal Green, trying to keep out of the way of the cops. They would be out, roaming. Going up the city. Knocking around, journeying over to Tottenham or further, at the snooker hall or arcades, making the city and playing it the way they wanted.

'Come on,' she called. 'We'll take a stroll around a few more shops.'

Neat windows and shop-fronts ranged: cafés with Formica tables, gift shops, clothes shops with reduced items, newsagents and bars. Outside Maguire's bar, she paused. If she wanted to go in, he wouldn't.

'I won't be long.' She rummaged in her battered fake leather bag, dragging a compact from the depths. She flicked it open, fixed a wedge of eyeliner across her lids and brushed on light blue eye shadow. He could not work out why she bothered. It only made her look worse. Or if not worse, older. In London, she slept most of the morning, before going out along the High Road in silky shawls, high heels, her nails painted, alert to the possibilities of the coming evening. She did not fit in there, and did not fit in here. 'Good. That's better.' She snapped shut the compact.

As they walked past a row of houses she pointed out hotels, Cushlawn and Moy Plain. They had iron balconies, flower pots, and fancy porches with neat doors and lace round the windows.

'I'd a friend, a maid in a big hotel in Kensington. She used to serve tea in a silver pot on a little cloth and was always saying I must call in and she'd treat me like all them other fancy ladies, but I never did and then she moved on to a place out the country...'

They passed shops selling clothes, shoes, a hairdresser and a luxury upholsterers. She peered through the large glass windows, smoky with reflection.

'Isn't it a wonder? The style of the chairs. I'd love a one like that.'

The men's shop across the street had a display of jackets and trousers. He crossed to it. Special offers. Three pairs of jeans for the price of two. As good as ones in Shepherd's Bush market. He would come back when he had got the money. He crossed back. He could not see her. He ran down the street but she was not in any of the shops. He ran up and turned right, coming down the other side. He looked through the door of two bars but she was not in there. He glanced up an alley between two shops. Shadowed and narrow, it caught him. A tall man stepped out of a doorway. He pulled on his jacket. Big Ian. Had to be. He had lost weight. It had to be him. He opened a packet of cigarettes and checked his phone. His thick quiff of blonde hair gave him away. Not Ian. Could not possibly be. Torin shivered and turned back to the street, oily with fear. He had lost time as well as his nerve. She could be anywhere.

She could not get far in high heels. Perhaps she had fallen. She might be lost. She might have asked a cop for help. He ran on.

A woman appeared in the distance sitting by the gates of a park. His mother.

'What are you doing?' he gulped, out of breath, reaching the bench where she sat, full of contentment.

Knotted and tight with anxiety, he was pleased to see her and angry.

'What's the hurry? I was taking a walk.'

'What are these?' He dug at the bulging plastic bags.

'A few things, only.'

He pulled out a tiny soft pink baby-grow. A yellow jumpsuit had a little pocket at the top in the shape of a horse. Pale green trousers dangled from his hand.

'What've you been doing?'

'Watch those things.' Her voice was worn. Whatever it was she had been up to had tired her out. She bent down and held a lemon fleece jacket up to her cheek. Tears had dried stickily on her cheek. 'I was only thinking.' She wiped her eyes with her cuff.

'Thinking of what, for Christ sake?' He bent to gather the rest of the dainty garments but the arms and legs of the baby-grows were rebellious and difficult to control. 'Let's get this tidied.' He gathered coats the size of his arm, a pair of mittens, a white cap and bootees into a bag. He had never seen clothes so small. He wanted to shove them in the plastic bag and dump them.

'You'll get nicked. We'll both be had,' he said.

Months back, Marcus had passed him stacks of mobile phones from warehouses, packs of cigarettes, silk ties, and once one of his mates rang him to look at a lorry-load of leather jackets and shoes from Spain. Marcus had been quick on his feet. The phones were scattered before questions were asked. They made a small pile of money out of the lot, but what was the point of these?

'Nobody saw me. You're making an awful fuss. And you're giving me a headache. Leave off. All my lovely things spilt.'

'Why've you got them?'

'I need them.'

'Need them for what?' He pushed a lemon jacket and pink leggings into another bag. She was getting more stupid the longer they stayed. 'We don't know anyone who needs these.'

A middle-aged man made his way along the gravel path towards them. He was dapper, his movements quick and neat as his goatee beard. He peered through thick glasses and raised his hat. Torin had never seen anyone do this before.

'You all right there, Missus?' the man called.

'Look at what you've done,' she hissed.

'It's your fault. Those bags'd make any one suspicious. He's probably a store detective.'

'He is not. They don't have them here.' She kicked a bag under the bench.

'How d'you know? He must've seen the load on the floor. He's not blind.'

Stiff with anxiety, Torin did not know why she took such risks. Surely she had put this caper behind her? He had hoped she was too busy and too sensible. The truth he knew was, she was not like the mothers of his mates who stayed in and cooked meals, there for them. He bent to gather in clothes which strayed out of the bag.

'They didn't used to have them. Shut up. He's nearly on top of us.'

'You've a big load. Would you like a hand?' the man asked.

'Yes.'

'No,' Torin tried to edge her away.

'It's happy for you, shopping for wee things,' the man continued.

He was too polite. They had to get away before he became suspicious.

'They're for a friend.' She pulled at the bags, drawing them in.

'Whenever the happy day is, I'm sure the child will bring great joy. My sister has six and though it's hard work, she never lets a day pass without thanking God he blessed her.'

'Thanks, but we must… be on our way.' She adopted a rare politeness as she struggled to gather the bags and the man walked off.

'Come on.' Torin took her arm.

'All right. What's the matter?' she asked.

'Look at what you've got us into. He might go to the police,' Torin said as he pulled her along.

'He would not. He's too nice.'

'How do we know? Hurry.'

She slumped glumly onto the narrow seat in the shelter at the bus stop. No one came. His grandad must have forgotten. Or got lost, if he hadn't been here before. Or he might be in a bar. He might even have gone without them. Worry niggled and strained in his chest.

'How are you? Did you have a good look around?' His grandfather slowed to a halt and wound down his window. 'Hop in sharp-like, or there'll be a pile of cars behind. Did you get the things you wanted, Eva?'

'I did. Thanks.'

Freed from the tight knit of roads, they were on their way. Torin sank in the front seat. His mum used to nick things when he was young, but not as much as this and not stuff she couldn't use. She couldn't even sell them on. They went around bends at speed without any heed for oncoming traffic.

'Are you all right in the back, Eva?'

'I am, Dad. Fine out.'

They hurtled along but the road looked different. The houses were not the ones they had passed earlier. They had not passed the school with the mural on the wall. Or the parade of shops with the tattoo parlour on the corner.

'Where's this?' Torin asked.

'I'm not sure,' his grandfather said.

'Are we lost?' Torin asked.

'Course we're not. Did you never want to take a good look at a place and drive around it?'

'We want to get back, Grandad'

He did not want to be on the road a minute longer than was needed.

'I might've taken a wrong turning. Only the one. You're hanging on like a scared pup. It's great to be out, looking around. I do never usually get the chance to see towns. What do you think of round here, Torin? Reckon you'll stick it?'

'I don't know.'

'Let's hope your mother does, because she can't be forever roaming the globe. I hope she doesn't go wandering off, getting lost the way she used. You see yonder? The mountainy parts. The kind of place, when she was younger than yourself, she'd be out on, whatever bit of the county we landed up in. We never knew where she was. Most often I'd find her, hours later. And I could, for I was the same, with a love of the open space. You wouldn't know what bit of a field she would be on or whether she would be scaling the rocks high up. She'd make my heart burst, the places I'd have to go after her.'

On a more familiar road, Torin relaxed. A straight run back. Until. A knock. A low, rumbling thunder against the side of the van.

'What's that?' he asked.

'I can't hear anything,' his grandfather said.

'Like something is dragging or fallen off.'

'It's nothing. Probably only the exhaust.'

'Something's come off,' Torin said.

'I don't know how. Everything was fine when we started.'

A heavy smell. Petrol. A dog ran in front of the car. They had surely hit it. Yet in the mirror, the dog barked and jumped in the middle of the road.

'Slow down,' he yelled.

'Jesus,' his mum said. 'I feel awful giddy.'

'Look at the speed. You're doing over eighty,' Torin said.

'Nothing at all. Them dogs are always in the way.'

He drove with a force.

'Stop,' Torin shouted.

Over his shoulder, a tall black girl with a head of tight curls jumped onto the verge, a flurry of a skirt swirling around her long legs. The car slowed, swerved into a bend. She raised her head, her smooth skin glowing as she frowned.

'The girl,' he said.

She stared after them, her hand raised to her brow, shading out the light.

'What are you makin' a fuss about? There's nothing wrong with my driving. It's herself who should've been looking out. I'm only trying to give you a good time. Amn't I tellin' you the girl must've jumped out from the edge of the road. She should've been looking where she was going. I slowed right down,' his grandad said.

'Not till it was too late,' he said, fear shivering through.

'You're exaggerating. You're a keen boy but you're not so smart over your old grandad.'

'What's going on there?' His mum pulled the plastic bags onto her knees.

His grandad jabbed on the brake, hard, and held it down. The air spun with speed as the car slid to a startling halt. The car was off the road at an angle, on the verge. If anything had happened. If.

Torin pushed open his door and got out.

'Are you all right?' he snapped in at the window on his grandfather's side.

'I am.' His grandad's voice was thin and whispery as he leant forward, rubbing the length of his right leg. 'If you get out, Eva, I can get the car on the road again.'

Torin's heart raced. If they had been a second faster... If the police had been called... Either the girl had been quick enough to dodge out of the path of the car or his grandad had seen her in time. He breathed hard with relief. Shit. No sooner here than getting involved with the police. His grandad might be the undoing of him.

He opened the door for his mum and they stood on the grassy verge as his grandad edged the car up and onto the road. The engine growled. He was hot and cold. Sweating all over. He looked over his shoulder. She had gone. Fled. Must have thought the driver was crazy. She had slipped from them as easily as she might have gone under the wheels, but he saw her face. The questioning gaze.

4

Gone midnight, light from other windows shone through the flimsy curtains, keeping him awake. Girls from the trailer next door passed by, wearing necklaces which glowed. If he was out there, it would mean being with his mum. A thud. The old woman from next door, making her way from the toilets, or the man with stringy grey hair in the trailer across the path. He slept most of the day and rambled around at night, knocking into things or cursing the water pipe for its poor flow. Footsteps in the dark. Someone after him. Following. Waiting. But the footsteps passed into the night and away.

A voice approached: '*Far away from the mountains, far away from the foam...* This step'll kill me. Let me in, can't you?' She pushed the door open. Droplets of blood flowered on her hand.

'What happened?'

'Nothing but a graze on my knee.'

'You've been out nearly every evening, since we arrived. And drinking.'

'I have not. I've only had a wee drop to wet my lips.' She loosened the stole from her shoulders. 'Blast it and a hole in my tights as well. Have we a plaster? Give a look in the tin.' With her foot she pushed a rusty biscuit tin from under the bed towards him. Over the last couple of weeks she had slept late in the day, livening up in the evenings, determined to go out.

'Here,' he said.

'Them high heels. Not a one'd help.' She kicked off the shoes. He supported her and managed to get her to sit. 'You're like your grandad, all fuss.'

'You'll probably be ill in bed with a cold.'

'Suits me fine out. Would there be a man with it?' she said with a low, gutsy laugh.

'D'you think grandad'll find us a bigger trailer?'

'I don't know. This isn't so bad. It's done us so far. We have to be grateful. And what harm is it, anyways, living here? It's warm and we're looked after. But I must be quiet or I'll wake the old fella. He'll be roarin'.'

'He isn't back yet.'

'He must've got stuck into a good night of it, then. Fair do's to him. I wish I could've, and not to be coming along wounded.' She struggled out of her dress, her arms stretching up as she wriggled and fought the arm-holes.

'Put out your arms.'

He let slip the zip. A bruise, a purple cloud on the thin pale skin of her thigh showed when she yanked up the dress. Her face twisted with pain, from the fall or remembering, he could not tell. She removed her tights and loosened her underclothes.

'I ran into a fella from Dingle, nice looking with fair hair. He lent me ten euros, said he was a plumber and thinking of building a house. Do they have plumbers in Dingle? I never heard of one. He'd lovely brown eyes and an earring on him.' Underarm hair fuzzed as she pulled a nightdress over her head. 'I'd have had an easier time if I'd headed for America. The gadgets there do save a woman's body. Put on a bit of music, for there's nothing else to make me feel better.'

He rummaged through his grandad's old CDs and slipped one in the player.

'The Way You Look Tonight.' She swayed as Sinatra washed over them. A sweep of hair fell from a slide at the back of her head. A cascading effect she used to say, for some blokes were worth dressing up for, especially the one who gave her the last cleaning job. He had been a good bloke. He had taken her to Great Yarmouth and she had been delighted, though she had only bothered with him, she had said, for comfort.

She lay down and he pulled a blanket over. Too many nights like this since they arrived would not do her any good. But any time he mentioned staying in she argued she could not. She had to be out. Enjoying herself. She dozed until she pushed herself up from the bed, reached up to the sink and vomited, grasping the washing up bowl just in time. A spray of mucky dregs fell on the two bulging plastic bags she kept her underwear in.

'God help us. My head's spinning,' she said.

Torin grabbed an old cloth from the sink and knelt to wipe the bags. He steered her feet out of the line of them. He cleared the mess, slinging out the cloth in a black bag. If he could just get her to sleep. In bed, at least he knew where she was.

'He said he had a good piece of land from his cousin who had the farm and could go back anytime. A few sheep and a dozen cows and a pig, or was it pigs, a dozen sheep and a ram? My head's pounding like a hammer's beatin' on it.' She sank back.

In the dope of sleep, squirls of tiny purple veins ran on her calves. Near her ankle, a deep blue vein stuck out like the wire in an electric flex. Getting old was horrible. He did not want to end up worn out like her. He folded in her arms. Her skin was soft as a puppy and she looked as though she was praying. A tattoo a Puerto Rican guy had made, a strange flower of grey and blue petals with three thorns, showed on her slack upper arm. Her breath stank, full and deep, from the muddle of blankets.

He pulled out his bed and lay down. It was cramped. He twisted and turned. If his mates in London knew about this, they'd laugh. They would laugh the way they did at films when they sat in the back rows stuffing themselves with crisps at late night showings. Or when they saw a stupid kids film in the afternoon just to get out of the rain. The way they used to before Harjit went. He could not see any of them laughing now. He could barely see himself enjoying anything again. Not films or food or good laughs. Harjit, so tall and clever with his dark blue turban. 'Top Knot,' Torin used to kid him when they all kicked a ball around the back of the flats.

Harjit's place was slightly bigger than his, but cramped because there were more of them. His mum and dad, three sisters and a younger brother. The girls had crowded around the door to see when Torin called to the flat one Saturday morning, collecting a game. Harjit's mum was cooking something that smelt sweet and strange. The youngest girl had passed him. She looked about ten, with golden skin and lively dark eyes. Sometimes Harjit had to take her and the brother to school. She had gone into her room without speaking, but from there a song rose. Harjit told him later it was a Punjabi tale about a bird winging its way over the seas to find a warm land. It was a dopey song, he had said, from a film. The song unravelled on and on. Without Harjit. Stiff with a kind of grief, Torin was very still. He turned, pulling a blanket up. His mum was lightly snoring. Night could not last. Soon as it was morning, he would be off. These days would run to an end.

Under the pillow his phone rang, muffled.

'Marcus,' he whispered, pulling it out.

'How you, mate?'

'How're things?' He pulled himself up to listen.

'The cops've been round again. Asking questions.'

'They won't ever give up. What did they do?'

'Took statements. From me and a couple of others. But it's their job, right?'

'Course. They're bound to.'

'Thought I'd keep you up to speed, but I gotta go. My charge is low.' The call ended.

All he could do was wait. But waiting was torture. One of the lads might say something. A stray word. A slip of conversation leading to someone else, leading to him. One person saying what they had seen. The shouts and cries, scuffles and jostling, fighting and pushing one another until it was too late. Too late for him to do more than run with a deadening numbness. Run while he could. Down the alley to the High Road, where cinema titles blazed and the windows of the chemists wept with rain, leaving Harjit behind.

His mum stretched in a difficult patch of sleep. Her closed eyelids flickered.

'Darling one,' she whispered, like wind under the door.

She should make the man bugger off, if one was pestering her. She had with others, uttering a few well-chosen words about a friend or a brother who was a boxer or who had a fleet of trucks.

She sat up to the window, parted the curtains and stared into the distance, letting in a dim flow of light before the fabric fell together. She lay down on the bed again. In the quiet, her voice came, like the way she used to draw a brush through her hair in the mornings, or like a whimper, someone in pain or the wind flying.

In the morning, he pushed away the edges of the scratchy blankets to find her face blotched from crying. The old man in his bed snored gollops of breath. He must have crept in when they were both sleeping.

'What's wrong?' Torin asked. 'Someone upset you?'

'They did not. I'm all right.'

A squall of blankets was heaped on her and the smell of drink came off her damp nightdress. The ribbons should have been tied in a bow, but instead hung down.

'You've been drinking,' he said.

An empty bottle rolled from under the bed into the streak of light from the gap in the curtains. The gold Jamesons label gave her away. He picked up the bottle and slung it in the bin.

'A wee drop only, to steady me.' She stretched to grab it.

'Get dressed. You'll feel better.'

'Better than what? I feel like an old sack of potatoes and no amount of dressing up will change it.' She perched on the side of the bed, twirling a brush through her hair. Strands stood on end, dry and frizzy. Nothing affected her; or if it did, she was doing a good job of concealing it, pressing everything she felt back to the bone. He kept in his words, for if she shouted back, they would wake the old man.

She pulled on a baggy tee-shirt. 'Jesus. My old heart's giving out.' She clutched her left breast. 'I feel a flutter.'

'It must be the coffee. Palpitations.'

'What?'

'Marcus said his dad... Oh, never mind.'

'Is something the matter with me?'

'You were up in the night.'

'Was I?' she looked around as though searching for someone, 'Must be being home. The strangeness.'

'You were talking about someone.'

'Probably a one I met who was blackguarding me.' She grabbed a cardigan and swept it over her shoulders. 'I'll be fine.' She tried to roll up her tights but her legs did not want to fit in.

Home. He did not know where it was. Here? Or the cramped rooms and flats they had left behind? His mates were not caught. They were free in the streets, outside the arcades. Knocking around Dubai Mall for when the man who owned it slipped to the back of the shop and they could make off with a stash of those floaty scarves before running to the park for a smoke.

'It was on my mind for years to come back. My old brain's having a hard time taking it in.' She edged off the side of the bed.

'Don't get up too soon, Eva. You said a doctor over told you not to overdo it.' His grandfather shifted up from under the pile of blankets. He pulled a worn cardigan over his pyjamas, got up and put the kettle on to boil.

'The scut. What does he know?'

Out of the small window, the quiet sky was airy, a soft blue; branches cast deep, thick shadows.

'Watch yourself, Eva, watch yourself!' his grandad called.

She slipped off the bed. He leant towards her, lying on the floor, a tipped heap, all arms and legs. Torin helped her up to the seat.

'I'm fine. Fine out.' She eased herself to sit and pushed a pillow behind her head.

He could not hang around in a place where he hit his head on the high cupboards every time he stood up, where he had to balance walking from the cramped bed to the front door. Those two could look after each other. He wouldn't have to sit in the smell of damp socks and tea cloths, or the sickly milk his mum had forgotten to put back in the fridge.

'Where are you going?' She stretched her arms after him.

'Out.'

'Out where?' Her face strained.

'Just out.'

'We could have a day together. Play Pontoon.'

'I can't.' He pulled back.

'Why not? We'd have a great time,' she persisted, her face pinched with the pain of knowing the inevitable. 'You want to watch yourself with these people. You don't know anything about them. There's a lot of wild people around. Remember it's your friends who take you out but your family who carry you home.'

He shut the door. Shut her behind. His grandad had her, and she him. They had each other and she had a father. His own had ghosted out of his life when he was so young he could barely recall him. He would not leave a kid when it was small. No way. He would stick around.

He ran past the yellow trailer up near the road. The brother of the woman who lived in it was in prison. Its side was dented. Had the brother caused the damage? Torin passed the black Mercedes parked mid-way along the track, making it difficult to drive up into the main part of the site. An abandoned mattress sank with the weight of rain; the hood of a rusty old pram was bashed in. He passed a heap of metal: the insides of an oven, a bent gate, piping and a radiator. He could not see how they made a living from scrap. Or anything. But it did not matter. They were passing through. Heading for somewhere else.

Somewhere better. He walked past a bone-thin terrier which kept circling the post it was tied to, a trail of a chain on the ground. A difficult dog he wondered, or dangerous? On scrubby land, two little girls yelped as they rode a small trike, balancing dangerously. Their silence when he passed told him he was a stranger. A girl walked towards him. She was not much older than Torin but her face was worn and grey-tinged. She carried a crying baby and she disappeared into the trailer with the rusty door, while he passed the field where the grass was scorched.

5

Puddles patterned with light splattered as he walked out of the site. The tracks of trailers were mucked up and someone had left an outside tap on. It dripped dark bullets of drops.

Guns were worse. At least he hadn't shot anyone. Not like Ace, Big Ian's mate swapping fire-arms between flats. Storing them until they were wanted. He could have had a loan. Ace would ask Finer who had a cousin who... he couldn't remember whether it was his dad or his uncle, but someone he knew had a stash buried in their garden. Bromley or Croydon. Somewhere like that. The blue roof of a trailer caught the sun, its edges angled hard against the sky. Being here was, well, he was getting used to it, he supposed. At least his mother was.

He threaded between trailers and vans, following the gritty main path to the entrance where the metal gate swung. The ground was pocked with holes. Tarmac which had once been a driveway was torn.

His mum didn't get it. How the caravan was too small. How he was always tripping over her things. He had stood on her brush that morning. The other day he had knocked over her talcum powder. What did she need it for anyway? They didn't have a bath. They didn't have anything. Living there did him in. She did him in. He kept knocking against the cupboard doors when they were open. And he hated the way she came in late nearly every night. She showed herself up. Showed him up as well.

The terrace of plain white houses was quiet. Too quiet. A man in a uniform—a Gard, a policeman—came out of a front door, looked up and down the street and got into a car. Torin stiffened. If there were trees to hide behind, he might be safe. But any minute the Gard would drive past, slow down, stop and recognise him and it would be over. He'd be slung in the back, driven to a police station, or whatever they called them here, and dumped in a cell.

The car drove off the other way. It slid up the road and on as easily as a sigh. A lorry passed, and other cars. The morning broke open with traffic in both directions and he realised he was no one but a body walking along a street and no one cared.

The Centre rose, stark and white. It had been a school, he was sure, because it had two double doors, high windows and looked crumbly and old. 'Up Kerry' was scrawled on the whitewash under the windows. He peered through one. Posters filled the walls like a kind of youth club, with a faint thud of rap. Two kids sprawled on armchairs, their faces blurry with light reflected from the sky. It was like looking into a puddle but it was him, Harjit, lounging at the end of a sofa. The way his lips curled and the half smile. His nose and the cut of his hair. Maybe he had recovered and was here. Just here. The boy rose and approached the window. The boy was white and wore a tee-shirt with an Irish football emblem. Torin kicked a stone. He was cracking up. He glanced into the room and the boy had gone.

He pushed open the main door and slipped in. It was quiet, with a long notice board announcing classes in knitting, keep-fit and photography, and times for the next information session on preventing scrapie, whatever that was. In the classrooms, girls sat over computer screens. The dry air hummed.

'Come in.' A tall woman opened the door. Her dark blue trouser suit with a long jacket was like a man's. He half-wondered: a woman police officer? Her sharply-cut blonde hair reminded him of a teacher who used to give him detentions for being late. 'You'd like a session?' The lines around her eyes were clearer as she leant towards him.

She had caught him. He had wanted to know what was going on at home.

'Fine. We've three free computers. Got your card?'

He frowned.

'Leisure Pass?' She held the edge of a chair, between him and the rest of the room. He shook his head. 'Forgotten it?' she smiled.

'I haven't.' He shuffled around in his pockets.

'I'm sorry. You can't use any of these until you have one.' She motioned with her hand to the interior. 'You have to apply to the Council and pay the deposit. Go up to the offices. You only need proof of address.' She smiled.

'Right. Thanks.' It was easy for her. Everything was in its place.

'We have to be sure you live here. Otherwise we wouldn't know what might happen.' She laughed lightly but her blue eyes were hard.

'Yes,' he mumbled, backing out the door, wanting to kick it.

She knew. Knew all about him. Could see right through, how he did not live in a house, had hated school and teachers like her. She would have noticed his worn trainers, the hole in his sweater. She knew he didn't belong. A tight ball of frustration sank in his chest. Shit. He did not ever want to see the woman again. But it would be easy to break in. He knew plenty of people who had. Nipping on the tops of roofs. Over garden fences in West Hampstead where stuff was worth taking. One boy had used a climbing frame and from it had gone onto a shed roof, dropping into a garden. Big Ian surely had. There wasn't much he hadn't tried. Slipping nicked iPods to his friends. Selling on drugs he got from a dealer in Bethnal Green. He had boasted about the guy's cover of using a wheelchair and told them how he used to push himself up and down the High Road under the noses of the police. He was able to stash all kinds of gear in the chair.

Big Ian had got away with stuff. Torin did not have the guts. There was good gear here, if he had the nerve. But if he nicked a computer he would be caught. Security numbers would give him away. He smiled nervously. Nicked just when he was trying to avoid this stuff.

He did not want to go back to the site. He did not want to go anywhere. Maybe Marcus had enrolled for the film-making and photography course. He had told Torin how he could make small films and set them up on sites. He could film their mates. Or make up stories about them, around the streets and down the market.

A sign standing on the pavement announced: 'Breen's. Saloon Bar. Lounge. Homecooked Food.' Larger than the other bars, it was not one his mum or grandad had mentioned. He went in. A couple of old lags stood at the end. On one of the upholstered seats an old man sat reading the paper. He looked like an old man, but he might have been an off-duty policeman. The old man steadied his glasses. Torin stared, as if to find some truth, and the old man coughed an old man's throaty cough and a little terrier emerged from under the seat. Wagging its tail, it trotted in front of the old fella, gazing with dark eyes. The old man put down the paper and picked up the lead.

'Good bye, my dear,' he called, walking out.

'Good bye. See you.'

In front of the row of green and brown bottles, her face was the face he had seen before. His palms were warm. He had too many fingers and did not know where to put them. Out of the open-ness of the road and behind the counter, her hair was different. It sprang out, brash curls trying to escape, emphasising high cheekbones which gave her an elegance which frightened him. She looked like a girl who knew what to do. Who knew her own mind. Who might be cleverer than him. His chest tightened. He ordered a beer and waited at the counter for ages, trying to avoid her eyes, before taking his drink to a corner. Tucked out of the way at a table, he sipped. It was cool and nicely bitter. He held the glass tightly, hoping she might not notice him.

She came from behind the bar. The way she moved, effortlessly clearing and sliding the cloth across the small wooden tables, stirred him. Her long legs were visible under the short skirt when she leant over. He had only had the pint but was cramped in his seat. He could not work out what she was doing there.

A girl from school had come from Dominica and her easy manner had disturbed him whenever he ran into her on the High Road. Girls knew something he didn't. Had a deep secret or knowledge he lacked. Knew what to say. She'd been good-looking, plus she was said to be clever, so there was no way she was going to be interested in him. The last he'd heard, she had moved to Leeds.

'Hello.' The girl smiled, 'I saw you looking at me.' Her eyes were deeply brown, darker than her light brown skin.

'No,' he shook his head. 'I mean yes. You reminded me of someone.'

'Okay.'

He hoped she would not recognise him from when he saw her from the car. But she hardly would, from the speed they had gone. He wanted to apologise, explain how his granddad was foolish and had not intended her any harm. But she might not recall. It probably meant nothing to her. They were just another car on the road going too fast.

A bulky man entered and called for a pint and crisps. The girl returned to serve behind the counter and the man told her he was from the north, had worked on barges on the canals.

Torin and his mum had lived in a flat near a canal and he had been fascinated by the lock gates cutting the water's flow. Slabs of light had glittered the surface and water had gushed through the slats until the level dropped on one side and they were equal. He had been a kid and balanced on the gates' edges, crossing from one towpath to another. A man from one of the barges had shown him a map of canals snaking the length of England. When they moved to London they ended up near a canal, a good place in the summer, watching the dance of flies above the water and the occasional barge as it crawled towards the lock.

The girl pushed three crates stacked on top of each other, scraping the floor.

'I'll give you hand.' He rose.

Bottles rattled and clinked as he pushed the crates into a corner behind the counter.

'Thanks.' The girl gave the crates a nudge with her foot to slide them in neatly.

She returned to the counter, putting dirty glasses into a machine for washing. Its light hum curled around in the air. Two old men with sticks entered. They pushed themselves up onto bar-stools, ordered and chatted. Cattle. The weather. A politician coming to the town to open a new extension at the school. Torin wanted to catch the girl's attention but she chatted to the men and they laughed, filling the bar with their shared jollity. A knot in his chest tightened. He had no hope of getting closer. But he hadn't the money to keep drinking either. The old men left. She wiped the counter where they had been, looked up and smiled. She passed out of sight and in the few minutes of absence, he missed her.

'Oh, no,' she gasped, returning.

'What is it?'

'The cooler's leaking. I need to find a switch. Where did Breen say it was?' She went to the back of the bar. 'I don't know what to do.' She frowned, looking older, greyed and lost in thought.

He rose and followed through a passageway to a room at the back. The chill inside nipped him. A light whiff of lager spiked the air. On the concrete floor, metal kegs and casks stood like soldiers. Apart from the runs of pipes, flexes and dials there was nothing else. A safe-room, he thought. With the valuable goods.

'I need to turn off the water but I've looked everywhere.'

He scanned the walls and looked behind the kegs. He pulled over a lone wooden kitchen chair to search behind the largest. Standing on it, he was face to face with a single dusty light bulb. Flexes tangled behind the containers. He climbed down. He didn't really know what he was looking for.

'Breen told me what to do but I was only half listening. God, he'll be annoyed.'

'I can't see a tap.' He peered by the kegs and casks.

'I must find it. I don't want to lose this job.'

She leant against the wall. He followed the slim and easy line of her leg. A red bulbous lever stuck out at the base of the cooler, hidden by a jungle of flexes curling beneath.

'This it?' He bent down.

'Must be, yes.' She yanked the lever to the left so it lay against the wall. Her hair, springy and light, brushed his face. He smelt...what was it? Flowers like his mum used. Roses? Lavender. They stood. She relaxed her eyes into a smile and stretched an arm to his. Such little pressure on his forearm. 'Thanks.'

'It was nothing.'

'I'd better get back out there. If anyone comes in and tells Breen there was no one tending the bar...' she laughed. 'But will you have a drink?'

'Thanks.'

Behind the counter, she took a clean glass and poured.

'Will you have one?' he asked.

'Daren't. I've a good few hours left.' She shook her head.

Carrying his pint, she came to his table and sat. The upholstery was a wild pattern of red and purple diamonds and squares. She crossed her legs. His cheeks warmed. His hands were hot and in the way. If he sat apart, he could see her face.

'The load is there since delivery and not a bit of help from himself or any of his lads. They're useless, the lot of them. He has three in college. It's what education does.'

Her left hand lay on the table, a stumpy finger in the middle.

'What happened?' he asked, unable to help himself.

She moved her fingers.

'One time in England, I was working on a fairground, well not working, helping out. We'd had a long day and I was tired. I sat down on the first thing I saw and wasn't it a chair for the clown? It collapsed under me.'

'It must have hurt.'

'It did. But they got me to hospital. I don't really think about it. It used to bother me because I couldn't play the fiddle any more. I was learning from an old fella who said I could've made a name for myself. I lost it all and it was awful having tunes buzzin' in me head and not being able to do anything with them. But it's past. Would you like some music?'

'Great.'

'If you do a selection, you get more.' She dropped in coins. A sway of strings rose. 'Sailing.' Rod Stewart. The old guy should be put out of his misery, but Torin would endure the old dog if it meant he could stay.

'We have it for the old fellas and Breen's too bloody mean to get in new stuff.'

Guitar notes and drums filled the empty hold of the panelled bar. Torin eased in the chair, stretching out his legs. She gathered glasses from the counter, running her cloth quickly over the top. He tried not to drink fast, to make it last. He could not hang out forever buying them. When she finished, she joined him.

'Are you local?' she asked.

'I'm not. But I'm around for a while.' He shifted uncomfortably and stopped playing with the beer mats. When he looked up, her eyes flooded him. The line of her lips, her neck. The way she held herself so straight.

'Visiting?'

He nodded. He would not mention the site for fear of putting her off.

'I feel I am. I started here a month ago. I wonder if I'll ever settle,' she said. 'Once I was getting off the bus and a woman from up the street shouted out, where was I from? When I said Caulnamore she was white with fury.'

'People aren't friendly?'

'The most are all right. It's just...' Her eyes were dark. She leaned over his table, her body slim and long, the line of her breasts rising. 'It'd be good to have a change.'

'But where'd you go?'

'A place I'd feel I belonged. Moved around a lot when I was a kid, but maybe it's time I moved on.' She laughed, her mood lightening. 'So where are you staying?'

'The site.' He nodded in its direction. 'Travellers' site. But I'm not one. I mean, not completely. It's somewhere to live. But loads of people around. Kids. I don't know where else to go.'

'Down by the shore are a couple of old houses. One of the old fellas who comes in said one of them has people in it.'

'Old houses?'

'You can see them from the path, the other side of town if you head towards the shore.'

'Okay. Thanks.'

He stretched his hand to pick up his glass but it toppled. Beer spilled over the table, smearing the wood to a golden sheen. It ran, darkening his trousers the more he dabbed the damp patch.

'Shit.' He pulled back from the table.

'I'll get a cloth.' She leapt towards the counter.

He had screwed up right and proper. He was losing her. He'd better leave before he made a bigger fool of himself.

'Thanks,' he said as she returned, skimming the cloth over the table.

'And you're...?' She looked up as she mopped a dry cloth over the wet patch under the table.

'Torin.'

'Caitlin. Call in again. I'll make up for that drink.' She crossed to the bar and squeezed the cloths in the little sink.

He headed for the door. He had made an ass of himself, frightened her off big time. The chance had gone. For company she would have the old lags who stepped in for a pint in the middle of the day from out of the factory, or a few who might pass from the farm.

6

From where he lay in the broken-down house, the dark sky seemed so near he could cut it. Through the tear in the ragged corrugated roof, pin-pricks of stars shone as they had the last couple of nights. He did not know their names but the circular cloud swirling around must be the Milky Way. There could not be so many stars in London. If there were, he had never seen them. They kept themselves shut out. He stretched his legs. Shane and Pauley were still asleep. Their plastic bags bulged with clothes, trainers, and phones. He could not see how this ruin of a house had ever been lived in, for it was one large room, stone walls strangled with clods of cement which had two square gaps for windows, one partly boarded up with wire and rope. Piss and shit wafted. His neck was stiff from squeezing into himself to keep warm, to forget he was lying on the ground. He had to believe this was a good place to be. He wished he could talk to Marcus, but it had been hard to get a phone connection. The first time he tried after arriving, he had to dance around to get a signal, his phone plugged to his ear. Nothing was like he was used to.

In the morning, a voice woke him.

'You comin' or what?' Pauley stood thin as a wisp of grass, blond hair falling over his forehead.

Torin turned blearily from the backyard of a dream.

'You want to stay here?' Shane asked. His bulkier frame blocked out what little light came from the window. Torin pulled himself out of his sleeping bag.

'If it's all right?' he said.

'What d'you say, Pauley? We let him?' Shane said.

'All right with me. If he wants to.' Pauley smiled.

'You gotta help get the oysters,' Shane said.

'I can do that.'

'We've to be on our way. Down early to get a good go at them.'

'Won't they know we've nicked them?' Torin crawled out of his sleeping bag into the chill air.

'No one could prove it.' Shane pulled a dark blue sweatshirt over his head, black curls crumpling down. 'No one'd know we did it if they don't see.'

'Okay. I'm with you.'

Torin rose and dressed. Beyond the grimy window, the sky and fields ran into each other and the continuous cry of waves was disorientating. Birdsong rippled the air. He rubbed through grime on the glass. The bird had wings so big, they might've weighed down any chance of flight. The haze of green and boggy land stretched to the sea where, according to Pauley, oyster-catchers and redshanks dived past midnight.

They ran out to the fields of lumpen cows laying down. Way out, waves threw themselves against rocks, showers sprayed, cascaded. So much nature, he was made small by it. Pauley ran ahead, so fast he could have been a footballer. He was as quick as the lads on the track at White City. Torin used to hang around it near the hospital and the prison, when he and the others jibed each other about how they might end up in one or the other.

Shane caught up, his eyes dark and sharp. Heavier built than Pauley, he could run as fast.

'You came over with your mother?' Shane asked.

'Yeah.' The sandy ground was falling apart. Wisps of stray grasses lingered. Being outside made him more aware of the inside of himself. It was empty, as though his outer part had fallen away.

'She's showing off her *gossoon*?' Shane laughed.

'She wanted to see her dad. And... other stuff.' Torin shrugged.

'Oh?'

'Nothing. I mean. Only a mate got knifed. This guy... he annoyed us.'

'It was your fault?'

'It was an accident. There was a crowd, so we're all treated as suspects.' He kicked a stone, skimming it through a whiff of dust.

'But you didn't do it?'

'I was holding a knife for someone. There was a scrum. Pushing and shoving. No one knew what was going on.'

'Is he dead then?'

'He's in hospital.'

'That's okay then.'

'But I'm afraid the police might turn up.'

Shane shook his head.

'No one ever comes here. Why would they? There's fuck-all going on.' He shook his head. 'Come on, we might catch sight of a rabbit. Catch one. Shoot it.'

'Shoot?'

'Only kidding.' Shane danced delightedly, a taunting smile on his face. 'See the holes?' He pointed to pockets of dark in the ground. 'In the evening they're all over the place. And if I'd a gun...' He raised his arms as though he held one, and did it so quickly it was frightening. 'I'd give 'em one.'

'Could you? Would you be able to get a gun?' Torin asked. It seemed a simple task. An easy target.

'Farmers have 'em, but I wouldn't get the use. Too bloody strict. My uncle'd one years ago. A Webley and Scott used to lean against the dresser. It'd lovely engraving around the barrel but I'd never get it off him. He had it to shoot rabbits and I was with him once when he shot one. He put it in a pot and we ate it. Nice bit of lean meat and good quality too from them running about in the fields, but there's an awful smell off it.'

'What d'you do with it?'

'Skin it. A good slit around the back and over the legs. If it's young. Easy. Great taste. We used get a good bit of grub out of them. The jug'd be warm after collecting the blood for the black pudding afterwards, and what was no good was left for the dog.'

Torin shivered. Blood had trickled from Harjit's nostrils as he lay on the pavement outside the kebab shop. Flashes ran from the film they had seen: the gang planning a break-in. The rush and madness of a quick grab. A get-away in a sleek car. But nothing was as scary as standing in the alley with Harjit lying on the ground. The Velcro of his trainers undone. His belt slipping. The push and shove of the others, as a girl tried to get close, to wipe his face. Nothing made sense. His heart pounded as they waited for someone to do something.

'My uncle gave me this when I was a kid.' Shane pulled a leather string from round his neck, where a stub of dark fur hung. 'Lucky charm,' he laughed, pulling it around and stroking it. 'From the first rabbit.'

He strode ahead, catching up with Pauley by the side of the ditch, and crossed a small bridge of worn planks. He raised the barbed wire on the top of the fence to let Torin through. They ran onto dry, rough grass, sand flying from their shoes. At the shore they crept among boulders fat and squat as toads. To one side, silvery shards splintered against the slate cathedral of rock, a looming presence. Spray from waves rose like a curtain. Padraig's Rock, Pauley said, after a fisherman clung to it for hours waiting to be rescued.

Black fishing boats, worn-out and old, were beached. The glass around the deck of a larger one was smashed and only the wooden section surrounding the wheel was left, though collapsing. It had been out to sea before it was banged up there. It had been in the deepest waters, exploring, taking whatever the waves hurled. What would it be like living here with mostly the sea for company? He might go mad looking at the same fields, the same kind of sky overhead. Even the cows moved like old women, their low-slung hips wide and thin legs walking leisurely. Torin walked around a sleek red boat, larger than the others.

'This is nice.' He placed his palm flat against the side.

'Some rich bugger's,' Shane said.

'I'd love a boat like this. Think where you could go,' Pauley said. 'The Caribbean. The Med. Your own master. Free for whatever the mood takes you. Go anywhere.'

'Let's head this way,' Shane said, taking the lead.

They followed while the sky was a silvery blue, undecided what colour to be. It melted into a grey horizon. Waves slithered and birds screeched against the sky; with each step, the sand sucked in Torin. This early, fresh light hit and the expanse of sea was shiny as plastic. They ran to the end of the pier, whooping and shouting in the smash of cold air on their faces. He could have a good time here; if they used the tabs Pauley had stolen, the buzz would be even better and he could forget.

'You gonna go in?' Pauley asked.

'It'll be cold.'

'No matter. It's a gas. Even if we haven't flashy surfboards like the lads up the coast, we can still enjoy ourselves.'

'Who are they?' Torin scanned the horizon.

'Lads from Dublin. Like flies all over the place in the summer, slinking around in wet suits,' Shane said.

'They must think it's the coast of California, the way they gather at weekends,' Pauley said.

'Come on. We've got this.' Shane ran along the quay.

He pulled off his clothes leaving on only his underpants and ran to the edge of the pier. His legs kicked in the air as he dived. His head bobbed. Torin took off his jeans and top. Swimming at the baths in Kentish Town had been good, the most sense of freedom in water he'd had. They all used to go swimming: five at the start, but two of the lads had moved up the country. Now only Marcus was left.

He took a breath and plunged down and down, cut open the cold darkness of the water. He heard his heart. Pressure compacted in his head as he counted seconds like years. The depth was deafening. Holding his breath in the slip of the echoing silence, he slid through, gave himself to the water. It soothed and swayed over his body.

Harjit. His khaki jacket over him. His dark hair slicked over his forehead. A girl pushing forward and saying, 'Leave him. You're supposed to leave them.' A cold, alarm snaked in his veins. Harjit had shifted. A murmur of movement. Someone said, 'You're supposed to put them in recovery position.'

Torin bounced up, water slipping off, his eyes full of it, gushing down. Dizzied, he shook his head. Slicks of hair in his eyes. Being in the water was wild and dangerous, even if it was colder than he had known. Waves roared in his ears while the salt taste exploded in his mouth. He made for the pier and pushed himself up. Pauley swam to the side; Shane was still out there.

Torin and Pauley sat with their legs dangling over the edge. The early morning was misty. Shane swam in, ran up the stone steps and along the quay to Pauley, grasping his waist.

'Come on.' Shane pushed Pauley towards the water.

'Oi. Leave off.' Pauley kicked back.

Shane pressed down on Pauley's head with his thick hands. An easy target, slighter built than Shane, Pauley was slow to anger but when it pitched in, it showed. Shane laughed, his broad face open with delight.

'Give us a rest,' Pauley yelled.

'Haa haa!' Shane danced barefoot up and down to the end of the pier where he stopped, balanced off the edge and jumped in. He was a bobbing, exuberant face until he swam strongly back and pulled himself up.

If Shane tried anything, Torin would sling him one, shove him in the water.

'Let's dive again,' Shane demanded.

'You know what I'd like to do?' Pauley said.

'What?'

'Dive off over there.'

Torin followed Pauley's gaze to a huge, grey rock.

'It's high.'

'That's why I wanna do it,' Pauley shouted, running to the head of the pier. 'You get a buzz.' He jumped in and swam far out to where the sea was preened and glossy.

Torin's heart turned. A flick. A murmur in the big silence. A trick of the light and Pauley's ribs were whispers. He was a lone figure among the waves, swimming near the face of the rock. He pulled up on it, was an insect crawling; his hands skimmed for holds in crags. Half way up on a ledge, he crept higher, drew in air as if to strengthen himself. A large gold cross on his chest glinted as he raised his arms. The tattoo around the top of his arm squirled a ring of thorns. He stretched up on the balls of his feet, his long arms aloft. In a flip, his thin legs were up. A flash of blue from his underpants against the open sky. He was semi-circling. Legs and arms in the fragile light. His body would break. He spooled into the air, coming down in a swirl. The expanse of sea was empty and he was gone, dunked deep into the heavy water. Torin could barely breathe. He missed a heartbeat. But Pauley hit the water, spliced it into circlets growing smaller. He bounced up, among scales of waves. A collar of thick foam spumed. An angular face bobbed up, smiling.

'Hey, you all right?' Pauley shouted, waving his arms.

Torin followed the voice.

'Okay,' he said, as if nothing was worrying him.

'Coming in?'

'Not there.' He turned to the side of the pier where it was shallower. He was as likely to go diving off a huge rock as go to the moon. Shane swam back. Torin said nothing. He did not want to sound too impressed but he wished he could dive as well as they did.

'There they are.' Pauley tugged him to one side and pointed into the sea.

'Those bits of metal?'

'Oyster beds. Sacks with seeds lie on the frames.' Pauley edged into the shawl of light foam thrown on the sand. 'Let's take a look.'

'Won't we get caught?'

'There's no one round. They leave this lot unguarded. They deserve to lose it,' Shane shouted, running towards them.

A strip of an old pier crumbled into the sea. Its steps were breaking away and bricks at the side were dislodged. It jutted out from a cluster of houses with roofs wavy from age. Shane said the fella who looked after the oysters lived there but spent nights in the pub, so he'd be sleeping it off. A fishy stink hung around. Ragged lobster pots, orange plastic ropes and roughed-up buoys slung on the side, but it was a stink he was getting used to.

They scavenged among black sacks laid out on iron frames, flat as drunks. Shane jabbed in, pulling off oysters, shoving them into plastic bags. 'D'you like 'em?' he asked.

'I've never had one.'

'You hardly will if you don't go to a fancy restaurant.' Shane scrabbled among the stones and found a reddish one. He lay down the grey ridged oyster, gnarly as an old man's hand. He smashed with the stone and the shell splintered in chalky white fragments. Pale as nails and a fine dust. 'D'you want it?' He held out the bottom half of the shell where a sludgy grey spit lay.

'No, thanks.'

'You get the taste for them.' He tipped up the shell, a delicate plate of light, and wiped his mouth with his hand. 'Wild salty. With a bite you don't forget.'

'Hey, you cut yourself,' Pauley said.

Shane raised his index finger where blood spotted.

'It's nothing.' He ran his finger across his lips but the blood came.

'Salt water'll help,' Pauley said.

Shane walked to where the waves ran and dunked his finger, pressing against the skin and the trickle stopped.

'Come on. Let's go,' he called and they headed for the road. 'We'll get a couple of hundred euros from the hotels for this lot.'

'You reckon?' Torin asked.

'A good few packs of fags out of it, anyway. D'you mind the time we were in Castleallen, Pauley? We hung around the side of the fountain until we could gather a good handful of coins.'

'Shane and I'll walk into town. You'll get a cut of what we get.'

'Okay.'

He didn't know it could be this easy but they knew the business. Would cut the deal and maybe he would learn something useful. Whether or not he saw any of the money they made, he didn't care. He knew where the beds were and could go back and gather his own crop.

'Keep it dark.' Pauley touched Torin's lips and tapped the side of his nose.

They rounded the head of the peninsula. Slithery grey skeins of light on the flat sea were so calm, Torin would never have thought it was deep. They walked along a rough track. A girl led a donkey around the bend. Caitlin. A fall of leather strap dangled between herself and the donkey.

'Let's go round the other way,' he hissed.

'Better. She might've seen us and we don't want the oysters wasted.' Pauley let drop the bag of oysters onto the pebbles.

'Perhaps she hasn't seen anything? How'd she know what we're doing isn't legit?' Shane asked.

Torin tensed. She might go to the police. He could be found out, hurled back to London. It would be over. Over before it had begun.

'I'll sweet talk her,' Shane whispered. He walked towards her.

'There's an easier way up there. Not as rough on the poor animal's feet,' Shane pointed towards the path.

Torin shifted out of her view behind a roar of fuchsia clambering on a stone wall.

'I know. But this lad,' she patted the donkey's back, 'likes to be close to the shore.' She let the rein dangle in a great 'O' from her hand.

'He's a fine animal,' Shane said.

'He's past it.' She stroked the donkey's grey ears. 'He likes a bit of a stroll.' She cocked her head towards the field of three chestnut horses.

'You don't see many around.'

'He's the last of any from the farm.'

A fist of rage clenched in Torin's chest as their voices carried. Why couldn't Shane leave it? She was the same height as Shane, who stood close. Shane clasped strands of grass from the dunes and offered his palm.

'Thanks,' she laughed.

'He's a lovely old fella. Lucky to have such a good-looking one to be taking him out for a walk.'

'Don't be talking.' She smiled and led the donkey along the roughened track, turning to pat its neck. Its long ears lay down against soft grey tones as she led it to a field and let slip the rope, setting the donkey free to roam.

'Who's she?' Pauley asked.

'Seen her around a couple of times. But first of her kind here.' Shane shrugged and laughed. 'But she looks the type you'd best not be thinking too much about. A cut above the usual,' he said, kicking a stone.

They went down the road in wet underclothes, their outer clothes a bundle in their arms. When Torin looked over his shoulder, Caitlin was sinking into the distance until she was the size of a pebble.

Templevane

1

'A lump of a lad sprawled in a heap when he's here. There's no knowing what the rest of them lads is up to,' Eva said, picking up two tee-shirts from the chair. She would take them to the laundry room in the afternoon, when she had gathered a load.

'He's enjoying himself,' her father said, rinsing a tea-pot in the sink

'Enjoying himself? I'd like to see him get a job. He could make a bit of money at a supermarket or garage.'

'You said he doesn't know about cars.'

'He doesn't. But he could learn. Hasn't he a brain in his head, even if he never used it much? He could learn something. And something useful. How to mend them. Put on a tyre or some such thing.'

'He's only young. Look at yourself, Eva. Leaving us with no heed on you. Rushing off and your mother upset.'

'I never meant to.'

'Ah, well. Let's not rake over the past, since there's little we can do about it. Have we any bit of bread left or did he eat it all?' He stretched to the empty plastic bag.

'I'd the last bit off the loaf. I'll have to get some and other bits from the shop.'

She grabbed her bag and jacket. No matter the load of food she brought in, it went. She believed he must be coming back from the old house in the dead of night, for he was never around to be seen eating it. It wasn't her father indulging himself: he was as thin as a bird. The years had clapped nothing on him, not like herself. Torin must be turning up with the other lads and eating it.

The new air slapped her to a keen alertness. She could do with a flood in her lungs. A rush of cold air into her, waking her up. She could not stay closeted in the tight box of a caravan. The woman in the long trailer swept the front patch of concrete. Two cracked cooking pots held an array of flowers. Lashings of bright pinks and reds. A neat front, her father had said. She would not mind one like it. She could do with the faces of tiny flowers to come out to.

Feather stood in the field, at a distance. Always a horse around. Her father had amused her as a child with his tales of galloping across every county in Ireland. He had said he had run off with her mother on horse-back, for she had been delighted, caught in his wild imaginings. In their early married life before he could afford the horsebox, the animal walked the road alongside them. She and her cousins rode bareback along the beaches, the wind streaming through them.

It was a wonder she threw off the blanket of her parents and crossed to England. But it was done. The damage, if any, done. She had been eager to get away. Away to what? Fields and a squat town which had nothing for her. The sea was what she preferred. What she would have run back to, if she could have. At least she had found her father alive and in good form. He was old and growing older. His deep blue eyes were smaller and lost in folds of wrinkles. His best days were over, though he was as stubborn as an old donkey for wanting to be out and about in the pubs with young fellas. But she could not blame him for it was in the blood; wanting of talk and deep need of company. To be out, free of herself. She should have come back before, even if he was happy with days full of new things: TV aerials, garden furniture, vans and cars. But she would make it up, for the years were telling on them both.

If her mother was alive, she would have seen herself and Torin in the crystal, journeying; a grey cloud shifting over the stream of light or the way a sheep is heard the other side of the hill or a cow knows its young. Her mother would have sensed their footsteps across miles of years. Seventeen or so was a long time. A lifetime. If Torin did the same on her, she would break.

She left for the shop. A man bent over the engine of a car, tucked up on the verge. His hair flopped over his forehead. He brushed it aside. There had not been talent in that department since she left London. And not such a lot there. No one on the site in the last month interested her. All families. Caught in their own concerns. She eased out the creases on her trousers. Not her most attractive clothes but she had not the same energy to dress up as she used. Perhaps she should have done what Torin told her and kept the hospital appointments. The doctors in England might have cured her, made her better, or at least got her over the damned pains. She never liked them places. They were strange and difficult. An awful smell. And the way the nurses looked at her. She crossed towards the shop. The fella, the way he held himself as he moved around the long brown car, had something. As she passed, he raised his head. She caught his eye but did not speak. Show some restraint, she decided. At least at the start. No knowing where it will lead.

On the way back, a plastic bag with the milk and bread at her side, he was stretching over the belly of the car. He raised his head and smiled, the corners of his eyes crinkling.

'Hello.' He brought himself upright. 'Nice day.'

'It is.' She capped her hand over her eyes. He was tall. She liked his openness but he was too assured in his manner to be interested in her.

'I wouldn't want to be inside. It'd be a waste.'

'A person'd want to make the most of the good weather,' she said.

'You must've just arrived to enjoy the good weather, for I didn't see a new trailer beyond.'

He had a quizzical look, taking everything in. A pungent whiff of oil rose as he wiped his blackened hands on an old rag. A hard worker. His tummy stuck out over the rim of his trousers and a thick leather belt. She should be on her way back to fix a fry-up.

'I'm with my father,' she said.

'Ah, I'm not on the site but on the road further out.'

'You don't fancy to live there?' she asked.

She would like to have put her arm around his waist, even if his hair was greying, running from the red it used to be, and the skin around his ears wrinkling. A little dog scampered at his feet, with dark, golden eyes; a red collar was around its neck. It wandered and sniffed and lay down near him.

'I do not.' He bent to stroke the dog. 'I'd rather be my own man. Head off on the road whenever I want. They've made up the sites pretty good though, with all the amenities. No doubt but the women love it better than what it was, with the outside tap and no proper toilets. If we'd them in our day we'd never have been out of the place,' he laughed.

'I'd say this one isn't as fancy as some, the way you'd think people were to stay forever.'

'It'd please the Gards, to have us rounded up like sheep. But it isn't natural for any person to be inside all the day. Did you hear of the young girl in Waterford, settled in a house? And no garden. She went out with a pram and the new baby, walked out into the sea, pram and all.'

'I didn't hear of that report.' She shook her head.

'I'd say it was how the girl had the walls of a house pressing in on her. She went into the waves, lonely as a poppy in a field. I'm the same way. I never could stick that yoke. I've nothing against ones who settle but I'm stopped up yonder in a quiet place.'

'King of the road, then?'

'I wouldn't say so. A man who claims I owe him money was after me. I never owed him a penny but I reckoned I was as well to move on.'

'You're on the run?'

'Not really. I couldn't hide myself.' He pointed to the dog. 'I get a bit of work from time to time. I'm no good at much but I can fix an engine.' He leant over the bonnet, closing it down and brushing his hands on his overall. 'Joe. Joe Murphy. What do you say to a drink and I'll give you the lowdown on these parts?' He put his hand on her shoulder, a steady weight, as they walked along.

'I will, Joe, thanks. I'm Eva.'

He made her heart burn with his eagerness, his spirit and talk. And a long time since it ever had.

'Corrigan's is small but I like it because you don't get so many coming in.' He led her to the small pub along the road. If the police were after him for the bother with a bit of money, how much more likely was it that they would know of Torin? Fear stabbed her. She had brought him all the way over but they might still not be safe. She fidgeted with worry.

'You all right, Eva? You're not tired with the heat?'

'No. Course not. This is grand. Lovely. I've been wanting to come into this bar since we arrived.'

They found a table and he ordered. His stumpy hands touched hers as he passed the glass. He sipped his beer. It was only a little brandy and would not do any harm. Brandy might numb the day. Heal her. The sweet aroma made her head zing. It was what she wanted, to be taken back to where she started and sitting in a bar with a man would help her feel better. He could not have a wife or kids. Or maybe he had and would spill it out, would tell her about the lot of them and how across the years he had little Mary and Johnnie. God help her. She could see it.

'... there's no call for work like years back when you could pick up jobs on the farms. All gone. Nobody needs extra hands. So I've learned meself mechanics. I can fix an engine, get a car on the road. Though I never did mind hard work. Being out in the fields, in the air, gave me the greatest pleasure.'

Joe had grit under the nails but she did not mind, for his eyes were soft brown, like turf.

*

While her father dozed outside in the late sun, she slipped away. Joe waited for her in Corrigan's. She sipped sherry and lemonade, vodka and lime. It was good to try a variety of drinks. Good to have the time and not be chasing from one cleaning job to another. Catching buses. Or missing them. Stuck in the overheated Tube, rubbing up beside some young man's bum and the ribs of a girl thin enough to be a model.

'So what was it brought you? Not the weather, surely?' Joe leant in.

'A few things...' She should tell him how Torin had been picked up by the police. Held at the police station where she had to collect him. How he was questioned. Questioned again, until she insisted they did the only thing she was good at, and they left the city one night on the bus for Holyhead, retracing steps she had made years back. Years so far back, it hurt to recall. But her body would not let her forget, and she had not had a decent night's sleep with conflicting worries about Torin and the day buried in the past when she had left the wee girl with her mother. How that day had sliced her, prising through the rock of years, the drag and scrawl of loss raging which she'd struggled to keep inside.

A family entered, the two little boys scampering on the padded seats, lifting up salt and pepper containers. 'Mum. Can we have chips? Mum, can we?'

'Sorry?' Eva asked.

'You were dreamin.'

'I was?' She blinked in the light. 'I'm sorry. I was far away. The thing is... my son was in with the wrong crowd in London. We left, for I was afraid it would get out of hand.'

'Weren't we the same ourselves?'

'I'd had a falling out with the fella I was with, as well. He was all for us staying but I didn't want to risk it.' She put down her glass.

'The husband?'

She shook her head. 'I never went down that road. It was a fella I'd met. We didn't get on. Not at the end anyways. There was him and oh, I don't know. A lot happened in England.'

'You held on over there a good while then?'

'I had to. Leastways, I thought I had to. I had met my son's dad there. Though I may have done as well to come home, for he didn't come from a family who'd been on the road, so there was none of the desire to be in the open air at the heart of him. And I didn't come back, for I didn't know what they'd make of me.'

'Were you never lonely, without your own people?' He sipped his beer, his brown eyes steady and bright as the glass.

'I was. But when I'd the young 'un, I'd to get on with it.'

'I could never have stopped so long.'

'Did you ever go to England?'

'I was there once.' He looked into the golden tones of his beer.

'But you came back. You'd sense. If a person didn't have anyone there you could get away. I was in a trap, for the fella I was with was able to force his view on me. But in the end I was afraid for Torin. He thinks he's smart but most of the time he hasn't two brain cells in his head. I couldn't stand the worry of drugs and the like. How'd I manage if he was caught up with that?'

'It's not much different here.' He brushed his mouth with his hand and licked his lips.

'If I found out he was involved in that caper, I'd break every bone in his body.' She gave a little laugh but it was the truth. She would be lost. Desolate.

'You've done right. You're a strong woman. There can't be many men who'd have the better of you.'

'Some did, easy enough when I was young with nothing in my head. You've a wife along, surely?' she asked, the weight of the glass in her hand. She set it on the table, ready to hear whatever it was he had to tell. After the drink, she could take it. A wife of course. And boys and girls. Maybe they were grown up and scattered around the world. America or England. Even Australia.

'I have not,' he laughed, 'for no one'd have me.'

'You weren't looking hard enough.' She forced a laugh.

There must be a woman. There was with every man, even if it was only a mother sitting in the corner, watching every inch of movement of the door. Her mother used say that there was a ghost of love around everyone.

'The women must've thought I wasn't worth hanging on to.'

'I don't believe it.' She touched his arm lightly. 'Wouldn't they be queuing up? A good-looking fella like you, must have had girls running after them.'

'It was not running after me they were, but hurrying off. To tell you the truth, I married once, a girl from Dublin. But I was young and braggish and after breaking up with someone. I fell into it like a bloody eejit. It's lucky for you, though. I've no son to keep company with. I've only myself. Even the old ones are no longer on the road but fixed up in houses. They're settled nice and cosy and we see neither hide nor hair of them.'

'Settled? Where?'

'New estates. A lot of houses were put up by builders and no one in them for a long time, so the Council handed them out to some of the old ones.'

'Old ones. How far away are they?'

'A few miles out the road. God, if I could remember the name of the place. Temple... Temple... vane. There are houses with two bathrooms. Would you credit it?'

'And it's old ones in it?'

'It is indeed. Why? You're not thinking of applying? You'd might stand a chance with your father if you want to put in an application.'

Her heart thudded. Delia. She hadn't seen her in years. The one true friend of her mother's who had taken charge of Caitlin when her mother died. Her father with the loss had wanted to be every which way on the road. Caitlin's face and hands. Those eyes. Lashes dark as an insect. Her luscious little body, smooth and soft. Not as dark as Kaybe but a lighter darkness which she had loved with a fierceness. A pinch in her heart which never ended. A cold thread ran in her veins. She had given away the years. Had not been able to manage on her own in London with no family, no mother or sister about. She had been young and stupid with only the sight of a man to bother her. The trouble. The nub. Kaybe's glowing dark skin had touched her with a kind of fire. He had told her they both came from a small island, though his was far across the ocean, but not distant enough to avoid colonisation by white men. His own inner night of sensing he had been passed over for jobs he could have done as well as any man, devoured her during their days. When she told him the colour of his skin was no concern for her, he seemed not to listen. But the more determined he grew in his sense of loss, the more she was drawn to him. She fell for him at the start and was drained when he walked out. She had been so empty of feeling or knowledge of how to cope it was no wonder a neighbour had phoned the Social Services. She had been hunted. Watched. All she could think was that everything would be all right if she could get to her mother. It had been a wild, bitter, dangerous thing with Kaybe, made more exciting by the fact he was unusual. Him from a people from across the Atlantic. He had told her about the land and the plantations of sugar cane running down the sides of mountains.

And the same thing happening with the next man. She had been furious with desire to be with Taylor. He had seared her life so she never returned to her own people. She might have. But he had burnt her out and left her with the shame of a child on her own. And given little enough time to see his own son.

'Are you all right, Eva? You're awful quiet.' Joe leaned in to her, fingers around his glass.

The dark wood of the table had coils in the grain. So many had likely passed through the pub. Friends, neighbours, those they had met on the road, made fun with, joined in songs with, quarrelled with. Delia might have been one.

'You sickening for something?'

'I'm not. I'm only tired.'

'Take it easy.' His arm slipped under hers. 'We'll get to know each other better soon enough.'

'To old times.' She raised her glass, attempting to match his optimism.

'No. To the future. We'll chase time over the hill.' He clinked her glass.

Out of the tiny bar, the sky looked down in perfection while so much was mucked up. She felt the warmth of him as Joe put his arm around her on their way back. His footsteps matched hers as they passed vans and trailers, a burnt-out car near the bins at the back, and bikes lying around. In sight of the trailer, she paused. Inside was a mess. No place for a visitor.

'I'd ask you in, but my father's after eating his meal and will be resting.'

'I know the way with the old ones. No matter.'

The next evening, as they strolled along the road by the fields, heading near the shore, she gathered her strength and asked him the question loaded in her all day.

'What way would you say I could get out to the estate?'

'A bus. There's plenty on the roads. Look for the one heading to Ashford. So I've put you thinking have I?' He squeezed her around the waist. 'I'd say it's tempting with the bathrooms and all.'

'It isn't for me. I was only wondering...'

'You'll be tired after our little walk and I don't blame you.'

She nodded, out of tiredness and a snaking apprehension as they followed a road back to the site. Templevane. So far and so near. A wild-goose chase would most likely be the end of it. He gave her a gentle kiss on the cheek. She spread her hands out on his back and drew him close. Through the trick and lapse of time, years fell away. She was young again and so was he. They were different people. The ones they wanted to be. She should have put on a bit of make-up. Mascara and lipstick would be an improvement. His eyes slid under folds within creases. He was weathered. They both were. But she was not the girl she used to be, running the length and breadth of fields. He was not the young man she might have crossed on the roads. His face was browned by the wind from journeying between trees and mountains, lakes and the sea. Inland places.

The sun glimmered on the sides of caravans. A gang of men and women stood outside the biggest trailer. The men drank from bottles, the women were seated and talking. Pity they never invited herself or her father in. The old woman of the family sat on a folding chair and leant to pat a black terrier. Eva walked to her own place. But Torin was ahead, aiming for the road with someone. A girl. Their backs passed around the corner. Gone. What way would it be with him? What had she taught him? Warm with shame, she put the key in the door but paused, letting it swing. She had done what she could. When the danger with the police was over, they would go back. Find a place to live in London, the two of them, and things would go on the same.

2

Rain started as he passed Dunnes, so he stepped into the doorway of a café, an old ladies' place full of tables with check tablecloths and tiny vases of flowers. The radio news talked on, 'and the Gardai are still looking for a young man seen leaving the house after the terrible murder of the young mother and her two daughters yesterday in North Dublin...' Torin breathed in deeply, not knowing if it was out of fear for what he had done or what he had not.

He needed to get out but there was nowhere to go. Nowhere except the bar. Even if she wasn't there, it was out of the rain. He crossed the road. Caitlin. Looking in the window of an expensive clothes shop. Handbags and flashy jewellery. Cool was the way to play it. Or perhaps he should head off before she had a chance to find out what an idiot he was.

'Hello,' she called, walking across, in between cars.

She was pleased to see him.

'You didn't come back.'

'No. I...' He was all too conscious of avoiding her and not wanting to.

'You coming in? It gets awful lonely with those old lads. How are the trousers?'

'They've dried out, thanks.'

Caitlin pushed at the door and went behind the bar, taking off her jacket and hanging it up. She called to Breen, letting him know she was back.

'What'll you have?'

'It's early. A Coke, please.' He tangled inside. He had lost it. Yet she drew him, had a solidity in those eyes. Her hair so thick and springy, he would love to touch it. Up close, her skin in daylight was lighter.

'You got back all right?' She wiped glasses dry, setting them in a neat row behind her.

Was it all she could think of, his messed up trousers?

'Fine thanks. I was okay. You… d'you live round here?'

She shrugged. 'A few miles the other side of town.' She pulled a fresh tea-cloth out of a cupboard and dried wine glasses and smaller ones that must have been for whiskey or brandy.

'In your own place?'

'You're kidding.' She gave a stifled laugh. 'I'm with a friend of my grandmother's. A bit of a *cailleach*.'

'What's that?'

'Irish for old biddy. She wasn't always like that. She used to have great energy and spirit. When I was younger, when we travelled around.'

'Can't you get your own place?'

'How? I've got nothing.' She clamped a bottle of whiskey into a clip above the bar, upside down in a perch where it shone hard and green.

'What about your mum and dad?'

She swung to face him, the tea-cloth over her shoulder as if she was a waiter in one of those fancy restaurants his mum was drawn to but never went in.

'Them. I don't know about them. From when I was small it's been me and Delia. Travelling all over. Even to England, once.'

If he kept talking, it would be all right. He would quieten inside and could listen better. Her voice rose and fell. Drawing him. The top three buttons of her shirt were undone and her lips were moist. But he mustn't keep looking at her.

'…near Bradford. We were there almost a year. She worked on a fairground. Then we moved to a circus. It had girls on the trapeze, their bodices sequinned with light as they flew in the air. Once, one lost her footing and slipped. I thought I'd die. I thought she would. But she was okay. She was quick enough to get a grip on a rope. It was a good time. We met lots of people and we were free. I liked it. I didn't think I would, but I did.'

A sharp wind blew through him. They had been in the same place at the same time. They might have touched each other's paths across the body of England. He remembered a song that Pauley had played, 'Paths That Cross'.

When he had travelled with his mum, the year of the coldest winter in Manchester, the sky was hard with frost. Icy. He and the lads had bunked school, daring to skate on the canal. Liverpool was the following spring, when his mum worked in a pub. Hull was another year. Another summer by the docks. The stench of fish clogging his throat. He had been glad to move on. They shifted to smaller towns, wherever the mood took her. Towns by the coast, run-down towns where the air sunk low on Wednesday afternoons with all the shops shut and all he could do with other kids, if they were speaking to him, was knock around by the phone boxes and do them in, if they got the chance. His mum might have found a job in a café, if it was the right season, and he played on the beaches. A landscape of slips of sand and low tides seemed to draw her, draw him, and he had not minded those places. She always knew someone or knew the friend of a friend as she tried to get from one small town to another. One night they had stayed on a lone station because the last train had gone but they had woken in the morning to take the first one out. It was going to Scarborough and she said it was a good omen, for the town was set in an English folk song. She said she believed it was meant to be, destined, and they would have a good time there.

One of the doors to the street flittered open. No one ever came in like that. The old men shuffled or coughed. Fuck. The police. Had to be. They had him. Someone had talked. Or whispered, or they had followed a chain of info. He stiffened. Palms moist with fear. He could rush to the kitchen door. Fight his way out through boxes and crates to the back way. He rose, knocking the table, sending the beer mats flying. But a tall scrag of a man slunk in. He had a goatee and spiky black hair.

'Give us a pint, Caitlin,' he called, striding to the counter, his arms spread open to her.

She slipped behind the counter, pulling the pump handle. The head of a pint came up zooming and creamy as she set it on the counter. Torin prickled with relief and fear.

'You do a good job, me darlin'.' The man's bloated belly hung out over a thick belt, though the rest of him was lanky.

'I should think so. I've been practising long enough, Sheridan. And don't call me your darling.' She stamped out the words.

'Why not, my dear?' His voice strained to a posh tone. He shifted to the other side of the bar as though it was his. He sipped from the glass but kept watching. The man leaned on the counter. 'Where've you been hiding these days? With your new friend?' He cocked his head towards Torin and laughed, a scrawly, ragged laugh.

'Don't be thinking any more about me.' She walked to another table where she gathered empty glasses on top of one another and put them on the counter. She gave a table a swipe of her cloth. The man neared, clamping his hands on her back. She shivered. Torin tensed. He should not be there. He did not want to see this. Women always had stuff to deal with.

'Come here, *a gradh*. Put your beautiful lips upon me.'

Torin fought to keep his hands quiet and not knock the man. Smash his face. What he deserved. He was a git. Like men his mum brought home after nights in the club, when she could not say 'no' or tell them to bugger off but let them steal her time and goodwill. Trample on her loneliness but give nothing back.

'Me heart.' The man leaned towards her. 'I'll sing you beautiful songs. I've been aching for you all the time since I first took a look at you.'

'I can get my own songs.' She struggled to get out of his grasp.

'I can do nothing to please you. What's happened? You doing a line with some other fella?' He smoothed down his jacket.

'I don't want the bother of any man.'

'You didn't mind the good meals I gave you. Come on. What's got into you, darlin'? We could have great times. What do I have to do to convince you?' He pulled her close and traced the shape of her face with a finger. 'You're a sweetheart. Wherever I am, I'm thinking of you.'

'Leave off.' She pushed him.

A U2 song clanged to an end. Torin rose, relieved there was a chance of other music. He jabbed in a different selection. Stone Roses. An old song. Gritty chords straining, lashed. He needed to drink up and get out so he pretended to read the beer mat, flipping it back and forth. 'Drink fills the void.' A blade like an Indian scimitar, decorated with squirls and leaves on the handle. Harjit had shown him one his father owned. A ceremonial sword, Harjit had said. Torin could do with one to slash through the man's crap.

'Come on. A dance for old time sakes. Put your head here. Don't fight the chance of a good time, Caitlin.' He pulled her forward while she tilted back

His eyes were darkly on her. What was worse was the way his body softened to hers. They moved slow as night, streamed dark as rivers. The man rubbed his cheek against hers though she pulled back. He swept around slow and firm. His hand was tight as a belt upon her.

'What are ye starin' at?' He turned in the slice of a second. 'Mind your own business. Don't be looking the way a cat'd be looking at a mouse.'

He was old enough to be her father. Torin was sick at the thought. The man had yellow teeth and his skin was grey. Jeans hung off his thin frame. His bony head looked too large. She untangled herself from the hold and walked towards the bar.

'I've things to do. Work. Some of us have to. Some of us don't mind it doing it,' she said.

'Come on.' The man pressed after, stretching his hands down her back, folding into the movement of the song.

The air was tense. Torin wanted to leave but he didn't want not to see her. He rose to turn off the selection even though he feared the man might raise a fist.

'You think I'm a sack of spuds?' She jabbed the man's chest. He laughed and pushed onto her. 'Get offa, you *druchtin*.' Her nails scrawled his face.

He let go of her with one arm and patted the reddening cheek. 'You'll have a good time. Just the two of us, like before.'

She leant over the counter, stretching for a tea-towel and whacked him with it.

'You b—! Stoppit,' he screeched, raising his arms to protect his head. 'You're no good but for cursing.' He brushed his cheek, wiping off blood. 'Ah, you're a tough one. Always were.'

'Leave her alone.' Torin shivered, while wanting to land the man one.

'What did you say, matey?' The man said the last word in a jaunty, taunting manner, squaring up. His nostrils full of hair, flaring.

'Get off her,' Torin said.

'Christ. What kind of place is your accent from? London?' His breath was thick with the fever of drink. 'The big city. With the big shites. Why don't you fuck off back there?' He lunged, attempting a blow. Torin dodged low and the man hit a chair. He rubbed his elbow. 'Little eejit.' He glowered. 'Friend of yours is he?' He turned to her. 'Ah, you're as bad as the rest. Taking a good look but no good to anyone.' He turned away.

'So bugger off.' Torin opened the door wide.

'You little fast one. I might've known it was all I'd get from you,' the man shouted over his shoulder.

The double doors slammed shut behind as he left. It was quiet with the depth of his absence.

'Thanks. He used to come in a lot. He bought me a meal a couple of times in the hotel. Then he stopped. S'pose I didn't do what he wanted.' She sat awkwardly on the edge of a stool, pulling down her skirt and smoothing her hair back.

'Which was what?' He did not want to hear but he had to. If whatever there was between her and Sheridan stood between them, he had to know.

'Oh, moving in with him. To some house he had up the country. I always forget he's likely to turn up and then he does. I should know by now.'

'It's all right.'

'He was telling me how the house has lots of land with a river running through and great sweeping trees to the side of it.' She kept glancing towards the door.

'Sounds good. If you want it.' He struggled to be enthusiastic.

'I don't. And I told him. He said he can do foundations, bricklaying, plastering, electrics, the lot, and will I go with him? Will I hell! He's old. The face of him, puffed up in places, wrinkly in others. Anyways, I don't want to live in a house.'

She gathered glasses with a sharp fury, running her cloth quickly over the tables. Her movements were stiff and awkward. He wanted to say, it doesn't matter. I know you're glad he's gone. I am. He can't touch us. It's over. But she worked steadily, as if used to intrusions.

The man reminded Torin of one of his mum's boyfriends from years ago, that one of her friends had described as a 'toe-rag'. He had taken off to Salford, leaving her desolate. She stopped eating and did not get up in the mornings until after three weeks, she started back to her cleaning job and she was his mum again, slumped in the armchair late in the evening after the jobs, gone in the mornings when he left for school. Talking of men she had met, men whose charms dazzled her and for whom she fell.

When Caitlin finished washing glasses in the machine, she emerged from behind the counter.

'My shift's over. Breen's seeing to the barrels. I can be off. I can leave with you.'

'Good. Let's get out of here.'

She grabbed her jacket and bag. The door swung behind them, glittering with light on the stained glass. Petals twirling was all he could make out, like his mum's tattoos. Rich and dark.

They reached a junction where two run-down garages competed for business and the mechanics hung around outside, wiping their hands with blackened rags or rolling tyres towards a car.

'I hate going back. Delia's got dirty clothes in the bath, soaking. I used to wish she'd be ill or struck down if I prayed hard enough.' She looked skywards. 'Whoever's up there, I don't mind who answers. I'm not fussy. The best times are when she's out of the way, gone to bed early. You'd need to in the winter because the night's so cold it'd cut a person. But I'll get my own place one day. And I'll not rely on luck from an old piece of dried shamrock in a saucer or the tooth of a cow going for slaughter on St. Bridget's day. And I won't be waiting for an old lag to take me, either. Sometimes, I fear I might hit her. The way she'd look at me, it'd make my heart split.'

The strength of her voice reached him, but she didn't look as if she would hurt any creature. The network of narrow streets led the main road, which opened to fields on one side and warehouses further down.

'Where can we go?' she asked.

'You wanna see where I live?' He was not going to take her to the house. Not where the others would take over and talk, making him look like an idiot. Not where Shane would meet her and talk his arse off. If he had to show her somewhere, he would have to go to the site, even if it meant meeting his mum. And if his grandad was there... Well, he had to hope she might be won over by him and his chat.

They walked under a sludgy sky the couple of miles beyond the town, past shops, offices and a run-down showroom which sold second-hand cars. In a field, cows bundled together under the trees.

'A good-looking horse.' She pointed to Feather.

'My grandad's.'

'You ridden her?'

He shook his head and laughed. 'I couldn't. Wouldn't know how.'

She walked towards the gate, where she lifted the latch and went through. Feather strolled over towards them.

'Hello, beautiful girl.' She patted Feather's nose and stroked the sheeny chestnut coat. 'D'you think I could get up on her back?'

'Now? Don't you need a saddle or something?'

'I managed without, the times we stopped in places with horses.'

'If you want.' He shrugged.

'Help me on, then.'

Feather neighed and nuzzled. Her nose was moist and her long lashes came down as Torin held onto the rope and hefted Caitlin on. She pulsed her legs against the sides of Feather and moved off in a steady walk. Feather livened, trotted, her coat glowing quick as a flame. Her step became a gallop as Caitlin took to the outer reaches of the field. She rode, leaning close on Feather's neck while the length of rope ran in her hands. Torin was dazzled that she knew what to do, yet feared that if she rode for too long and too furiously, Feather might become restless and spring her off.

Bringing Feather back, she jumped down. 'Beautiful girl.' She stroked Feather's side, her long fingers spreading over the dark coat.

They reached the bare strip of land beside the site where two little girls shoved and pushed each other and tumbled in a heap, squawking and laughing. 'Sally at the bus stop, one, two, three,' they chanted, starting another game. Three plastic crates dug into the ground. He wanted to say, I didn't always live in a place like this. I lived in a nice flat, once. Well, not nice. But not as bad as this. It was flats where we weren't allowed to kick a ball against the walls and lifts which roared at night and bins overflowing with rubbish.

A collie sniffed the green plastic bag of rubbish his mum had put out. The revolving washing line was buckled and his grandad's horsebox waited forlornly to be repaired.

'This is it.' He put the key in the door. It was quiet and he wished hard that no one was in, and no one was.

Inside, he cleared magazines off a chair and pulled his mum's clothes from the bed into the wardrobe, already bursting and the door not closing tightly. Two pairs of trousers fell against the bin and a pile of dirty clothes splayed on his bed.

'Your mum's?' She picked up a pair of silver shoes with tiny straps around the ankles. A silvery flower glowed on the front. She slipped her feet from chunky, mucky boots into dainty shoes with silver bows. The impression of her toes was visible.

'I wouldn't be seen dead with her if she wore them out.'

'The heels are crazy.' She took them off and lifted a thin layer of fabric from a dress hanging up, her fingers visible underneath. 'Mmm. Beautiful.' Silky purple slid like water. Red fabric flowed, rich and dark. A V-neck plunged and fabric flowers clustered at the centre. She fingered the petals, stroked them. 'I'd love clothes like this, even if I never wore them.' She lifted a dress balancing on the door of the wardrobe and held it out. The neckline curved in a heart; the sleeves were cut past the elbow with seed pearls at the edges. She took it off the hanger and smoothed it over herself. 'This is lovely. Oh.' She folded back the fabric, showing the underarm inside mottled with the trace of dried sweat. 'It doesn't matter. It doesn't show outside.'

'I don't know why she brought these. She won't need them.'

'You mean there's nowhere nice to go around here?' She kicked against a bag stuffed under the sofa bed. 'What's this?'

'More of her stuff.' He kicked the plastic bag under the bed. 'But we'd better head off.' If we don't want to meet her, he could have added.

His mum had too much stuff. She had stumbled along on platforms and on the boat with two fat cases on tiny wheels but he had no idea the amount of clothes in them. The red dress drew him, but the sweat and stains were embarrassing. He might have shown off too much of her. Made her look mad or odd or both.

He shoved a packet of chocolate biscuits into his pocket and they left. Vans and cars were parked close to each other and the ground was muddy. A woman hung out clothes on scrabby bushes. White and green blouses blew, billowed fat stomachs. Trousers draped and little girls' dresses danced.

'I'd better be getting back. I'm expected and I can't face another row with Delia.'

He saw her off the site, walking up the road to where she could catch a bus.

'I'll be fine the rest of the way.'

'Okay, see you.'

'Bye. See you,' she said.

Empty, he headed back but there was nowhere to go to. He walked past the site into town, as if seeking where they had started from.

In a man's fashion shop he riffled through rails of expensive stuff, clothes he would never wear anyway. But he knew the music in the background: a garage mash by Trojan Index. Marcus's brother had played it at a party, a celebration for a video one of his mates was an extra in. They had bunched in the tiny kitchen on the twelfth floor and looked down over the balcony, out of their heads. It was a wonder no one had tipped over and landed on the pavement. He slipped out of the shop, past racks of tee-shirts for fifty quid and vests costing even more.

The internet café was open, the shop window showing the screens. He went in and sat at a screen under the humming strip lighting. He scrolled sites and messages for news. 'Ripthestreets' would tell. Marcus's mate had started it. Torin clicked in. A photo of the park they used to roam around. The scuffed football pitch and worn-out play area for kids. The dark blue roundabout they used to ride. Another shot showed the canal at the back of the flats. On either side, beyond strands of tall grass, blocks of flats and houses rose by the railway line, a liquorice-black streak against the dusky horizon.

He followed the thread. Going deeper. Into old posts. Delving. Going under. A calendar of what he had left behind. Dates drawing him. Names. No one was ever who they said they were. He clicked on. Going in to the messages. Two people had been online. Babyface and Firecracker. He didn't know who Firecracker was but everyone knew Babyface knew Big Ian. The round-faced boy who followed after him.

Firecracker – That boy still in hospital?

Babyface – Think so

Firecracker – He'll get better.

Babyface – He might.

Firecracker – You been out and about?

Babyface – Not much. U couldn't go no place. Freakish. Only went round my friends in South London.

His eyes strained as the words stared back. Little hammers hitting. That night all over again. His palms were sweaty on the mouse and kept slipping. His neck was hot with an ache as he leant into the screen, as if he might hide what he read from anyone passing. They had argued over getting a bus to Finchley and which film to see. He had not cared. He did not have much money but they ended up straggling the pavement of the High Road while red lettering glared 'Stavros' from the kebab shop. They had waited while he checked his money. They even discussed getting a Chinese from Fragrant Harbour. They were still talking when Big Ian's gang appeared. Sifting behind. Shadowing. He had thought of scarpering. Next thing, it's over. Over before it began. He clicked to a link for the local paper and ran through. A headline posted up said the boy who had been stabbed was still in hospital. His condition was worse. The doctors thought he might make a recovery but he was in danger of sinking into a coma. The weapon had yet to be found.

His heart thudded and he was dizzy. He held onto the table, making himself breathe deeper. He had not meant it to be like this. He pushed through the rest of the paper, pictures of flower shows and kids from a local school showing off their paintings. Nothing else. But he knew as much as he needed. He saw the police closing in. Someone letting his name slip. One of the gang who had stood around. Who had been passed a knife. Who might have done it. Someone would mention his name and where he was. He shifted in the chair, as seconds slipped out of the box at the bottom of the screen. His breath tightened. His face warmed. If the police did their job right, they would want to talk to him.

Harjit's mum had glowed in her flame orange sari. Harjit's dad, stocky with a dark moustache, had driven past one evening in a dark green ages-old Nissan. But the car was gone. Quick as a flash of light on chrome. Quick as his son went down.

Time was up. He had no more money. Words were not enough, anyway. The guy behind the counter, in a check shirt and beard, like a student, glanced up.

'See you,' he called, as if Torin was an old pal. A light shower began as if the rain before was not enough. The world was tumbling and it was difficult to know where to go.

3

Because Pauley had to go to his dad's to pick up trainers and jeans, they called to his house. The pebble-dashed terrace stood in a treeless street. A deep blue Rover stood on a scrubby patch of garden of the house next door, and on the other side a pile of black bags sprawled. A cat or dog had bitten them. The houses faced an old gravel pit made into a lake, absorbing the grey light, where Pauley said he had seen golden plover and teal. Torin followed his gaze to the sky. He could not see the birds and wondered how Pauley knew so many from simply their wing markings.

Two scrawny black-and-white sheepdogs scrabbled for food on the dry grass at the front. They nipped at each other. A shuffling of feet behind the front door. It opened slowly. The man in the bar. Sheridan. He stood in the hall, glowering. Torin shook in his bones. An unmistakable trail of scratches ran down Sheridan's cheeks. Caitlin's fingers. He saw her up close to Sheridan and wanted to run.

Pauley was already in the hall, stepping over piles of old newspapers and junk mail. The oddness of Caitlin linked to Pauley's father stuck in his throat. He wanted to know but this wasn't the place to find out. Avoiding a broken chair, they shuffled past bundles of newspaper and undelivered leaflets clogging the hall along with a bulk buy of baked beans wrapped in polythene. Pauley said his dad had been in the house for years but never got used to being settled. He had only come to live there after his leg was broken one winter. Two electric fires, a bicycle and a cooker were abandoned in a corner. A stench betrayed stale bread and beer. Crumbs were brushed to the corners of the kitchen or crushed underfoot. Up close, Sheridan's eyes were a dirty blue. Thick black hairs stuck out furiously from his nostrils.

'Where've ye bin?' he growled.

'Out.' Pauley pushed on to the kitchen.

'Jesus, I know you were out. I'm asking what you were doing? Where've ye bin the last couple of weeks? On holiday?' He leered, smelling of spirits, his stubble rough and the rims of his eyes reddened. He trailed after his son, persisting. 'Who are these ladeens?' he slurred, attempting to push Pauley against the wall. Shane stepped back; Torin cowered. 'And who, may I ask, is this fella?' The thin, bedraggled face looked down. 'Don't I know you from some place?' He smiled with dull yellow teeth. 'What's yer name? D'you have one or are ye always like this, without a tongue in yer head?'

'Torin.'

Pauley cut in, taking his father by the arm and leading him to a chair in the kitchen. Torin hung back. Empties littered the floor along with stacks of old newspapers and two black bin liners which had collapsed, the openings falling away to reveal a load of clothes. Pauley led them to the room at the front. It was cold. A long whitewood room divider took up most of the space. Shelving displayed photographs, and plates with lavish red flowers. A leather sofa which had once been white was stained and scuffed. The television was on and two women with stiff blonde hair gabbled in front of a display which showed parts of a word beginning with 'B'.

'Let's see what's on the other side.' Shane leant across to get the remote.

Torin sank back in the sofa. The flat screen, which took up a good bit of the room, was one good reason for being there.

'This film's started,' Pauley said.

'It's old, man. Black and white. I can't watch that.' Shane slumped down.

'There's nothing else.' Pauley skimmed through the channels. 'It's all kids' stuff.'

Torin didn't care what they saw. If they kept watching something they might forget about Pauley's dad. He might forget about when he had first seen him.

'Hasn't he got Sky?' Shane asked.

'Course not. He wouldn't pay for it,' Pauley said.

'Then it'll be rubbish.' Shane pointed to a man on the left of the screen. 'Look. It's a Western. Really old.'

A man in a cowboy hat rode into town. Two mean-looking men were at the station with a ticket collector who looked terrified. The land was bare and open; scrubland with a couple of stark trees.

'You all right, Pauley?' Torin asked.

'Yes. But I wish I knew what he was up to.' He glanced to the door edgily and fidgeted on the sofa. 'It's too bloody quiet.'

'Don't worry. He might be drunk, or sleeping,' Shane said.

'Or dead,' Pauley laughed.

'Yes, well. Hey, Torin,' Shane said. 'She looks like your mum.'

'Does she?' Torin frowned at the screen.

'Kinda oval face,' Shane said.

The woman on the screen, riding in a carriage, was slim with a quiet, pale face. His mum was chunkier. Not fat, but not as slim as this woman. She placed her hands neatly in her lap. Everything about her was trim. The cowboy looked great with his big hat and holster. The woman sat up straight. Shane was right. The woman was prettier than his mum, but otherwise was like his mum in the way she held herself. He leaned back in the sofa. A guitar rested in the far corner, its slim body curved and gleaming.

'This yours?' Torin asked Pauley.

'Yes.'

'Why don't you have it down at the house? Can you play it?'

'A bit.'

'He's pretty good,' Shane said.

'I've never seen anyone play the guitar. Not close up in real life. Can I hear?' Torin asked.

'All right.' Pauley stretched to turn down the television. He picked up the guitar, holding it as if it was a baby.

'You still here? Having a wee bit of a sing-song?' Sheridan thundered into the room. 'You're going to give us a song, lad. Good. Give us "The Parting Glass".' He sank to the sofa, crushing in.

Pauley was pale and frozen. Torin hoped he would play, that he would not think they were too demanding. Pauley leaned into the guitar. The notes came swimmingly as his voice coiled into the empty corners of the room.

'... her rosy cheeks and ruby lips, I own she has my heart in thrall...'

Caitlin. The shape of her cheeks, her ears. The sweep of her neck. He wanted to hear more but Pauley turned away and rested the guitar leaning against the wall.

Sheridan slumped in his own darkness. His face was scraggy and wasted as if he had barely been listening.

'Have you any money?' He leant into Pauley.

'No.'

'You've a bit hid somewhere?' he bellowed, his face tight with irritation.

'I haven't got any money.'

'I don't believe you. You've something, ye bugger.'

Pauley twisted away his arm, freed himself from the grasp.

'What are ye doin' here?' Sheridan turned and glared at Shane and Torin.

Torin wished he had the nerve to smack him, give a jab in the gob and scarper, but Sheridan kept his eyes fixed on Pauley. Shane got between them. Sheridan turned. Torin was sure he would go for Shane. Instead, Sheridan gave a last thrust at his son and turned away.

'You're no good, the lot of you. Annoy the dead you would, gathering up every kind of person on earth and bringing them along here to be pestering me. And this one the worse, for I've met him before and he's not the sociable type.' He slurred and swung a jacket over his shoulder as he stumbled out, up the stairs.

'Let's push off.' Shane edged to the front door and Torin followed.

'You go on. I'll collect my stuff. I won't be long. He'll soon be off out for the night,' Pauley said.

On the thin road out of the estate, when Torin looked over his shoulder, the house was small and dark in the fading day but a light shone from a window upstairs. Pauley watching, looking down.

'He's a bastard. How'd he get like that?' Torin asked.

'Pauley says it was drink. And his wife going off. Pauley says he was never the same after. He drank when she was around, but he drank more afterwards when she wasn't.'

At least Pauley had a dad. And knew where he was. His mum had not given much away about his own.

They walked down the main street and passed the internet café. Torin slowed down.

'What's wrong?' Shane asked.

'Think I'll go in for a bit,' Torin said. 'Catch up. See what's going on.'

Shane glanced towards the greasy glass and the cramped tables with screens. In the back, a man was serving at a counter.

'Okay. See you later.'

'I won't be long. Shit. My money's in my other trousers.'

'Want a few euros?' Shane pulled a scraggy ten euro note from his pocket. 'Here.'

'Thanks. See you.'

The café was full and he had to wait for a girl to finish on a computer. He logged on, clicked onto ripthestreets.

Firecracker – What's the scene?

Babyface – Nothing doing.

Firecracker – Quiet round here, ain't it?

Babyface – More than used to be.

Big Ian must still be around. The police had not got to him. He was liable to do more damage. Torin searched through back pages but there was no reference to the night of the stabbing. His stomach lurched. He clicked and let images of the park and street parties, someone's rave and a skate-boarding competition run away.

He looked for what was on in Islington and Hammersmith. He crawled to a site for Arsenal. The shop had shirts, mugs, scarves. New gear for the season. Stuff that cost, that he could never wear unless some of it got lifted. Harjit used to go with his dad. Lucky bugger. If Torin could not have his dad physically he would trawl him, trace him, track him down on sites. The least he could do was chase after him and try to find him.

He keyed in 'John Taylor'. All his mum had given him and the fact he had come from the west of Scotland. The screen opened to a roll call of names. Mostly people in America. Estate agents, lawyers, an actor. Some living in Australia. He ran through the links. Too many people in too many different places not giving him what he wanted. He should not have started this. He should be satisfied with the bare facts. Ten minutes left. Photos spilt onto the screen. Unspoilt beaches. Hills. Fields climbing mountains. He pressed on, racing. Images streamed. Sand dunes, wide plains of light, men on bicycles leaning into a wind. It was similar to where he was, the same but different. Expanses of land. A wavering line of hills. This was where he belonged, what he was meant for, but his hour was up.

At the old house, he and Shane took down the tent Shane'd got from his old man. It had seemed a good idea, a couple of weeks back, but they had not used it. Falls of rain had found a tear which leaked. Shane cut the lip off a can and while they waited for Pauley he opened a packet of fags he had nicked and offered Torin one. They smoked outside until a light shower sent them in. A thin net across the dirty windows, torn in places, gave a drizzling light and the shimmering side of a mountain with a sprawl of bog.

Sitting on a box, Shane hugged his knees. They smoked. Sounds of the evening rose: long moans of a car in the distance; a lonely dog; children's fading cries as they came in from play.

'I'll wear this tonight to keep out the cold.' Shane pulled a big coat from a nail by the door.

As he spread it on top of the mattress, Pauley crashed in, his face pinched white and bruised around his left eye. Someone had left their mark.

'You all right? Sit down. Have some of this,' Shane offered a can and produced a sandwich of limp bread with a sliver of cheese falling down the sides, a squeal of tomatoes dangling.

Pauley took a slug of beer.

'I shouldn't've stayed. He kept going on about money. I won't go back. Not ever. I've got all my stuff, shirts, trousers, jackets. He's full of shit.'

A cut above his eye looked sore. A streak of dead blood stuck. His cheek had the impress of fingers. Sheridan had done a good job of doing him in.

'He hit you,' Torin said.

Pauley nodded. 'And smashed my guitar.'

'Why?'

'Cos he's mental. He threw a bottle at me. It missed but got the guitar and broke it.'

'Fucking awful.' Shane put down his can.

'I've thought about getting a gun. It'd be easy. But afterwards…' Pauley said.

'It'd be prison. Life.' Shane stabbed the ground with his toe.

'How long's life?' Torin asked.

'Twenty, twenty-five years.' Shane wiped the top of the can with his cuff and sipped.

'Could I bear it? I'd say I could.'

'A friend of my dad's, years ago, did some woman in and was lucky to get eighteen years. He went to Mountjoy. Said it was a terrible place. That's the trouble. Killing screws up the rest of your life,' Shane said.

'It's no good then. Not worth it.' Pauley sank back against the wall and pulled his jacket around him. When the rain stopped, he went outside and walked to the edge of the field.

A shiver ran through Torin and he followed after. He wanted to ask Pauley about Caitlin, but Shane was around. She was probably working. He would like to step into the bar but he wanted to be on his own when he next saw her.

'Will your dad come here?' he asked.

'He wouldn't dare. Doesn't know where I am, anyways.'

'What'll he do?' Torin asked.

'I couldn't give a shite. He can do what he likes. There's nothing for me to go back for. Nothing he can give me. Soon as I can get out of here, I'm off.'

'Where'll you go?'

'I'd love to go to London,' Pauley answered starkly. 'Be a hairdresser.' He smiled. 'Good money. Get in with a fancy salon. Do an apprenticeship. Soon have women chatting, becoming regulars.'

Yes. Women customers would go back to him. He would chat and make them feel good, his slim fingers wafting around their hair.

They went in and Pauley lay down on a bed of old coats and blankets. Shane got out a pack of cards, greasy with wear. Shane dealt. Torin's King and Knave looked up. A low throb of a techno beat pulsed. Shane had more stuff than they did, though it was really his elder brother's, who had headed off to Dublin. Torin shifted to get comfortable on the scratchy blanket. At least with his mum he could get round her, and she worked to get what she wanted, even if half the time she did not know what it was she was after. You needed someone to stick up for you. He should go and see her, not for the food but to see how she was. A week before, his granddad had said she had to go to hospital to have tests. He had not known what for but said she was a fighter, whatever was wrong, adding that there were all kinds of medicines doing great things nowadays.

Night came down. Empty lager cans piled in the corner. Newspaper spread on a battered case for a table and dusty rags of lace curtain covered the windows. The other two were sleeping. Torin went out for a piss. His phone pulsed and he scrabbled to get it from his trouser pocket.

'How you doing?' Marcus.

'Okay. Any news?'

'The court case's been adjourned.'

'Why?'

'Some technical thing. They have to get more evidence.'

'Anyone go to it?'

'No. Keep away's what I say. News'll get out soon enough. Thought I'd let you know. It's not good. But it's not bad neither.'

'It's all we've got then? They question any more people?'

'Not sure. No one's saying much. I'd better go, now. S'long mate.'

'Thanks.'

He sank back to the mattress and lay down, trying to settle, pulling up the worn blanket over his shoulders. He stretched out his legs. He turned, shifting to get comfortable. Marcus's voice took him back. Torin saw him slinking around the streets they both knew, kicking a ball around, hiding out in the park, meeting someone who had grass in the cemetery. Going by the canal. He didn't know if it was any easier being at a distance. If it made him safe. But what was going on over there was huge and encompassing so he was best out of it.

4

Caitlin led Torin out of town, past newsagents, small pubs, the two supermarkets both proclaiming good value, the used car garage and the church. Early morning rain had ceased and the air was fresh, showing up the fields in the distance. He felt naked with the gang but this was different. She seemed to fill the land and sky, his whole view. The angle of her head when she spoke, the run of her voice and her burnished skin. They reached a road of new bungalows, with double garages and well-laid lawns showing an easy wealth. This side of the town was new, with identical houses in rows.

'I used to wish I lived in a new house with everything shiny and in its place, but then I'd see the people who lived in those kind of houses and realise I'd never last.' She pushed a strand of hair behind her ear.

In her baggy trousers and boots scuffed with mud, he could not see her living in one. Her tight curls of hair had sprung loose, revealing the whisper of a scar, a crescent moon on her left temple. The skin was lighter, where it tried to heal. Sheridan might have done it but Torin was too scared to ask.

The road eased to fields and scrubby, dry land, then a row of bland white warehouses and superstores. In the distance, the shriek of a police siren tore through and he paused, shivering.

'You okay?' she asked.

'Yes, fine.'

They were coming to get him. It was over. He couldn't go on pretending. The air had fallen quiet. Caitlin stood in front of him, frowning. A bee hummed. The air sank in its own weight of silence.

'You sure?'

'Course.' He edged a smile. 'I'm fine.' They crossed a ditch and pasture with nettles and dock leaves. 'It's so open and bare. Nowhere to hide. Looks like no one bothers with it.'

She laughed. 'This may not look much but it's worth something. Each plot is identifiable and handed down through families.'

The bog was flat, with rolling differences in the level of grass or soil. Inconspicuous land but worth something and whatever it was, was passed on through the generations. Is that how it was with everything? Being outside was disorientating. He had thought he was getting used to it but he was tipped off centre. Nothing was what it seemed and he was not part of it. Deep tracks cut the earth. Brown turves piled like the slabs of chocolate cake his mum used to buy from Shepherd's Bush market. She used to arrive when the stall holders were clearing up and they got to know her. How she loved sweet things. Maybe that was what was doing her in. He didn't know. Sometimes he didn't know anything about her.

A breeze lifted. A rough, bleak field had long grass and trees whose branches were frenzied in the distance. Pastel-shaded mountains rose on the horizon. A slide of a silvery river, catching the light.

'You haven't been out this way before?' She led on.

'No.'

'I'll have to make sure I show you around, then.'

'What's that?' He raised his hand to shade his eyes and pointed to the sliver of river on a hilly outcrop.

'The Argideen. It flows down the other side. Breathtaking views.'

'You been up there?'

'Once.'

'Not sure I could do it. The highest I've been's the twentieth floor of a block in Hackney where my mate Marcus lives.'

Marcus. He hadn't heard from Marcus for a while. Life was going on without him. It meant bad news. Or was it good? He was strung out on a line, dangling. The police must have questioned everyone by now. Was it likely anyone would split? He didn't know who knew and. if they did, what they would say.

'You all right?' Caitlin asked.

'I'm okay.'

'You're far away. What is it?' She faced him.

Strokes of dry grass rustled in the wind. Bare patches, then reedy parts.

'The police might come here.'

'Why? What'd they want?'

'A mate was stabbed. I mean, he was there at the wrong time. And I was.'

'The police are after you?'

'Maybe. I ended up with a knife. Someone handed it to me. It all happened so quick.'

'But they don't know where you are?' she asked. He shook his head. 'Good.' She grasped his arm, squeezed up to him, running her fingers over his cheek. 'I won't let them get you. I'll hide you.'

He smiled. 'Thanks. He didn't deserve it. If he hadn't been there... If I wasn't, it would all be different.'

'Did you know him, the one who got stabbed?'

'I knew him. And it wasn't meant to end that way.'

Stairs and a passageway had led to Harjit's front door. It was streaked with sun from a gap in the lift shaft. How would his sisters manage? His mum? His dad? All the different parts of his life. Bits which fitted.

Caitlin led the way across the bog as the mountain ranged higher, streaks of silvered rock. 'Whatever went on, you're safe here. Let's go along this way. Try to take you away from all that stuff. If we follow the track down the other side, it leads to a beach that's great for swimming. And it's warmer, as the bay's protected, but you can't get there any other way than climbing.'

Rock slammed the horizon, blocking the sky. A person could hide in the mountains. His grandfather had told him of when there had been a war in the country and families were split with the fighting. His grandfather had said his own father had been caught up in it. A young man of seventeen, he had taken to the hills, travelling dirt tracks with the sky for a ceiling. The land could protect, if he knew where to go. For days and nights, he could be secreted away. However long it took. If he knew how to ride, he might have been able to escape on Feather.

'The boggy earth crumbles, so be careful. Especially if you're on your own. One man from England was killed last summer. Lost his hold and fell into the waves.'

A jagged line of rock. Cloud shadow filtered to one side; on the other, the sun picked up sharp ridges.

'You're doing a good job of putting me off.'

'This way,' she smiled.

He followed along a wide slit of bog, sliced down on one side into a sheer drop. He picked up a dark piece of wood lying in the dry grass. Slim and angular at each end, two triangular parts opened like wings. He ran his fingers along the length. Knotty, leathery bark coiled away. He pulled it to reveal sleek whiteness. The wood arched like a naked shoulder. Pale as bone. Taut and slim, the way his mum's arms angled as she hung clothes on the small line strung outside the trailer. Her constant bending and stretching. She never complained of pain, but in the months since Christmas she had not been well. He put the wood in his pocket where it sat, an awkward, difficult shape he could not hide.

'The roots are thousands of years old. Dark ones are oak, older than the rest.' She knelt to a tangle exposed by a cut into the earth.

'Like the land's asleep.'

'Not much sleeping if you're working. I used to help when I was a kid, when we stopped places and there was work. Once, it was awful dry and I didn't have gloves. So I put on socks to cover my hands. The farmer'd only a big pair which kept falling off me. Bloody tough work it was, and any time we got we'd jump and run at the big pools in the drains where they used to keep butter years ago.'

She walked ahead and knelt at a pile of stones in front of a scrabble of bush. It was wiry and stunted, branches leaning, pulling towards the light. She crouched low and removed a thin cover of slate from the middle. A hole held a pool of dark water. The pool reflected their faces darkened with shadow. The sky's light was behind them.

'A mountain spring. Supposed to be a holy place. People prayed here in the old days. They'd hang bits of rags on the bush behind, kind of gifts to the saints.'

'What on earth for?'

'Special intentions. Prayers.'

'What? Prayers?'

'Yes. They worked. Seemed to. Once, a minister arrived from England, giving relief during the famine. He set up a soup kitchen near the well. The kitchen was said never to have run out because of saints guarding it. So you see, they say if you pray from here, your need'll be answered.'

An old story. The same as his grandfather had. Tangled and webbed so you could not tell one bit of truth from another. The ground was ragged, offering nothing except nettles and dock leaves. What was the use of it? Even he could see that nothing much could be grown but a tangle of weeds, thorns and thistles, grasses and reeds.

'Where'd you learn this?'

'Delia.'

'You can't believe it?'

She shrugged.

'I often came here with a worry and prayed and it turned out all right. You know, there might be something you could pray for?'

'I don't know how.' He could not drag out any words. Not prayers. More like questions. It was ridiculous, gazing at a crust of dried grasses and wilting flowers. 'What'll I pray for, anyway?'

'You must have something?'

'My mum's not well. She takes a load of tablets but she won't talk about it.'

He sank onto his haunches, grasses sticking. This was weird, but if it pleased her, he would do it. He closed his eyes. Shimmerings of scarlet. Blue streaks. Fidgety particles of orange showering.

He stood and they walked on, to a field where a bike lay, all angled and upturned but in one piece.

'Let's try a ride,' she said.

'But it looks crap.' The cycle was clunky with leaves of rust flaking. It had a weight of no other bike he'd come across. He'd last ridden a bike near the flat, when someone nicked a mountain bike and they'd all had turns until it got chucked into the canal.

'It's got two wheels. What more do we want?'

He steadied the bike. The leather saddle was ragged but he got on. She sat on the cross-bar. Up close, he was warmed, uncertain, but he reached round her and grasped the handle-bars.

They set off, crunching over stones and grit. The bike was lumpen and he strained to get control to raise speed, for there were no gears. As they swept on down a slope, she swung out her legs.

'I love this,' she said.

He was charged by her words. He might have said the same, but meaning more. Love itself, or something like it. He didn't know what had happened, but this was bigger and warmer than anything he'd known and he was pleasing her in a way he had not expected and he wanted to go on, with her against his chest, her hands between the span of his own, as they creaked along. Careless. Delighted.

The chain crunched and slipped but the bike ran on. They kept going and going and their speed increased until they toppled, landing in a heap. He lay against the frame, the wheels spinning.

'You all right?' he asked.

'I'm fine. We landed on grass at least.' She stood up. 'It was a blast,' she said.

He raised the bike. The oily chain was slack and the saddle had shifted out of place.

'Come on,' she said. 'Maybe we should head back.'

'You working later?'

'I always am, it seems.'

'I'll be along with you.'

'We can shove it off the path. It was dumped when we found it, so no one'll be after us.'

He pulled the bike into longer grass, where it sprawled like a thin drunk. It might have been a good bike once but its day was done.

*

'It's really blowy.' She pulled her jacket close, as he came to stand beside her. 'But I like the rough weather, keeps visitors away.'

'I don't hate it,' he said, sensing her judgement. 'It's just different. I don't know it like you do.'

If the lads at home could see him, they'd double up. They'd think... He could not imagine what they would think.

'Follow this path towards the sea,' she said, running ahead against the swell of the wind. Her voice battled through the gusts. 'I like it wild. I feel part of the place.'

He caught up and they took the path through a cleft in the dunes towards the shore. She strode on, possessing the land, while he hung back. Pale sand softened underfoot. Tough grasses fought each other in the wind and lashed his legs. The salty air caught his breath. At the edge of the sand lay shells and dried seaweed. Where did all these dead things come from?

The shell was dry, seaweed cracked and fell, disintegrating. He walked towards the sea, where rocks were larger and shimmered with light.

'Mind the wrack. It's lethal when it's wet, if you step on it,' she called.

At his feet a flow of bright green algae trickled around rock pools. He threw small grey pebbles into the sleep of the sea where scrags of seaweed splayed. Wind pummelled his face. She was a bit screwy, but if she liked being there, he did not mind. He hugged his jacket, wanting to feel her, her dark eyes, her warm skin. She was unlike any girl he'd met, and there had been plenty. But this was different. Wanting Caitlin alarmed him. He was lost. She disturbed his being. Filled it. He was more alive and alert, as if whatever she said or thought sank deeply in. He moved after her but she climbed through the dunes to get further down.

'What's wrong?'

'Sand in my eyes.' He rubbed them, feeling the grit on his skin and under his nails.

'We can go back, if you want?'

'I'm all right.' He blinked, fearing she was making fun of him. When he opened them, the wide expanse of beach was still there. 'Ugh!' He stepped back from a pale globule muscling fluid in and out, at his feet.

'Only a jellyfish,' she said, while he shied away. 'It won't eat you.' She laughed, bending to pick it up and holding it out while he flinched and felt foolish.

They walked into the endless sky, passing boulders and smaller rocks near the sea edge.

'We've come miles,' he said. The town was a smudge of indistinguishable buildings.

'We have.' She shaded her eyes, looking up the coast, and he followed her line of vision. 'But I come here a lot. Especially at night. I've seen the drowned moon. One time it's coasting the horizon, the next it's gone. Laid down on the water and drowned.'

He didn't quite get what she meant and started to go on, but his foot knocked against the maggot-ridden body of a sheep. Half of the body lay on its side, prey to a flurry of flies hovering like a gauze. They were a continuous haze around the curve of ribs and the knuckles of joints.

'Sheep fall over the cliff edge. Especially old ones, when they're blind and there's no fence.'

'What'll happen to this?' The dried skin and whitened bone was a mad tangle. He wanted to kick it out of the way but was scared it would break down even more.

'Nothing. It'll be there 'til it's eaten.'

'How long'll that take?'

'A few months. The sea'll wash it off. Take away those bones, spread them somewhere else and leave another pile of rubbish. One for the other.'

She walked towards the sea and a clutch of boulders. When he caught up, she was hunkered down at a broken bird sunk in the sand. It shivered, trying to fly. The fibres of the wing separated in places, like lashes, and flecks of mud scattered its wing. She leant to stroke the tiny body as it trembled; its beady, dark eyes were bright as she cupped it.

'Can you get it some food?' she asked.

'How?' He did not even know what they ate and was surprised the bird did not struggle.

'Pick up a stone and knock off one of them limpets on the boulder.'

He searched the big rocks. Strands of seaweed unravelled. He pushed the trails aside and scraped until the shells squelched off. A sickening green slime. He pushed it onto his hand. The squadge of flesh made his stomach turn. She lay the watery food near the bird.

'We can't do any more except leave it and hope it'll have a scrap of a life before it becomes dead meat.'

'Something'll eat it?' he asked.

'Some old dog or cat. Maybe a fox.'

This outside world overwhelmed him. There were no limits. The horizon slipped into the sea, one merged into the other. It was difficult to know where one began and the other ended. Where anything fitted. He was small against the hugeness of the waves. They fell back into the belly of the ocean, while a flurry of white spread at his feet. He was lost against the vast sky which swept down, brilliant and gaudy in its silver and gold light, exposing him.

Up ahead, Caitlin bent to pick up a clutch of pebbles. Turning back, she waited for him to catch up.

'What've you got?'

'Only these.' She opened her hand.

'They're nice.'

'Gems. Kind of.' She slipped the stones in her pocket. 'Well, as near as you'd ever get here.' Her face was open with pleasure, while he pulled his jacket close. 'Are you all right?' she asked.

'I'm freezing.' Raw wind was on his face, an echo billowing in his ears.

She ran along the shore and he chased after. He could barely catch up, unable to get a steady footing on the slippery sand trying to trap him. He fell, his hair messed up and his eyes tired with sand and light.

'Come back to the house,' she shouted against the beating wind.

'What about the old woman?'

'Delia'll be at the clinic. They collect her on a Thursday and it takes all afternoon to deliver her back. Please. She doesn't like me going out and she doesn't want me to see anyone but she can't have a hold of me all the time. I have to keep some piece of myself that's mine.'

They walked over the dunes to the small road. He did not want to meet the old woman. They could be difficult. The old lady on the site had shouted at kids who played around the trailers, and the one in the trailer near his grandfather had moaned into the night.

'Come on.' She raised his hand to hers and played with his fingers.

The idea of being coiled up beside her warmed him. He thought he had put her off but he wanted her, and either she wanted the same or she did not.

Leaving behind the beach and fields, they walked until they came to new houses in an area he did not know.

'Where are we?'

'Carlington. Not much further.'

She led through a network of roads of new houses to one at the corner of a square. She slipped a key in the back door and led him upstairs. Her room held the barest of furniture: a bed, a dressing table and a wardrobe. Dried seaweed draped a wall and pieces of driftwood stood in a corner. The air was salty. Her bed was under a window showing mountains in the distance. Oyster shells littered a shelf, along with shells long as knives. Chalk-white pointed skulls and coils of rope and netting lay amid tangles of branches, stones and shells.

'A sheep and a goat. But they can't hurt,' she smiled.

'Yours?'

'Yes. And this,' she dropped a stone into his palm, 'is yours.'

He opened his palm to a pale stone. 'Quartz. You liked it.'

'Did I?'

'You said so.'

'Thanks. How'd you get all this up here?' he asked, lifting the netting.

'Carried them. Had to, to make it the way I wanted. I've nowhere else. Delia doesn't want my stuff downstairs.'

She looked pained and it scared him. Whatever was going on with her and the old woman, he could not help. He could barely help himself. He was useless, wishing he could offer more, understand what she understood, what she was going through.

'I suppose I've to be grateful. I've little else, except maybe this. Give me your hand.'

He let her take his fingers, curving them round, making a ball shape. Opening them, she placed his palm within her own, looking at the pads of grubby skin, the rim of dirt clogging his nails.

'I see a figure in grey. A woman. I'm not sure. There's pure, clear water flowing across the rocks.'

His palm was grubby, with a graze from when he had scrabbled on the rocks for the oysters, and the beginning of a blister.

'What does it mean?'

'I don't know. I've only pictures in my head. I didn't ask to be able to do this. Often I feel a right eejit.' She removed her fingers, beautiful pale handcuffs. He wanted them around him always. For a long time, at least. 'I've told you all I can. You'll find this place far from here and there'll be peace.'

'What place is it?'

'I've no idea.'

'No one's ever done that to me.'

'Most girls have tech skills or are into beauty and make-up or are good at cooking. They might have a brain in their head and go to college. But I never stayed in one place long enough to learn anything. That's the most I have. Delia says it was handed on to me from my grandmother. All I know is, lots of people pretend they can do it and it's easy to play on others.'

He lay back on the bed and took her face in his hands. His eyes were liquid as he moved easily on her, pinning her to the bed, his arms locked over her head. She loosened herself and pulled off her top. On her upper arm, in squirls and lines of pinks and red, with others of blue merging, the wings of a butterfly spread. On her forearm, feathers of red slashes and pink weals criss-crossed. Scarred tracks. A flare of violence stirred and frightened him.

'How'd it happen?' he asked. She sat up, hugging her knees, rocking back and forth, deepening her impression on the bedspread. 'Was it him?'

'Sheridan?' She shook her head. 'No. A guy from Brazil. He was married. He said it didn't matter and he'd go home to sort it out. But I couldn't face it, so I left. I always run when I'm in a mess. Except he had a hold on me, but in the end I did it. I walked away.'

'That was good.'

'Part of me wants to keep walking. Walking out of here. Far away.'

He pulled back then leaned over her, his face to her arms and kissed the soft skin.

'Couldn't you leave?'

'Where'd I go? I've lived so much of my life with Delia. Travelled the length of England with her. Been in Scotland in the winter. Seen the mountains capped with snow. Gone to Cornwall. Worked on farms there. I don't know how I'd manage alone.'

'What about the time with those other men?'

'It was different. Delia and I'd big rows and I took off with them, though I was dependent on them and I didn't like to be. But you're different. I like you.' She rolled close. '*A leanh.*'

'What's that mean?' He rested his head in her lap, in the dozed warmth of the room, sealed in.

'Sweetheart. Or darling. Loved one. Delia used to say a word can heal but sometimes silence is better. I keep hoping love will save me. Save me from myself.'

He didn't know about that. He didn't know anything, except that being with her was the only place to be; she resting against his side, he stroking her hair. The world was bigger out there and she had seen more of it, had a firmer grasp of it than he did. He wondered what it would be like to travel with her.

*

Afterwards, he turned to her sleeping, her skin richly dark as the night breathing. Although she didn't think so, she was homed here, in a way he could not imagine. But being with her was the nearest thing. No one could get him. Not Big Ian. The police. Anyone. He had lain on his bed in the top flat in Kilburn, adrift among roofs in the listening dark, the breath of traffic below and calls of men working late in the garage across from their flat. A powdery smell from childhood among a tumult of blankets. A light, fragrance which soothed and the dangerous, unbalancing sensation of being alive.

An engine outside drew to a halt.

'Oh no! It's her.' Caitlin leapt off the bed towards her jeans.

'What?'

'The bus.' She pulled on a tee-shirt.

He jumped up, leaving a trail of sheets. He scrambled to put on his trousers. He slung his jacket on his shoulders.

'They're early.' She searched the floor for her knickers. From the street, a woman's voice rose, giving directions. 'Go out the back, through the garden.' Caitlin pulled on a sweater as she led the way downstairs and the door of the van thudded shut.

She opened the kitchen door while a key sounded in the front. He slipped out. The old lady was surprised to see Caitlin and a woman's voice said she would call the following week. He ran out the back through the stubbly abandoned garden. He nearly caught himself on a straggly rose bush as he pushed open the gate. When he had cleared the houses, he stopped to tie up his trainers.

Torin was hot and sweaty, gulping for air, unable to get enough. He hurried, gathering pace until he pounded the concrete strip leading to the garages and onto the main street.

Ceol na Mara
1

During the warm night, giving only broken rest, Eva threw off the duvet. It muddled with a sprawl of blankets on the floor. She woke in the early morning, out of a slug of sleep which had eventually trapped her, even if the dreams were ragged and torn and she saw a train cutting through the countryside, long carriages with endless doors and small compartments that she tried to enter.

A whiff of cigarettes hung in the air. She coughed. Her father must have been up a while.

'Is it food you want?' he asked.

He wore his tweed jacket over his pyjamas and might have had it on in bed, for all its creases. He shifted and covered his ways. Never liked explaining himself, so she had no clue when he might go out or who he was with. He had said he knew no one, yet he had spent time with a couple of old fellas he had met up with in a bar in town. She did not ask. It was his life. She had left him to it the day she took off.

'You don't look well.'

'I'm grand.' She rose, tidying the blankets.

A smell of fried bread and bacon wafted. She would have loved a cup of sweetened tea.

'If your mother was here, she'd have you better. She'd great healing...'

Only too clearly, she saw her mother making cures for any they met on the road: a woman who had headaches with a child coming; a man with a rash on his face; an old woman who lived in a small house by the sea, complaining of pains in her back like the waves. It was unsettling, bringing back her mother too vividly. The past clamoured. Fell on top of her like a shower of bullets.

'Is it the new fella you're thinking of? Are you a wee bit gone on him?'

'Course not.' She combed her hair.

'He has a notion for you, surely,' he declared, sitting on the edge of the bed and munching a sandwich of bacon and egg. Gloopy bright yolk dripped; curls of overcooked rind hung down.

'Why not? Are you surprised?' She flattened the blankets with a swipe of her palm across the length of the bed and folded it up to make a long seat.

'Any fella'd be glad to have time with you. I always said, you didn't give the lads who were your own kind a chance. You were gone in an instant with them foreign fellas when there were lads over here'd have you... There were plenty who asked. And we'd no way of knowing where you were, until the few bits of news back from whoever might have run into you over.'

At the table, in her nightdress, she spread hefts of butter on a slice of bread. If only she could sleep; let the pains of night drain out. She knew too well how she had left in a hurry, not giving the briefest care to him or her mother. If they had been waiting for her to travel home, she had not known or cared. The day she left Caitlin with her mother, she vomited in the ladies toilets at the bus station in Cork, wiping away the puke before the tetchy woman who looked after the place noticed. She had fought back tears, wanting the bus driver to go fast as the wind on the rough road to Dublin.

She dressed, keeping open the tall cupboard door to separate them. She would have some piece of modesty at least. Show her father she had standards, whatever about the past. She must not let him trawl over the old days. It would smother her, the way a blanket would be thrown over a one to keep out the cold. Lord knows, after all the running, she had not wanted to be landed with a young one on her own in England the two times.

'Joe'll look out a trailer.' She smoothed down the front of a blue sweater which should have been ironed.

Her father pulled on his trousers and a check shirt.

'Good luck to him, so. But you might have a notion and go off with him.' He shuffled the newspaper back and forth, searching for the horse racing pages.

'How could I, the state I'm in? Fit for nothing. Those damn tablets, I don't think they're doing a bit of good.' She rubbed her stomach as a lug of pain shot through her.

'You want to look after yourself. You worrying about the lad?'

She shook her head. It was not him, though she wished he was not gone so many days. She had no way of knowing where he was or what kind of people he was with.

'I won't be long,' she shouted, going down the steps.

'Why are you leaving so fast? Anyone'd think the banshees were after you. Can't I come?'

'I wouldn't want to tire you. I'm only going for a walk.'

'For the love of God.' He waved his arms distractedly. 'The doctor said you were to rest. Where are you going?'

The door clattered and swung. His words trailed until she no longer heard them, but when she glanced over her shoulder, he was still looking after her.

She passed the small blue caravan and the red trailer. A woman drove a van out. Bony and fierce, the woman had no sign of a man by her. Eva would like to have driven, taken herself all over the country. Visited places she had only heard of. Giants Causeway. The mountains of Mourne. She wanted to put places to the songs. Duneen. Dungloe. Tipperary. But she could just about tell one end of a car from another.

Beyond the fence, she was free. Tired, but free. Light-headed with relief, she walked off the clodding ache. A bare light picked out every living thing. A rage of spring, the hedges thick with leaves and the nips of hawthorn buds. The breeze refreshed her, though her feet were heavy as lead. She would go on, like the times she had walked into the sea with a giddiness and delight in the spray of waves. If she found Delia, what would she say? And if Caitlin was with her, what could she offer? What words after so long? Her throat caught and she could not breathe, but she pressed on. 'Keep going,' she thought.

For months after she had left Caitlin with her mother, she had seen her own child in every one passing. Her heart lurched towards them. She had to keep a hold on herself so as not to rush forward and take the infant out of its pushchair. She used make-up every day, but inside she was falling apart. She saw Caitlin everywhere, in the blue check dress with tiny embroidered flowers and the white collar. As each day passed, she had wondered what way her mother dressed the child. She saw the run of dresses and cardigans Caitlin might have worn and longed to touch them, but they were gone, packed in a brown holdall with a broken zip. All the clothes Caitlin used to wear were ready for wearing on all the other days running to a future she would not be part of.

Fields glistened, leaving the grass sodden. She walked in scratchy sandals, fleshy leaves brushing against her. The curve of the bridge to the shops rode over the river like a sigh. A man passed on his bike and a boy played with a stick and a dog. The land unfolded in stretches of small farms like those her father worked, fixing walls, mending pots and pans, sharpening shears, or to bigger houses where he might find a job for a week or so digging potatoes. Getting used to the walk, to the stretch of it, she could go miles.

A twenty minute wait for a bus. How did they manage? She had forgotten how few ran, but a bus arrived heading for Waterford. The driver told her of housing developments along the way. She would hang on until she arrived and he would tell her where to get off. The bus wove through villages and fine-looking houses, some with grey stone like those she had called to years back with her mother. She recalled a story of her mother's. A woman, Elizabeth Worthington had lived in a big grey-stone house, brought over by her husband, who was often away in London. Elizabeth was lonely without the social life she was used to in London. She missed the round of parties and dances and being able to play the piano, for her husband would not allow one in the house. He had a nervous condition from the Boer War and could not abide noise. Elizabeth saw few people except her husband's groom, a great horseman with whom she fell in love. Her husband returned from London and found them together. He was so full of rage he brought out his shotgun. The groom ran off and, knowing the lie of the land, escaped easily while Elizabeth, chasing after, fell into a river and was said to have drowned. Eva heard the hooves cracking along the road at speed.

She should have come back when her mother was alive. She should have borrowed money and come. Or stolen it. But this time would be different. She would watch herself and not go on with the drinking. It did her no good, the doctor had said before she left. He had told her to change her lifestyle. Lifestyle. She did not know what it was and did not want to disappoint him by asking.

Beyond the town, when the driver indicated, she got off. Near a network of roads, a couple of teenage girls hitched. No one would be bothered with her if she attempted it. She might have once, smiling, giving the glad eye, her skirt riding up. She walked on towards rows of new houses. An estate, surely. No. Dead end. Up here, a right turn, then left. One road leading to another. All the houses looking the same, it was confusing but she would keep walking. Even if it was dark when she arrived, even if Delia was not there, at least she would know. Her bones ached. She had little breath but walked the rise of a hill and made out a cluster of signs: Roseland. Broadfields. Templevane. Even if Delia was not here, Eva would keep on looking. She would not hide in the back roads. She would move up the country, travel around, find her.

The houses were tightly packed tiny boxes, clinging to each other like toys with white wood cladding at the front on the upper parts. Some had drawn curtains. Three cars were lumped on grass verges where tyre tracks made muddy ridges; one had a dented side, and the front of a dark green car was smashed. In a garden, an ice-cream van had 'Antonio's Exclusive Ices' and 'Watch the Child' spread on the back windows in worn-out lettering.

She knocked on the nearest door, but no one came. The neighbouring door, bashed in at the end and a crack in a square of glass, brought a woman in slippers, dripping a fag from her lips.

'Yes, missus?'

'Is there an old woman living round about?'

'There's a few, yes, that took up with houses a while ago. Were you wanting one of them?'

'I am.'

The woman looked over her shoulder and yelled, 'Stace. D'you hear that? Seen an old lady around? No? No, she didn't. I didn't either, sorry.'

'Thank you, anyways.'

On the next row of houses, the gardens were as small as stamps; a scrub of green but no flowers. A baldy man in a white vest came out of a front door and got into a car. There was barely room for him to drive, but after several goes he swung round until he edged the car off and came to a halt.

'You all right, missus?' He peered out of the car window. Nosey, the way everyone was if they got a chance.

'I'm fine thanks. Would there be any old ones around here?'

'Who you after?'

'A one by the name of Delia. Delia McArdle.'

'There were some put in the houses and one man died a month back. You'd not see them much would you, if they're old? You could try the blue door near the corner. I seen an old one in it a few weeks ago.' He nodded towards the end of the row.

He put his head back inside the car, glanced over his shoulder and the wheels squealed off, leaving squelchy mud. She went up the path of a straggly looking house.

Her heart was a brick thumping. She raised her hand to the half-open door. She should run away while she had time and before she made a fool of herself. She took in short breaths, unable to stop the shake in her legs. All this was wrong. She should not be here. Delia was clever and neat enough to have found the chance of a house in a place like this. To have taken up the offer with the Council. And yet was as likely to have gone off travelling, abandoning the house for the summer. Eva could see her slip out of the house early of a morning, a dainty handbag with her, her face made up, devilishly charming, having found a lift with a man who was going up the country.

'Hello,' she called. 'Is anyone here by the name of Delia?'

'Who's wanting her?' a dragged, worn voice called.

'Myself. Eva. Eva Finnerty.'

A pad, pad on the floor, inched near. A whistle of wind along an alley. It was all wrong. Wrong place. Wrong time.

'Who did you say you were?'

The crabbed voice took hold, spun around as a ball of wool passed through women's hands on evenings when Delia and the other women sat by the side of the wagons, singing quiet songs, an evening when one or two mothers keened for a lost or broken one who had died on the road before a doctor would come. The voice took her back to when they last met, when her mother was living, when the world was open and new, and travel and freedom, love and the tie of it, all things she had known under the sky, were possible.

'It's me. Kate's girl. Eva.'

The old lady clutched the door frame with one hand.

'Indeed, it is. Eva. And you've the one you're seeking in front of you.' Delia leant on a stick, around which her striped skirt fell to the ground, so no one would guess it hid a wooden leg in the folds, beyond the muddied hem. Her face was grey and creeping with wrinkles. The past roared. She was smaller and more delicate than Eva remembered. Years drained out. Eva was weak. She was soaked with longing to hear of the past and the present, but this was not the woman she had known. Where was the youthful woman, the lively woman who had been the close friend of her mother? She had let too many years slip.

'I wouldn't know you,' Delia grabbed Eva's hand, 'but don't they say the calf always returns to where it got the milk? Come in.'

The hall led to a kitchen with a table and two plastic garden chairs. A cooker stood in one corner with a worn saucepan of stew cooking. An electric fire blared with two bright orange bars.

From the basement of memory, Eva saw gold hoops of earrings and dresses with lace trim, others with velvet, and violet eyes the envy of other women. Until her accident, when she was run over and her leg damaged, Delia moved with grace and ease through the body of dances by the side of the road, the eyes of men and women upon her. She had an energy which had taken her door to door, carrying baskets, or helping her husband bend the metal for pails, washing in streams, cutting turf or peeling a sack of potatoes.

'Come in and sit down. You were great to come a-finding me. And not in the old places but in these new houses.' Under a dark blue scarf, Delia's black hair straggled, flecked with grey. 'I'd a longing to come.'

'You'd great *gradh* for your own people. It's how you must've been taking after your parents, the way they ran off together, making their own road, for your mother'd a blighter of a husband and they were lucky he didn't come after.' Delia sat in front of the cooker, from where an aroma of overcooked meat and vegetables rose. 'And here you've the benefit of good fresh air blowin' on your face. Living in cities did nobody any good, with never a bit of green but only old factories and shops. At least it was the way in England. D'you mind when we were on a site near Staples Corner?'

'I do.' Eva tensed. Her calves were tired with walking but she could not force this, could not push on to what she wanted, no matter how hard the road to arrive here. She had to reveal herself and what she wanted slowly over the grain of time. The fact struck: Delia could lay her out firm as any boxer might. Eva had let years fall and gather dust.

'You would, of course. The *creature*. It was good for the scrap from the factories nearby and it had three toilets and basins even in those days. I long for when we were on the road. Now it's only me and my old leg and this crutch. I see no one since I came into this house. Even the girl is little company.'

'You took her on after my mother passed. You were a great woman. Few'd do the same.'

'Your mother would've for me, if I was in need of help.'

'And how are you keeping?'

'Not so bad or so good. The truth is, since I came to this place, I was barely out of it for the pains in my old leg. I wasn't at Mass once.'

'Were you not?'

'I do say my prayers between these four walls.'

'So you like it here?'

'It's good enough for the while. I was glad for the house when I was put in it and I've come to be used to it. I've put myself out of the way of things amidst strangers, but I don't mind.'

Hot and sweaty, Eva fidgeted on the plastic chair, straining to make herself comfortable and not knock against the old boots lined up by the wall. She had expected meeting would not be easy, but not like this; a beguiling friendliness, the tangle of facts leading her on a strange path. She was dizzy with answering. Answering and questioning. And the remembering, like a spring bursting through stones. She sat with the question she longed to ask, huge as a boulder.

'But I'm not complainin'. I've a roof over my head after the years of travelling and I have the few comforts I want. I'm past noticing any staring eyes on me, the times I'm out, the way we'd look at a *gombeen* long ago. The way these people'd think we're exotic birds landed out of another continent. When I arrived with my bags and clobber, they strained out the windows to look. But ever since, nothing. They're all too pleased with themselves with new carpets and cars in the driveways. So they don't bother me. Put on the kettle and we'll have a cup of tea.' A crumpled black kettle sat near the cooker. Eva rested it on top of the gas. A battered saucepan with blackened sides gurgled on another ring. 'The years have done little to you, not like myself. I have the look of wars about me.'

'You have not, Delia.'

'A woman's years is written on her face but we're only down this road the once. In the good light I see y'are the spit of your mother but there's the trawl of the years on you. And no doubt you're wondering what way the girl is?'

Eva's throat was dry and tight. The words she wanted to say would not slip out easily but she had to know what there was to know.

'How is she, Caitlin?'

'The wee one's no longer wee but she's grand. With great energy, though with every year passing she puts ten more on me.'

'She's not been any trouble?' Eva feared the worst, but would have to put up with whatever way things had turned out.

'Oftentimes she has the better of me. I've tried to do what I can, though she cannot see it and we do be arguin', but isn't it the way with youngsters?' Delia shuffled in her skirt pocket, producing a small tin and filled her pipe. 'The truth is, I've not had it smooth with her and she can be a worry to me. I do wonder what's in her, for she's taken off from me twice, going off with men.'

'She's brazen, is she?'

'There's a bit of that way with her. She went off for weeks when she was no more than fifteen. I'm worried no father of any young fella'll come for a match, and I haven't the legs to chase and bring her back.'

Had Caitlin turned into one she would not recognise? The early years of her own mother's care gone in a wisp, far as the mountains. Eva wanted to cry for the child she had lost. Wanted to grasp her, hold her shoulders and look into her eyes.

'I done the best I could, no more than your own mother. Caitlin is often out. I've no heed of her but she's with every *glincin* around.' Delia held the pipe with yellowed fingers and sucked. She had always smoked along with other women on the road.

'I'd love to see her.'

'You would, of course. She'll be along in a while, though I wonder would you know her, for she's the height of a cane for stalking beans, towering over me.' Delia put down the pipe and slurped her tea. Her knobbled hands wrapped around a mug decorated with a swirl of flowers.

'Did she ever ask after me?'

'She did not. After your mother died and she came to me, she missed her of course and I'd the devil of a job to ease her, but she settled and there was never a peep out of her. She was happy enough, a mild creature, but deep. I'd never the measure of her, for she walked around with her own thoughts.'

'Like my mother?'

'Your mother was awful lively and good natured. Isn't it how she got hold of your father? Quiet and shy, till she caught him by the sleeve and pulled him off to dance. But herself is musical the same way, with a beautiful voice for singing.'

'If I could even hear her...'

Dragging herself up and rearranging her skirt, Delia shuffled towards the window.

'Come over and take a look. She's on her way,' Delia whispered sharply.

Eva stood at the window. A girl of about eighteen walked across a line of houses. A wrench of confusion rose in Eva. Her eyes were playing tricks. The dark flurry of hair and the face. This could not be Caitlin. Grown into a person. A person away from her. To be so near. At once a mother and a stranger. 'She's lovely.' Eva held the sill to steady herself.

'And why not? Her father must have been as good-looking as Omar Sharif. But what does it matter, for aren't we all descended from the same two in the Garden of Eden?'

'I'll go out.'

'You've no need, for wouldn't it be a fuss? Wait till she comes in, as she surely will soon.'

'No. I must. I've got to see her.' She ran out of the kitchen, sweeping past the chairs and table, setting a stool to wobble, hurrying down the hall and up the path, heaving in gulps of breath.

Caitlin had gone. A stitch rose in Eva's side. She rubbed but the pain persisted. Flooded with not knowing where she was, she stopped. There was no one to see. No person. Only the rows of houses. A bike flung down in a garden. Bins. A cat slunk by. She was lost. A wave of the past blew through her. Was it a vision? Had she walked into some dream of Delia's? Eva drowned in looking and looking for a version of herself. And him. For might not Caitlin have the same walk as her father Kaybe, his self-assured casual walk? She wore his skin, carried his eyes and face, but Eva did not know the inside of her. She did not know how she liked her food. Was it fish or meat she was fond of? If meat, was it the juicy tender flesh of the lamb like herself, or beef? Did she sleep well and what made her laugh? She returned to Delia. The mistake of her youth hit, the way she was struck with a stone. But there was no bandage.

'You're pale with running. You're not used to it.' Delia rested her hand on Eva's arm as she fell to a seat. 'There's no hurry. Come back some other day earlier and I'll have her here for you surely.'

'I will. I'll be back soon.'

'You've time enough. Are you all right?'

'I do find a sickness comes on the odd time.' Eva shifted in the chair, to avoid the blast of heat from the electric heater.

'What way's the sickness?'

'Awful pains in the stomach. I've had them a while but the doctors can do little.' Eva rubbed the soft mound.

'Ah, doctors. You don't want to be holding with only them. Let me look around. I could make you a drink.'

'I don't want to be any trouble.'

'It's no trouble. Why wouldn't I help, the way your own mother helped me, and myself and Tomeen not able to bear a child.'

Delia pushed herself out of her chair, gripping the sides, and stumbled to a cupboard. She searched through tins and jars, raising each to her ear and rattling it. She took out leaves from one and from another a scatter of dead spiders and flies, placing them in a bowl. She carried them to the sink near the back door. Water ran, slopping and falling.

Returning, holding a jug and a spray of grass, she stood at the dresser and mixed the liquid in a small bowl. She poured it into a china cup with delicate pink flowers on the side.

'It'll ease you.' Delia offered the cup. A puddle of dark liquid caught the light. Eva drank; an acrid, bitter taste. There might be nettles in it, for her mother had boiled them for sickness. 'We'll say a prayer to settle it.' Delia foraged in her pocket and produced a rosary. She spread it on her knees. The beads trickled in her hands. 'Glory be to the Father, and to the Son, and to the Holy Ghost,' she said in a low voice. Unheard for years, the words fell into Eva until Delia drew to a pause. 'I'll put the rest of it in a little bottle for you. But be sure to keep on with the drink for the next seven days, and whatever ails will pass.' The craggy caves of eyes were heavy lidded and screed with lines. 'Is there any more I can do?' she asked.

'I'd like things to be straight,' Eva said. She wanted to put her arms around Caitlin, to see the shape of her eyes, their deep brown, her mouth and nose.

'You do of course, but don't annoy yourself with old stuff. Give yourself a chance. Leave time do its job and come up on the girl slowly. In your own time, lest it not be a shock.'

Delia was right. She must bide her time, come in close, the way her father would handle a horse: a light touch with the rope, a tug gentle as a breeze, and before he knew it the creature was reined in, able for riding.

'If she's too much, I'll take her. She can come with me.'

'She has a home here and no cause to be going any other place further than this door.' Delia's voice broke in, strained and harsh, in a manner Eva had never heard. She was stung. She twisted her hands like a cloth, wished she could see the rest of the house where her child lived, where she slept. 'We don't want to be making rough roads for ourselves.' Delia shifted her chair and talked about the price of meat, the noise, and her neighbours who left the house every morning at six, before ever she was out of bed. Taut with reproof, Eva sat back. It was difficult to breathe, the heat of the kitchen smothering. She was lost to all but the call of Caitlin.

Eva had clutched her shoulders on leaving the child. Her hands pale as sand, raised to be carried, her eyes following as Eva went out the door. The metal slamming closed was a knife in her back. The way her father slipped his blade along a line of metal to make a handle for a bucket. She had gone out down the steps and not turned back but kept walking, past vans and bicycles, washing lines and chairs left out from an evening's talking.

'I'll say goodbye.' Eva set down the cup on the table. She clutched the bottle with the liquid.

'Come another day and I'll make sure herself is here.' Delia stood at the door while Eva walked out. Trees in the distance were women frenzied, their arms straining heavenwards, but the gulp of cold night air and its very darkness revived her.

She would take Caitlin shopping and buy her chains, earrings, beads. Combs and clips for her hair. They would go into shops and she would buy her anything she wanted: a blouse, a nice skirt or trousers. In new clothes, Caitlin would turn around in front of a mirror and know her. They would be together and Caitlin would understand all which had been held in, hoarded, like a bundle of clothes in the back of a press for years, in a long narrow street, in a room in a far city.

Eva's eyes sparkled as she walked back, her pace slower with the pull of remembering and want. The muscles in her legs were riven with aches. She rubbed her thighs. She had done too much, walking all the miles out of town and beyond when she should have caught a bus the whole way. She crossed fields and came out on the lane leading to the small road and onto the road for the site.

She rounded the bend, walking between trailers and vans for their own. Torin was inside checking the fridge.

'Hello, love,' she said. 'You haven't been around for a while. You're still down at the old house?'

He nodded.

'It's only fit for cats and dogs and sheep. You want to look out for yourself with all them droppings. It wouldn't be good to be bringing them along with you.'

'I haven't seen any sheep.'

'You wouldn't know one end from the other, if you did,' she said. 'Stay. You'll enjoy yourself. There'll be a good crowd later.'

'I can't.' He pushed into his sports bag tins of peas, mushrooms and soup, a pair of trousers and two tee-shirts.

'Why not?' She wiped her cheek quickly with her cuff.

'Is there any milk left?' He bent to the little fridge to check. 'You all right, mum?' He stood, sweeping hair from out of his eyes.

'I am, of course.' She wished she could blow her nose.

'You've been crying?'

A plastic bag hung from his hand full of the bits of shopping: tins of beans; biscuits with the jam. Bread. She had no strength to scold him. 'Let the lad alone,' her father would say when she told off Torin for the food disappearing, 'He's growing.' He was indeed. Growing away from her. Away from what he knew. What she knew. And all she did not, but which she wanted to and would reveal to him soon. Soon. In the breath of time. She was weak with regret.

'I have not. A bit of grit in my eye, only. Are you coming in? I'll put on a good piece of a chicken and you can have it fried.' She twitched her cuff for a tissue.

'Can't. I've got to go'

'When will I see you?' She stretched an arm towards him.

'I don't know. Soon. Later.'

She stood at the door as he sauntered along the muddy path between broken skate boards and water butts, under the branches of trees by the field. A slide of contentment rode within. She would see him. Make things good. Introduce him to Caitlin. The three of them would go on together, easy as a path through fields, stretching through the years. The time would come like the breath of summer rising.

2

Caitlin said the community centre was the only place where local bands played decent music.

'Decent if you define it as live and loud. Or there's a Sunday night DJ and band at the Paradiso Hotel. Old boys in from the farms who can barely hold a guitar,' she laughed.

'No, it's fine. Whatever they are.' He gritted his teeth.

At the entrance, she pointed out the carved lettering, '*Ceol na mara.*'

'What's it mean?' he asked.

'*Ceol* is music. So it's music of the sea. Music is the best of it. Usually they have evening classes, or information sessions for farmers,' she laughed. 'You sure you want to see this band?' She broke into a bar of chocolate. 'They might be rubbish and you'll think we've nothing around here.'

'I'm happy to. A couple of hours out of my life's all right.' He put his arm around her shoulder and bent as she fed him pieces of fruit-and-nut chocolate.

Drips smeared her fingers. She licked them then gave her fingers to him to suck. Even though he had not taken anything, he was high and buzzy. He could climb a ceiling. Touch the stars. He was with her. Anything was possible. The evening opened in front of them. All he wanted. More than he had expected.

His phone shivered. Marcus.

'Sorry.' He pulled the phone from his pocket.

'How're things?' Marcus slurred. He must have been drinking. He had the freedom to roam in and out of pubs, probably had a bit of money.

'I'm all right.' Torin backed from Caitlin.

'Least you don't feel as bad as me.'

'What's wrong?'

'Game at the weekend. Didn't you see it? QPR slaughtered. Bloody Spurs.'

He had not seen a match all the way through for weeks. If he was there, he'd be going if he got the cash together or be able to see at in the pub at the corner. His life was slipping away.

'What was the score?'

'Three bloody two, to them. They'll go down the table... Ricardo was useless. The new manager has no idea what to do with him.'

'Is there anything else?'

'Harjit's still in hospital. Critical Care.'

'What's that mean? Bad news?'

'Must do. We ain't heard any more. But I've gotta go. Someone's ringing on my other phone. See you.'

Marcus had probably run down the street, past cars and flats, houses and offices, crowding out where they lived, free to go where he liked.

Torin saw the knife on the pavement. The blade in a flicker of light and the girl in the sequinned top saying to ring for an ambulance, but as its siren ripped through the night air he was running. He tore down the alley stinking of piss and fags and drink, onto the High Road. He had slowed, so as not to draw attention. Walked as if he had no cares in the world while neon tore in the night in the video shop, 'Two for one offer. Last fortnight.' All he had known was that the night was over before it had begun, and he and his mates and some others were standing around useless as kids in a playground while Harjit lay until they scattered.

Caitlin leant against a wall.

'Everything okay?' she asked.

'Everythings's fine. Fine.' He forced a smile and shoved the phone to the bottom of his jacket pocket, never wanting to hear it again. Not the rest of the evening. Not ever. He put his arm over her shoulder, drawing her in. What went on in London was not happening here. Could not touch him.

A gang of lads bunched around the main door, either side of two burly men in dark suits. A couple of girls in short skirts smoked, and three boys kicked a ball near the chip van. Boiled eggs in vinegar stared from jars on the van's counter. A sharp tang of salt in the air. He was hungry but Pauley and Shane were at the side of the van. Shane strode over, his hair brushed back. In a dark jacket with his best shirt, the grey one, he looked neat.

Torin should have realised. A tee-shirt was no effort. He looked like tat. Caitlin laughed at a joke Shane told. Her face was bright and smiley. She had probably noticed but not wanted to say anything. Shane held out his wrist while she admired his watch.

'I got chicken as well,' Shane offered.

She put a big, fat chip in her mouth. The golden skin glistened, made Torin more hungry. But he didn't want to spend his money on chips. It was low enough and he had to watch how he spent it. The internet cost. Drink wasn't free. If he rode on a bus it cost more than in England. Money was a nag which never left. Never got better.

A sour, vinegary smell wafted. His throat was dry and his stomach queasy. That evening, it had been his idea to get something to eat. They could not decide where to go. He would not have minded an Indian but one of them said the smell of onion bhajis made him sick. They had walked up Palmerston Road, edging in and out of shops. The evening had been chill and he would have gone in somewhere to get out of the cold. They might have tried a Chinese, KFC or a Big Mac but instead they had stopped at the kebab place beside the alley. Fat oily chips had been stamped to the ground, a mushy splurge under their feet.

He pushed into the crowded hall, hot with talk and sweat. Pauley struggled to carry three glasses from the bar, so Torin helped.

The band straggled across the stage to their instruments and excitement crackled. Lights dimmed. Keyboards thundered against the low bass of a drum, the sharp strains of a guitar. Notes strained and thrashed. His hands pressed Caitlin's shoulders as they danced in drifts and waves of yellow, orange, green and gold. He was quiet with pleasure. Slabs of music pummelled the walls, hardened. He wanted to go on, but the music rose in a torrent and she broke away, heading to the Ladies.

On her way back, she chatted to a tall, slinky girl, then Caitlin leant towards Shane. Torin's palms sweated around the glass. She had nothing to talk to him about. But he had to keep calm. Keep breathing. His mum used to say it was all about breath, repeating the words of a yoga teacher whose house she cleaned. You live longer if you take deep breaths, because the body produces a certain number and if we use them all up, we die. By this calculation he would go early.

'They're giving away samples of a new beer.' Pauley tugged Torin's arm and pushed off through the crowd. Shane and Caitlin did not shift.

'You all right?' Pauley asked.

'Fine,' Torin said, pushing out into the crowd after him. He took two glasses from the girl at the counter.

'I've got you a drink.' He raised the glass as Caitlin arrived back. Cool it, he told himself. 'Beer. A new promotion.'

'I don't drink beer.' She frowned with disdain as she sipped. It was true. She had told him. He may as well have offered her dirty water. 'It's awful.' She shook her head, moving her lips in distaste. 'I'm gonna throw up.'

'Is it the new one, Avondale?' Shane forced Torin to face him. 'Cat's piss, as my gran'd say. Probably why they're doling it out to anyone who'll take it.'

Torin put the glass on a sill. He need not have bothered. He looked worse than useless. Two guitarists strummed; one, tall with long brown hair, stood solemnly. A drummer in tight trousers fiddled with drum sticks and took in the depth of the crowd. The guitarists checked sound levels, while in the distance, cool and calm, Caitlin and Shane gazed at them. Shane leant towards Caitlin and murmured. She smiled and nodded seriously. Heat rose in Torin. He hated her. Hated them.

'Hey, what's wrong?' Pauley asked.

'Nothing.'

Torin's heart pumped. His legs were stiff. If they kept talking for any longer, he would not be able to continue to stand. He would... he would... He did not know what he would do. He pushed towards Pauley, wanting to crash into the swarm of other people to get to them.

'Hold on,' Pauley said. Caitlin and Shane had gone. Slipped out. He could see them down at the old house. Could see it all and the way it was happening. He pushed past the couple next to him. 'Hey man. Hold on.' Pauley grabbed his arm, to pull him back. 'They're only dancing.'

'Are they?' Torin stood on tiptoe to see her among others on the floor. And Shane. The bastard. Her body turned to him, while he moved in front of her. They weren't touching but they could have. As good as. Torin strained to see. 'Caitlin. Caitlin,' he called.

'Isn't that her?' Pauley pointed to the far reaches of the hall where a gang of people clustered.

'Course not. The girl with the handbag doesn't look like her.'

'I mean the one at the bar.'

Bar. Fuck it. What was she doing there? She sat on a stool at the bar, as though she had been drinking cocktails all her life. Shane was beside her. Inside, Torin was falling. The world was crumbling. His chest tightened. Shane put his hand on her shoulder. From a distance, he was thin in the face. His hair was blacker and longer. Slinky. Sly.

'Want some?' Pauley's voice came from far off. 'Crisps.'

Torin shook his head distractedly, though his gut churned.

'I don't.' He wanted to leave but he pushed through the crowd, and called, 'Caitlin.' She took a long time turning, pulling on the straw in her drink.

'Where were you?' He was not gonna let this go. He was not gonna lose ground.

'We went round the side for a better view,' she said.

Shane's eyes narrowed like a fox Torin had seen the first evening at the old house. Rusty tailed, the fox walked slowly, waiting for them to catch up and then it turned and looked at them, green-eyed, hard and centred in the soft night. Until he shot off. Gone. Clean out of the place leaving a hole in the dark.

'What do you think of them, then?' Shane asked.

Think? He could have bloody smashed his head in.

'The band? Crap.'

'The bass is too heavy and the drummer hasn't any rhythm, but they're only starting out. How many of us'd have the gumption to stand up in front of a crowd and knock out a song? My uncle used. He was a guitarist in a show-band in America. But he got shot in the leg in a bar and came home. He was always moping around at home, trying to get work. He'd bring his guitar over and show us how to play...'

His voice cut. Shane knew everything. Torin tried to look interested but Shane's voice ran on. 'I learnt a lot watching him.'

'You coming back?' Torin asked Caitlin. This was coming out wrong. All wrong. He sounded curt and bruised. He wasn't. He was not upset. Nothing wrong with him.

'Now?'

She wore more make-up than when they had come out. Her eyes were bigger and darker. Green streaked the lids and the brows looked finer. Her lips were more red.

'Yes.' He was edgy. He sounded pissed off but he didn't care.

'They're getting good,' Shane shouted to a man in the crowd.

A clutch of lads carrying pint glasses barged through. With the thrust of the crowd, she was forced closer to Shane.

'She's with me,' Torin said.

'So what's the problem?' Shane shot back.

Behind Shane, Caitlin ran a finger along the rim of her glass, round and round. Torin was stung to silence.

'We were talking,' Shane said.

'You think I haven't got eyes in my head? I've seen you. All evening.' His body closed up to Shane. The flame of a fight spat out. If Shane faced up to him, he would back down and they could all move off quietly. Everything would be as it was, as it should be.

'Seen me? Seen what?' Shane's face became mean. His eyes were a snake's. He had set this up. 'You want to go outside?' Shane jabbed Torin's chest with his index finger.

'Right.' He tried to sound casual, the way he would answer if he was asked if he'd like a few cans back at the old house, while all the time he wanted to smash Shane's face against the wall.

'Hold on.' Pauley grabbed him, an arm between them. 'Keep calm lads.'

'I meant what I said,' Shane called over his shoulder.

Goaded, Torin followed, breathing fast and shallow.

Round the corner from the main entrance, on a dusty road in a cul-de-sac to new houses, was not where he expected to square up to anyone, least of all Shane. While music thumped out, dense with menace, glutting with the thud of a drum, his calf muscles tightened. A vein on his temple beat. The notes were battering him. In collision. Blood heating.

'See this?' Shane held out his fist. 'Go on with your nonsense and you'll get it in your face.'

Torin slung out a hit but before he could land the punch, Shane moved in. He smashed Torin's cheek. Torin staggered back, knocked a couple of wheelie bins. They skidded towards a pale girl who was leaning against the wall and a stick-thin guy who sipped leisurely from a can. Murmurs of laughter rose from a couple of girls chatting in a corner.

Torin gathered his force and lunged, catching Shane on the nose. He gave him a thump in his gut and made to grasp around his neck. If he could only screw off his bloody head, but a right hook from Shane caught Torin's eye. A glint of blood trickled. He knocked Shane. They fell in a bundle on top of each other.

'You want her don't you?' Torin struggled out of Shane's hold.

Shane pulled himself on top and sat astride Torin, pinning him down, keeping his arms spread out.

'What are you on about? Coming over here with your little fantasies. Go back if you can't take the pace.'

His hand was on Torin's chest. Torin gasped, jerked his knees up, hitting his foot against Shane's back as he lurched forward and fell to the side. Torin's legs ached. His eye throbbed. The world was bleary. The rough concrete area around the Centre had cracks and strangled grass. Brown rubbish bins stood in the distance. The girl and the skinny boy were over by the crates. They had seen everything. Everyone had. His head was heavy. His throat was dry and his knee hurt. Someone was bound to ring the police. The notion suffocated him. They would ask questions. He would be hauled off. Chucked in a cell.

A pained screech of a siren ripped the air. As he lay on the ground a car drove in, starkly white, with 'Garda' on the side. His time was up. This was it. He pulled himself onto his knees while a thickset officer got out of the driver's seat. A younger, slimmer man left the passenger side and crossed to Shane and the others. He was covered. The police would nail Torin. No escape. He could not even think of a line to string them.

'Hello, there,' the big officer said, approaching, as if they were old mates. Strands of ginger hair showed from under his cap. He knew. He had to. The police in London would have alerted him. Easy. Press a button. Information flying all over the place. 'What happened here, then?'

'I, he...' Torin rubbed his stinging eyes.

'You'd a falling out? Come over to the car, will you?'

Driven away. Over before it had begun. Not a chance.

'This way. I've left me notebook on the seat. Sit in.' The officer held open the door. The car was warm and sweaty. The wrapper from a tube of sweets twisted on the floor. Coming around on the driver's side, the officer edged in his bulky frame and sat.

'So. Tell me what went on there.'

'I was in the centre with my girlfriend.'

'Her name?'

Her name. Her name. The questions came. Time they arrived? Who they had met and spoken to, where they stood. Torin answered quietly and tried not to sound too English.

'All right.' The officer tapped his pad as he listened. 'Sounds like you had a wee scuffle. Nothing the pair of ye can't fix over a pint. You can get out.' He leaned over and let slip the latch for the door.

What else? What would happen? He dare not ask. He stumbled onto the yard of the centre in a blur. The younger officer walked towards the car.

Shane was talking to his mates. They shot quick, sharp glances. Torin went back to where he had been standing and slumped down to sit on the ground.

Caitlin was chatting to some girls. Her heels were scuffed. Had he messed up the way she looked? She walked towards him and a mixture of relief and fear flooded his veins. At last. She understood. How things had screwed up. How he only wanted her to talk to him. He pushed up to stand, brushing the trickle of blood away from his eye. He had to look decent. He wiped his bloodied hand on his trouser leg. Her eye make-up was smudged and her eyes flickered with a cold light, colder than he had seen before. Had somebody gone for her? His blood rose. He would get them. Seek them out. Do them over. They had no right. No right.

'What was that about?' Caitlin came over.

'Sorry. I never meant—' he began.

'Sorry? You were crazy going for Shane. And you look a mess. You made me look foolish, too. Don't bother coming after me.'

'What?'

'I don't want to see you. I need a break.' Her bag dangled from her shoulder as she stomped off.

'Caitlin!'

She walked away, while from inside the centre music thrashed the walls as night wore on. Too drained of energy to stand, he slumped and closed his eyes to cut out the light.

'You okay?' Pauley leant down to him.

'Yes. I mean I don't know.' Torin opened his eyes. 'I don't understand anything.'

'Who ever does? Let's get out of here.' Pauley tugged him up to standing.

In the old house, laying on the mattress, the throb was worse. He eased out his legs. A dry run of bushes ran by the field and in the distance two gnarled trees fought for light. A van passed on the narrow strip of a road, climbing to higher reaches, past lumbering rocks and boulders.

He was dizzy and closed his eyes. He was in two places at once and they were closing in on top of him. He needed to get back to London. Whatever was going on, he may as well face it up. At least be there. But Caitlin. His heart rammed. If only it would slow down. He wanted the night to wrap around him and take him in but his body was strangled into a form he did not know. He saw Harjit's blood staining the ground. Big Ian lived in Gainsborough Tower, the flats due to be done up. Had the police gone there? They must have. Must have climbed the stairs or got in the piss-stained lift which always broke down. Had Big Ian said what had gone on between them? Someone would let slip his name. Soon the police would make connections. They weren't stupid. They would come after him. Harjit had been too good. He was due to start a business course. Used to talk about his mum and dad and his sisters. He had proper love for them. They were a real family. He had felt that for Caitlin. Or something like it. Bigger than himself. And he had thought she felt the same about him. The question tore at him until he fell asleep, exhausted.

He woke knowing only that Pauley had heaved him like a sack of potatoes, helped him to lie down and be comfortable. He smelt mouldy bread and stale, sweet biscuits, or was it himself? He was disintegrating.

'How you feeling?' Pauley's thin face strained with anxiety. Delicate silvered veins ran on his temples.

'Like crap.'

'Your face's pretty smashed. You were flat out.'

'Did the police come?'

Pauley shook his head.

'No. Why would they? They've seen you and weren't bothered with the two of you. They were asking who'd rung to bother them in the first place.'

Torin sank back. The bone around his eye hurt. The police in England might come calling. Crawling like insects in the house. Ants outside the walls. Spider hanging in the chimney. A mate of Marcus had got six months. Aggravated Attack. Or was it Grievous Bodily Harm? Public Affray. Public Afraid. He was afraid of them. Shane. His mates. The police. Everyone. Caitlin. Time would creep up and he might be found. Hauled down to the station. Charged. And charged in a different country, where he did not know anything or anyone.

'My head's bustin' all over. A firing squad in there.' He closed his eyes.

Shane's face scrawled in front of him. His pudge of a nose. Beads of blood on his cheek. His sheer bewilderment.

'He did a right job on you. You should go to hospital.' Pauley knelt by him.

'I'm not going there. Not like this.' He touched around his eye.

'You'll have to put something on it. Like ice. I'll see what we've got.' Pauley said and pulled a towel from a hook, dipped it in the bucket of water which they kept for drinking and wiped

Torin's eyes. The moist rag of a towel was comforting even while anger crawled inside. He did not know what time it was or how long he had been sleeping. The old house was so dark, day and night crashed into one.

'What do I look like?'

Pauley helped him to sit and gave him the small cracked mirror. Holding a torch near, Torin's pale and shocked face looked out. He turned on his side, wanting to hide from the shred of light through the windows.

Pauley sat back on his haunches.

'I know how it is. You meet someone you're crazy about. You have a good time but in the end they're off. You've taken a few mighty punches. But no girl's worth it.'

3

In the overheated trailer, when he woke up, the afternoon had already started. He dressed and pushed the bed against the wall.

Two small boys were kicking a ball and dodging in between vans. He and the lads had hung around the bins at home, hiding lighter fuel until one of the bigger boys found out and they had to change the place to a gap in the wall by the lifts. They had taken turns to look out, until one of them moved to Liverpool to be with his dad. A journey he wouldn't have minded making, even if he had to go to the other end of the country.

Feather chomped grass near the fence, her rope tied to a brass bed-head his grandad had found on a skip. The veins in her legs were prominent. Even he could see she pulsed with verve, the desire for movement. He stroked her nose and patted her neck. She turned, a flick of her head, tail lashing.

'She's a beauty, but I don't have energy to be looking after her and I can't afford her. Your mother's needing taxis to the hospital.' His grandad approached, an old rag for cleaning the car dangling from his hand. Feather's dark eyes flickered recognition. 'I used let go of her into any field I might find for a few days, but that time's gone. Any farmer finding I'd done so now'd call the Gards. She's lively enough but she needs room to roam and more looking after than I can give at my age. I'm hoping to get a good price for her.'

'You going to sell her?'

His grandad nodded.

'No other way out. You can't look after her, can you? With all your skills of horsemanship.' He laughed. 'Much as I'd rather keep her with me, she's getting on. I'm getting on. I'll take her to the fair at Moynard's Cross.'

'Where is it?'

'Up the country. You fancy a trip? You've been in bed for days. I'll show you the countryside. Many's the good time I had in the town. Trees as tall as the sky around the green.'

He could go. Get away as far as possible. It was distant enough to help him forget. He might run off to the most isolated place in the country, a den in a woods or a cabin at the edge of the sea. He would like to tell his grandad he needed distance, how there was a girl and before, someone he knew who he had injured badly. But it might alarm him. Or his grandad might tell his mum. As long as he got away. Anywhere would do. Anywhere to hide.

'I don't know whether you should be going anywhere, Dad, and I don't see this lad travelling. The furthest he's been is up and down to that cess-pit of a house.' His mum appeared in the doorway in her red dressing gown. Her pink slippers were stained and dirty. Nothing stayed the same. She was ragged and tired, her skin slack and grey.

'You trying to tell me I'm past it? Is this what you've come all the way for?' his grandad asked.

'It's not what I meant. You could be robbed or have a heart attack or fall down in a ditch.'

'I'm as good as ever I was.'

Early next morning, Torin checked the horsebox before they chained it to the car. He had an impulse to stay, for his mum had become slower and weaker, but he would be back. Soon. Too soon. The open road was best. It had attracted his grandad for years. It might do something for him and keep him happy. Torin blew up the tyres on the horsebox with a borrowed pump and checked the axles. The battery in the car was gunged around the top and his fingers were blackened from cleaning it. Dark green paint flaked above the wheels and the door was loose.

His grandad said not to worry, to clear out the ropes and cans and it would do fine.

'I had good times at the fairs. They bring great fun. Myself and the lads used to enjoy ourselves. If you can't do so when you're young, when can you?' He slapped Torin on the back.

He was like a child with his rush of optimism, but raw, wrinkly skin fell over itself around his neck, betraying his age. Torin could not believe the old man wanted to leave but, if his granddad had any desire to, he would go too if there was a chance. He had to get out of the place and he could put up with his grandad. Travelling with him would not be as bad as waiting for Caitlin, with his pulse for her running through every day, every hour.

The sky cleared and lifted after the night's rain as they drove out. A narrow road overhung with high branches led to the main road. They gained speed and his grandad hummed an old tune. The day grew fine and warm. They headed for town and, once out the other side, took smaller roads going between towns and villages. Some looked the same, with bland squares in the centre or a statue of a priest or soldier. Many had houses in shades of pink or blue, yellow or orange, a variety which surprised him.

'The road over there'd take us to the castle your man Essex besieged. The beggars had no chance and were left with nothing,' his grandad announced as they passed a crossroads, leaving a spreading town. His mouth sank, the lines around more pronounced. His hair was white in the sunlight.

'Essex who?'

'The man of Queen Elizabeth.'

'The Queen?'

'Not the one now. The other. The one a long time before. The first one. Do you not know your own history? They fought for five days and nights. Didn't your mother tell you?'

Torin shook his head.

'She should have. Only right you should know where you come from.'

Torin sank back. There was no stopping his grandad. He should have thought of how he would be trapped. But it had to be better than being on the site, hanging around, in fear he would run into Shane or Caitlin. The rubber mats under his feet were worn. The plastic fascia was scuffed. If he had a car he would make sure it was decent.

'Did she teach you any songs, either?'

'No.' Torin shifted, leaned forward, distracting himself with the contents of the glove box. A piece of string. A cloth. A worn medal of St. Christopher.

'I'll do it so, before it's too late and I'm over the hill.' He took a deep breath. '*The minstrel boy to the war is gone, in the ranks of death you'll find him...*'

Despite wishing his grandad would stop, and straining to find interest in the fields they passed, the tune soaked in. Torin saw a boy, light glinting off his blade. A field rugged with ploughed mud. Hooves raging. The minstrel might have walked or had his own horse.

'I'll make a scholar of you. See, if we went west from here I'd get to the rock where Grania and the young fella jumped into the sea. She must've been awful taken with him but in those times perhaps one would.'

Torin saw a couple on a headland. The crash and sprawl of waves as the young man jumped in. He had limp blonde hair like Pauley's, lifting in the breeze, the day they found the oysters. The day he saw Caitlin.

Moynard's Cross, when they arrived, turned out to be a drizzling little town overcome with crowds. A strict-faced grey building stood on the outskirts. He wondered if it was worth coming.

'What's that?' he asked.

'The prison. You wouldn't want to be landing up there,' his grandad laughed.

Torin shivered and rolled down the window for air. If the police wanted him. If they knew where he was. He needed to keep moving. Weeks had passed since he had left. They might have found him if they had wanted to.

They drove through the narrow streets of the crowded little town to a green at the centre. Surrounding roads were overtaken by vans, cars and horseboxes. The grass was full of horses and men holding ropes or reins. A dark brown horse was led around the green.

'Beautiful creatures. Fine good necks on them. They came from Spain years back. You can see the strain in them,' his grandfather said as the horse raised its head.

Haughty. Proud. He was right. Something about them.

Rough voices crammed the air. Men shouting at each other, at the same time. Nobody listening. Some with flat caps moved between the animals, pausing to examine them. He could stay. Get a job. Whatever the town was like, it would shield him. He would be lost and could forget. Forget Caitlin was serving men in a bar, how she knew Shane and the others, how she belonged and he didn't. Forget about the tight hold of her room which was not a room when he was there but a world, a land, a continent, with life forms and offerings from the beach and the shore.

'I'm glad to arrive. I don't want her agitated.' His grandad stroked Feather's forelock. 'She must be shown for the beauty she is, docile and well pleased with the world, the way I first saw her, on the side of a hill in Connemara. No need for mustard in her backside to make her lively.' In a snug pitch, the far side of the green, he loosened the rope on Feather and tied her to the horsebox. He threw down straw and slapped her hind-quarters.

The houses opposite were blue, green, pink. A ripple like the summer. A light breeze ruffled the trees. Torin gave Feather a drink and her fat tongue slurped.

'I'll take a look around,' he said.

'Do. Make yourself at home.'

He walked across the green as it filled with horseboxes, vans, and old cars looking as if they could not last a drive down the main street. The late afternoon warmed. A police car was parked near the green. Two fat policemen sat in the front eating chips. Of course. Any big gathering drew them. Coming had not been a good idea. What had he been thinking? But he was stuck. He crossed the street, out of their sight, quickened his step, walking in the opposite direction. Boutiques and craft shops lined the road. He turned a corner past tiny cafés and their queues running on the pavements outside. An old lady with a shopping bag on wheels tried to pass a girl in a flowery skirt with a buggy. The girl pulled the buggy over and smiled. With her cap of curls falling about her ears and one arm angled on her hip, she was like Caitlin. His heart gasped. He wanted to stretch out a hand to touch her, to test if it was.

Further down, a larger, modern, glass-fronted bakers was emptier; he bought a can of Coke and a doughnut. He walked to the lower slopes of the green, which fell away to a church and its frontage. Groups of people sat drinking and talking. He lay back. Coming was easy. His grandad's chat partly filled the gap inside him but he did not know how he could go on when they got back to the site. His mum was likely to make demands on him to stay there.

The girl in the flowery skirt pushed her buggy onto the grass but the baby was crying. He hoped they would sit at a distance, but she sat near and released the child. She rocked him, his chubby little face turned up, and gave him a bottle. Quiet fell. A simple need, Torin realised, for when she had finished the bottle, or the baby had enough and was content, she tucked the baby in the buggy and walked over the grass to the street.

In the evening, his grandad said they had to ready themselves to settle for the night in the back of the car, an old jacket for a pillow, two worn blankets over them. He said, he expected the following day to be fine and they were likely to do good business.

'Feather'll be well rested and in fine humour. We won't hear a peek. She'll be quiet as ourselves.'

'This is old.' Torin pulled a scratchy blanket over his shoulder.

'Don't mind. My mother had it off a farmer's wife we used to call to. She made it. Had the wool from her own sheep and spun it herself. It may have a few years done but it's pure wool. You couldn't find better.'

'Okay.' He wanted to sleep. For the night to sink in to his bones. Out here, it would be easy to let go. No police. No Shane. Nothing to remind him.

The next day, they were up and ready early. His grandad brushed down Feather and plaited her mane, saying it would never be as good as the way Kate trickled in a red or gold ribbon.

'She has a good smooth coat and her muscles are strong. Look at the big rump. I'll get her to stand tall, the full sixteen hands,' he urged, tapping Feather's hind leg with a stick. She shuddered and stepped forward. Muscles moving over bones, fluid as water.

Crowds pushed and melted in between horses; men with stubble, boys his own age who might be jockeys. He stared into the distance, certain it was Abdul, Harjit's friend who had long hair. His brown face was distinct in the crowd. Abdul out of loyalty had followed Torin. Come over and trailed him. Torin turned, attempting to hide.

'What are you doing, lad? Stand out there and let the crowd know you're selling,' his grandad said.

He fell back to where he had been standing. It was too late and didn't matter. Abdul would have seen him. It would be over. But no. It was, as he gazed on, not Abdul or anyone like him. The face of a woman was before him. Her tanned, bony face was her own. He turned to Feather. Wanted to cry at his shrieking anxiety, stripping through. If only the day was over. All the days were over.

In the evening, as the crowds left, they strolled across the field to a pub. His grandad recognised a face and talked to a couple of men. He was always talking, not letting go of people, as though afraid of being alone. He found the man was not one of the McMasters from Kildare but another branch; horses were fetching a good price this year, a gangly man said on his way to the bar.

'Some buyers are over from England. And Scandinavians here too. They love the coloured ones to stand the bad winters,' a man shouted, his brown eyes sharp in the dim light. The bar was brash with loud voices. A young man played an accordion and another sang, but Torin could not take in the words. He strained towards the door. Anyone might come in. The police. If Caitlin was there, he would be all right. Protected. Safe. Everything which had passed between them would have passed and they could start again. With every movement of the door, he fidgeted. It opened and a girl swung through. Caitlin. Someone had told her where he was. He hadn't expected anyone would, but they must have. She had chased up country and everything was going to be all right because he would forgive her, and she him. He had been stupid and rushed to the wrong conclusions.

But the girl leaned up at the bar and chatted to the barman; up on her toes as she stretched to point out a bag of crisps, she flicked her dark hair behind her ears. He was seeing things. What was he thinking? She had black hair but it was straight. She was not Caitlin and could never be. The evening fell flat and worthless. He did not deserve to see her. He probably hadn't deserved her anyway. Laden with hollowing emptiness, he shoved on over to his granddad.

Torin's head buzzed as they bedded down in the car. He lay awake and saw Caitlin riding bareback on beaches, a bit of rope for a rein. He saw hooves soft and clear in the sand. He saw her on Feather taking in the length of the field. He would never see her ride again. Not Feather or any horse, and all those days when he had been new to the site and the town were like an age back. Belonging to a different part of him.

The next day, he woke to the stink of shit and urine from the green. Too many horses gathered, and a fear that they may not sell Feather snaked in him. He followed his grandad out to the animals. A police car lurked nearby, the window down as an officer spoke to an elderly man who pointed his stick to a fine black horse, taller than Feather or any horse Torin had seen. The two laughed. Some joke. Was it about him? Torin pushed into the crowd to lose himself.

The air was thick with the crash of voices. Shouts about prices. The height of horses. Men arguing. Numbers hurled in the air. Deals made with a slap of the palm and spittle. Business was money laid down in another man's hand.

A man examined Feather and slapped her sides. 'What age is she?'

With his brown tweedy hat tilting off, he was like a gangster. But half the folks around could be, from what his grandad said.

'There's a good few years left on her,' his grandad said.

'I've seen a couple of mares but this one is more the kind I'm after.' He walked her length and pushed back his hat to get a full view. Feather raised her head, eyes dark. She was unused to the noise of strangers, their hands upon her. She had no room to move. 'She's placid enough.'

'She is for sure.'

'Does she like kids?'

'Gets on well with all of them. The young lads used ride on the bare back of her,' his grandad answered.

'I've a daughter. She's been at me to get her a ride.' The man ran his palm over her flanks, along her nose and slipped his other hand quickly under her chin, and opened her mouth. 'What're you asking?'

'Five thousand,' his grandad declared.

He was a chancer. Had dared too much. They would soon see the journey home the same way they had coming, and Feather not sold.

'Pricey. Will you take four and a half?'

Torin glanced at his grandad, who looked at Feather. He did not want to let her go. Jesus, they would end up with nothing to show for the couple of days' venture.

'You won't get any horse better for the age or temperament. Make it four thousand and seven and she's yours.'

'You drive a fierce bargain,' the man said, looking in her ears.

'There was never a broken bone on her.'

His grandad had said that years ago Feather had knocked against the trailer, trying to edge out to the field, and there was damage to her leg. They needed to get the deal done and clear out quickly.

'And the tack too?' The man put his hand into his pocket, drawing out a crumpled envelope, fat with money.

Like taking the shirt off of his back, he could hear his grandad say.

'All right. All included.' His grandad slapped Feather lightly.

'I'll take her so. You've a deal done.'

The man pressed worn notes into Grandad's palm while he counted them down with his eyes. 'And one for luck,' the man concluded.

Quick as a handshake Feather was gone. Into another life, another field, other people riding her.

His grandad loosened the rope and she and the man walked across the field to the other side, where the large horseboxes were parked.

'They're all the same. Clever scuds from the cities. But our business is over and we didn't do too badly out of it, did we?' his grandad announced on their way to the car. 'Enough here for a good drink or two when we're home.'

They cleared the car of old paper and shook out the cushions.

'I'll go up by the shops a while,' Torin said. He might see Feather one last time.

She was over at the far side of the field, tethered at a blue horsebox along the ridge of the green, one of a number in a row. She looked restless, uneasy. And then, with the crack of an engine swerving along the street, she broke free of the rope, ran into the crowd on the green, hurled herself in. Thudding in blind panic, her big muscles kicking, she set a pushchair flying. A baby's wail gathered with the gasp and cry of the crowd as they fragmented and drew to one another. The girl in the flowery skirt screamed. The pushchair lay on its side, the wheels spinning.

Torin shied away, sickness in his gut. With energy only to leave the place, he staggered backwards. At a distance, when he did not fear he was seen, his step quickened. Hot with the stink of sweat and alarm, he ran. Ran until all breath was out of him.

Dizzy and faint, he walked up the street, following the trail of terraces leading away from the main square. He sat on a bench outside a church to get his breath back. He needed a drink. Anything to settle his head, to relieve the fear. He went into a bar. A gaggle of men burst around the counter, blocking the place, suffocating the entrance. A man with a beard declared that the mother of the child who was hurt on the green was from Cashel, and wasn't it a great pity?

'Weren't you with the fella'd sold the horse?' a rosy-faced man jabbed at Torin.

He shook his head in fear a word might slip.

'Someone like yourself,' the bearded man joined in.

Torin's fingers fluttered on his glass. He needed to get out of the place. He put down his drink and edged from the counter.

'... broke her foreleg with the force of it,' said another man.

'The bastard of a man, selling an animal doing no one any good,' a gruff voice barked.

Either it was the drink or the hour, but the mood was dangerous. You could cut it. Torin had to clear off but he must not hurry. A man with bulging eyes looked him full in the face. 'You wouldn't want anything to do with a creature like that?' the man growled.

Torin couldn't breathe and his legs ached. He needed to go.

As he crossed the green a man in a dark coat, carrying a large bag, walked towards a crowd. A second later Torin realised: Feather. They were putting her down. He pushed through the crowd as elbows poked in his sides. He got near enough in to see Feather lying, dull-eyed. Quietened. The man opened the bag and stroked Feather's head. The needle sunk and blood flowered on her brown coat. She tensed. Her limbs shuddered in a spasm. She was alive and, with a jerk, was not.

She slumped. Her neck collapsed. Her eyes were open but she could not see. Her legs shivered and folded in. She passed out of reach, trapped in a deep pause of sleep on the straw. Her mane was still in its tight plait, with a strand of red running through which Torin realised his grandad must have threaded.

4

He lay on the sofa bed while his mum sat at the table with a cup of tea and an opened packet of Bourbons. She played with a teaspoon in her cup while flicking through a magazine, probably searching the horoscopes for her sign, Aquarius.

'When are we going back?' he asked.

'Back? Back where?' She turned a page and popped a biscuit in her mouth.

'London. Home. You know.' He pushed a dirty tee-shirt into the plastic bag they took to the laundry room.

'When I'm ready.' She ate another biscuit.

'We've been here a couple of months,' he snapped.

'You don't want to rush away,' his grandad said, eating a slice of toast.

'You've seen your dad. Why can't we go?' Torin whispered.

'We'll hit the road in a while.'

'I think I'll head back.'

'You will not. You don't know what's going on over there. Besides, I need you.' She was pale, with grey bags under her eyes and her forehead furrowed.

'What for?'

'To...' She shrugged. 'Keep an eye on things. Be here, with himself. Wait a while and we'll be back together and I can sort out a flat. It'll be easier for both of us if you're along with me. We're likelier to get a bigger place.'

She rose, rummaged in her toilet bag and smoothed beige cream on her face. When she put on make-up, he could not tell if she was ill. But something about her was different, and it wasn't her face. Her voice. Strained, harsher. Drink, he supposed.

She had never learnt to limit it and must have been out the previous night. She was lined and her skin seemed paper thin. She pushed away the magazine, searched through her handbag and found three bottles of tablets.

'What ones are you on?' his grandad asked.

'Some damned kind. I don't know but the pains raddle me.' She took two from a bottle and threw them into her mouth. 'I don't think those doctors know what they're doing.'

'What did they say last time?' He sat at the table and slurped from his mug.

'That I should go to the Marie Curie Hospital, wherever that is.'

'The other side of town. I've heard you'd get great care. They must have good nurses. Anyone who goes in is well looked after.'

'You make it sound like Marie herself is there, but I never did like them places.'

'But it might do you good to try there.' His grandad swept up a rind of bacon in a curl and slipped it in his mouth.

'Whatever way I am, work has to be done.' She took his grandad's plate off the table and put it in the sink. She washed and stacked cups and plates on the drainer. She opened the fridge, putting away the milk along with the scraps of bacon, two dried sausages and half a black pudding. 'Torin, have you taken the bread, for there's only two slices?' Sitting on the stool, she put on her shoes. 'You greedy lad. I haven't money to be buying food for you and them monkeys down in that old house.' She rose and brushed her hair.

'Where are you going?' he asked.

'Only out.' She twirled in front of the mirror, angling her face side to side for a good look. 'Meeting Joe. Goodbye. Bye, Dad.'

She leant over her father and kissed him on the top of his head.

'Will I see you later?'

'Of course. I'll be back.' The door flicked back as she left.

The pair. Him and her. They had each other. He should get back to London. He had nothing here. He rose, flung his jacket over his shoulder, pushed out after her and called, 'I'll see you too, Grandad,' as the door snapped shut.

He passed the Mercedes whose back tyres were let down. Two women from the green trailer were chatting as they hung clothes on a line. No cloud in the sky. Only sheer, blinding light as he left towards town.

In London, his mum used to go out without explanation. Out for the night. Coming back in the early hours. As if he did not live with her or belong to her. He had to get away from here. Could not see what drew her. Though she was right, London was too uncertain. And he hadn't heard from Marcus in a couple of weeks. Anything could be going on. The fear was like drums beating, never letting go, a rhythm he might hear from a flat in the summer at home when the low beat of a sound system hung over the roofs.

The shore was clumped with wind-blown grasses. The old house was in sight but he would avoid it, going the long way round at the back of the fields.

The tide was out. He clambered over rocks. In the distance, a couple were walking. The woman turned. His mum. And Joe. She sat on a boulder while his attention was solely on her. Torin was struck by how innocent and girlish she looked. She stood and they walked towards the waves. Joe's trousers were rolled up. His mum gathered in her dress, revealing chunky thighs. They walked separately and drew together. Their bodies merged with the waves. His mum cried out in delight, dancing in the water. She leant forward and dabbled her hands in. She jumped little steps and walked towards the shore, bending to scan the sand. A trail of seaweed draped from her hand as she showed a cluster of shells to Joe.

She moved with ease and lightness, made splashes flicker against her skin. She was alert and lively. She had never been like this with him. Never so free or content, but caught in worries about whether she had the next cleaning job, enough money for rent or food or a trip to the pub. Joe's dog ran, scattering shakes of drops. Joe threw a stick and the dog ran into the glittering waves, splashing back. Joe and his mum belonged to each other in a way he had never seen her with anyone before.

Torin made his way past boats, to the old house. Dared himself to approach, see if anyone was around, though he'd scarper if he came across Shane. It was deathly quiet and he did not know if this meant no one was in, or they were there but were zoned out, stoned beyond heaven and hell. He listened for Shane's voice, or the music he played. He waited for breathing and peered through the window. Nothing. No sound.

'Hi. What you doing here?' Pauley sat up and rubbed his eyes from sleep.

'Hi.' Torin pressed at the door. Dry wood flaked under the worn seal of paint.

'How you doin'?' Pauley stumbled into the light.

His face was tanned, hair hanging down flatly, as though it had not been washed for days. Torin sat on the ragged plaid blanket draped over a couple of plastic crates, while Pauley re-arranged himself on a mattress, his long legs stretched out.

'I'm okay. Shane around?'

'You kidding? I've not seen him for days. He's headed off. Always his own man.' Pauley flicked open a packet of ham and loaded a slice into his mouth. 'You can't go on hiding from him forever.' Torin kicked a stone. It shot off into an empty can. A dint of a ring and then silence. Pauley was right. Shane belonged here as much as him. More so. 'Want some?' Pauley held out the half empty pack.

'No, thanks.' Torin shook his head at the lank pink slices, curling at the edges.

Pauley threw the pack into a black bag in the corner. 'These'll make you feel good and alive.' He handed over two tablets.

Torin hoped they might, or else bleed sleep into him. 'Don't think anything will.'

'They'll help you forget.'

'What are they?'

'My dad's. Keep him sane.' Pauley laughed.

Torin slugged down the tablets with a can of Coke. A thirst rose, itchy and raw. He needed more drink, any kind of liquid. He finished the tin, kicked it away, lay down and fell asleep.

Late afternoon, he opened his eyes and tumbled off the mattress. A long numbing sense had taken hold. The day had passed without him knowing.

'Get up,' Pauley said, looking down, laughing. Shane must have shown up. Or be on his way. 'You coming?' Pauley stood with the height of two rods and a canvas bag hanging from his shoulder.

'What? Why? Fishing?'

Pauley nodded.

'Now?'

'This time of day's best.'

Torin rubbed his eyes. If Shane was not around, there was no need to get up. His head was dizzy. The most he knew about fishing was a person stood on the side of a bank for hours, waiting for something to happen.

'Okay, mate. Hold on.'

They took a stony track leading outside the town, beyond the bridge, to the slack bank, which tumbled away to the water. In the distance, cattle heaved and settled, clustered like boulders. They passed a ripple of a stream, lapping over stones of rust and lavender. A door lay across, bank to bank. Bushes covered the lower bank and further down, the gnarled roots of a tree and its branches were falling in. Pauley drew to a halt. He sat against the tree and its fingers of dried roots grasping the earth.

'This'll do,' Pauley said. 'We'll catch something because there're plenty of gnats and flies. The fish want to eat. Hunger drives them.' He set out jam jars of worms squirling behind the glass. Torin sank to his hunkers. Embers of a fire spread on the bank. Pauley said that fish scarper if there's noise. The water level was low and fish beneath the surface darted like electricity. 'Ssh. They'll be frightened.' He removed the lid from a jar and took the maggot between his fingers, pale and long, and stuck it on a hook. The wriggling shape was stunned. All it could do was hang. 'Watch after the jar. They'll like these. Anything resembling food. The little blighters. I'll get a nice fat brown trout. The maggots and worms took all morning to dig.' He moved forward and cast out, letting the line drop in a shadow. 'You can tell 'em by their tail. Plain with no spots. If I get one you'll see it jump like an acrobat.'

Torin leaned over the bank, touching the water, its flickering waves warm with the fullness of the day that had passed. Pauley stood with a halo of midges swarming the skim of the dark surface of leaves from overarching trees. He was intent, patient, the way Torin could never be.

The line strained out and pulled. Pauley rolled in a fish fighting itself.

'A lovely wee trout,' he announced, delight wide on his face as the fish came up in a curve. He splattered it down on the grass and banged it against a stone. 'Good isn't it?'

'Yes,' Torin said, unable to fathom the mysteries of the river but impressed. 'Where'd you get the rods?'

'In the house.'

'Your dad goes fishing?'

'He nicked them.' The dark came down as Pauley turned to the heart of the river, darkly resting under the spread of tree, shadows underneath.

'You went fishing together?'

'He wouldn't take me if you paid him. Well, maybe then. It was a lad across the street. He gave me the odd meal and took me with him.'

In another life Pauley could have been a sniper, earned a packet abroad as a soldier. Maybe he still could. There were armies he could join. Groups of men who went out fighting.

The silence was heavy. Torin could not do this stuff. No use kidding himself.

'We'll go further up. But don't make a sound and we'll get a few more of those fellas. And you have a go.' Pauley held a rod aloft.

'Me?'

'Go on. Won't hurt you.' Pauley passed over a rod and the spindly weight stretched over the river. Minutes passed. This was useless. Torin could not concentrate. He only did it to please Pauley. A flutter. He heaved up the rod. A fish twisted and turned to free itself from the end of the line. 'Hang on there,' Pauley called. 'Don't move.'

The fish tugged. Torin stepped back. The fish jumped off and he fell backwards.

'Sorry,' he gasped, wiping the taste of dust from his mouth.

'Shhush. Stand still.'

Pauley picked up his rod, stepped along the bank and continued fishing. In the dusky distance pinpoints of light shone across the river and a van's engine ran. Three figures shadowed between the trees, voices carrying.

'What's that?' Torin asked.

'Keep your head down.' Pauley lowered to his haunches, tugging Torin with him. ' Lie low.' He put his hand on Torin's shoulder, pressing him to the blanket of leaf mould and moss, twigs and the crinkle of leaves.

'What's up? This illegal or something?'

'It is if you haven't a permit.'

'What?'

'Only a bit more than gathering the oysters.'

'Bloody hell. Who are they? Gards?' Torin hissed.

'No. Guys from the estate. As if we shouldn't be allowed a few of these blighters. Not like we're depriving anyone.'

'What estate?'

'The Brien family own the river and lakes.'

A door slammed. Someone coughed. Voices rose and laughter fell to quiet, the quiet of lighting a fag. Minutes passed. He had not even liked fishing. The van's doors opened and shut.

'They've gone.' Pauley said, rising. He pressed Torin's arm. 'Just have to be careful. A couple of years ago, a lad got nicked. He was only carrying a bag with three fish over.'

'Oh, right,' Torin breathed, not knowing whether to be more alarmed or relieved. This was crazy. 'You sure they won't be back?'

'They won't. Got three more lakes to check.' Pauley handed him back his rod and they stood on the river bank.

'This is so slow,' Torin shrugged. 'I might take a walk while it's light enough, if that's okay?' He lay down the rod so it overhung the water. The further away he got from those guys, the better.

'Hadn't you down as a quitter. But if you see anything, get back here.'

'Course.' Torin shifted off, the leaves softening and twigs breaking underfoot, crisping into the evening. He had disappointed Pauley. But he could not hang around. Especially if he was likely to be nicked.

Upland, a path led towards grey rock which rose boldly, a jagged line dragged across the sky. Evening was darkening. If he had to, if he had to escape out here, he saw how he might do it. Bring a tent. Get one from somewhere. If a person had to hide, this was a good place. Branches and rocks would screen. Far back, his grandad had said, men running from the English had lived among the mountains. They had hidden stashes of guns, watching the roads and passes, eager for the sight of British Army trucks. At one corner his grandad had driven around, he said they had landed shots and lugged half a dozen soldiers.

Eager to get to higher ground where it was light, he crawled up a bank, moving across rocks, and followed the lie of the land. He never had a dad who did things. Even if the most of what Pauley's father did was drink, he had one. And knew where he was.

Up high, he pushed onto a broad ledge opening out to higher ground. Among gorse, a rush of silver fell against the rock. A hiss and a spill of vapour across stones, glossy with light from the head of water bursting over. His feet struggled on boulders while the river crashed and ripped the air. He leant down, touching the water, and splashed his face. He rose and walked, ranging over spongey grass where heather was flecked with tiny purple flowers. A breeze blew across sunken, mouldered moss so thick it drew in every filament of sound.

Jumping down, he came into complete, open silence. The whole of nothing. He could be lost. The notion thrilled and alarmed him. A flicker of a brush against grass. A rustle and shift. Fox or a stray dog? But no. Caitlin. She stood there in a black, sweeping raincoat, too big for her, the edges flapping open.

'Hi,' he said.

His fingers were edgy. Nothing to hold onto, so he put them in his pockets. He might be an intruder, but seeing her face gave him a release from feeling he should not be there and his eyes were playing tricks. He needed to focus.

'You,' she said.

He nodded dumbly, as if responding to a teacher.

'Why you here?' Her voice rose stiffly. She took a cigarette from a pocket and lit up.

'I like it. Wanted to get away.'

She squinted, not believing. Of course she didn't. She could see he lied.

'I often come,' she said sharply, ignoring whatever attempts he was going to make to explain himself.

'Right. Yes. It's good. The quiet and the trees. The river.'

'Not many people come this way.' She sounded strict. Of course, this was her place. He should have known. He was too eager. She would make an excuse and go. He gave the wrong signs. 'Too rocky. Even for sheep.' She threw back her head, flicking ash from her cigarette.

He couldn't explain. He was not there to fish or to hang around with Pauley, but to get away to somewhere different. He wanted to say, 'I've been empty without you.'

'Though I'm not sure where this is?' He glanced around. He may as well give in. She knew this place was strange to him.

'North of Coolne.'

He had heard of it but the name meant little more than a name and he dare not ask her more for she had an air like a flame. Could burn him.

Unnerved, and zoomed with a dizzying pleasure, he had to talk. Keep talking. He had read about getting mugged, when you should keep the person talking. You were more likely to get a hold on them and be able to slip away. If he kept talking he would have space to think and if he kept talking she would have to stay.

She crouched, hugging her knees while a swathe of fabric swam at her feet. The edges of her mac were dirtied. Further out, mountains loomed and hefts of rocks scrawled the sky.

'What've you been doing?' she asked.

Calm. He had to keep calm.

'Nothing. Nothing much. You?'

'Working. What else?'

Any minute, before she swept away, she would let fall stuff about her and Shane. He didn't want to hear it. He was hot and cold. He did not want to know. Yet he did. He wanted her to keep talking. To tell him.

'You didn't need to get mad that night.' She stamped out the fag, crushing it into the soft ground with her heel. 'You don't bloody own me.'

'I thought he and you...'

'We were talking.'

'I'm sorry.' He hated her being right. Knowing what to say. 'Sorry, I...' The path was ragged with tufts of moss and scraps of bark.

'You looked stupid. You made me look pretty much the same.'

'I didn't mean to.'

'Shane told me how he'd a brother...' Her voice melted against the rage of the river so he could hardly hear and not caring if he didn't. 'A twin who died of meningitis.' Her voice was rasping; strange and dangerous, as though she was drawing it out from a well within. She bent to remove a load of leaves scuffed and stuck to the sole of her shoe. 'He said it affected him, more than he thought.'

'I guess those things do.' Torin shifted, easing his weight as he stepped close. Twigs snapped. Underfoot the rustle of leaves. 'I lost my mum, once.'

'Oh?'

'She'd to go to some clinic. She was always coming off drink. Often at home there'd be nothing to eat unless I went to the shop. So she went there and I was put in care.' He was relieved he had said the words and they were out in the air, freed.

'An orphanage?' Her eyes stilled and widened.

'No.' He shook his head. 'I was fostered.' Her eyes darkened but he would take the chance. He could tell her anything, all the tangled bits inside. He may as well. He screwed up with her, lost his way and there was nowhere to go back to. Either way, it would not make things any worse between them. 'I was treated okay but I hated being away, even though I hated the way it was at home. She came out but every day after, back home, I was afraid I'd come in from school and she'd be gone. And it was never the same again.'

'I guess things that happen when you're a kid, happen to you forever.' She came close and stroked his cheek.

He put an arm around her and they locked, close, closer, until she untangled herself and stepped back.

'Have some.' She took a paper bag from her pocket.

Slices of cheese dripped and butter melted as corners of the bread drooped.

'No, thanks.' He shook his head.

'What's wrong?'

'I'm not hungry. What I'd really like is to get away.'

'We could do.' She finished the sandwich and scrunched up the bag, putting it in her pocket. 'We could go away, if you wanted?' She moved to a broken tree with grainy bark. The roots were upended, harsh and dry.

'How? And I don't know where to go.'

'Can you drive?' she asked.

'I know how.'

'But do you have a licence?'

He shook his head.

'Then we're stuck.' She picked up a pebble and threw it.

'We could go to a big town and get jobs.'

'I could work as a waitress. What could you do?'

'Anything.' Far out beyond trees and rocky outcrops the blister of sea was calm, metallic. 'And we could get a car later on.'

The wind blew and flecks of dust got into his jacket.

'You wanna go up this way?' she asked.

'Okay. You go on.'

A range of boulders loomed. He could not see how it was going to be easy. But he had to stick with her. She clambered up, her legs stretching, the mac hanging down. Breaking away, she skimmed the surface of the rocks, able as a lizard. She moved across rocks onto higher ground and he was disappointed at the distance between them. They walked among trees on dank leaves. A dark coolness soaked through the soles of his trainers as he slushed and slid.

'This is the best land around for miles. You can see it, for there's nearly every species of wild flower,' she said. Bushes and long grass brushed him as they broke a path through.

He put out a hand to steady himself and pressed on, scrambling, letting his weight carry him. She stormed over rough, difficult rock until she was out of sight. Rocks thundered, tumbled in a storm and he could not see her.

'Aahh!' She was calling in the wide air as earth dislodged, running away with itself.

It was everywhere, filling the light, the air, but he could not see her. He followed the line of her call and rushed to the edge of the precipice. She stood on a grassy ledge, clutching onto the tangled roots of a tree. Disturbed soil showed the path of her slippage. She raised her arm but he could not reach her.

'Torin,' she wailed.

'Don't worry, I'll think of something,' he said, stiff with fear and not knowing what to do.

He was useless. Pauley would know what to do, he always did. But he needed a rope. He could not escape from his own body, his uselessness. He pulled off his belt. Tied it to the nearest tree. With his face against the dusty soil, he lay down and while one hand clung to the belt he stretched towards Caitlin. No good. The belt was too short. He was too fucking short.

'Torin,' she called, her voice fading.

'It's all right,' he lied.

Night would hurtle down on top of them. His heart raced. He pulled off his top and knotted one end to the belt. He made another knot in the arm for a loop to hang on to and lay down. His neck strained. This wouldn't work. This was stupid. But all he could do was go on. Go on with it and convince himself and her that it would work. He should have run back to Pauley. Run fast. His gut churned. Calm. Keep calm. He had to. For her. If he panicked, everything would spiral out of control. He wrapped his feet around a tree near the ledge and leaned over. He pushed close, dragged himself near. He was hot and numb with panic. He breathed fast. A sharp pain charged his leg. His fingers stretched. A shower of soil fell. His legs shivered with the strain and his arms ached.

'Keep holding,' he shouted, as much to remind himself what to do as anything.

Far below trailed the faint line of a road. If she moved suddenly, she would fall.

He tried to make his legs work and pulled against his weight. Twigs and a scrabble of dried leaves pressed in. His mouth was dry and his throat parched. He feared the pressure of the rock against his chest would break him and he would tumble over the edge, but he kept pulling as the fire of exhaustion surged through. A fist of might.

She was up. Over the edge in a heap on top of him. All arms and legs.

'What happened?' he gulped, untangling from her.

Beyond the curve of land lay the horizon. Easy. Peaceful. Why had he let her bring him here? He hated the space. It scared him. A person could be hidden and lost in it.

'I lost my footing and the earth crumbled away to nothing. The path ran out.' He read his own fear on her face, rubbed sweat off his nose and grabbed the side of a tree, to sit. A hole gaped in the knee of his jeans. A graze and a trickle of blood. 'It's my fault. I shouldn't've brought us so far.'

He was winded. His eyes were itchy. She could have lost her grip. Fallen down into a place he could never reach. Her face was pale with a mask of dust and her hair was all sticking out as she tried to get up.

'I've an awful pain.' She rubbed her right leg.

'Try the other.' He held onto her, his fingers weakened, all his strength drawn out of him as they edged forward.

He slowed to her pace. He had left Pauley in the lurch. He should've gone back. He couldn't even get a signal on his phone.

'You must've had enough of this place,' she said.

'No. No. It's all right.'

He leant her against a tree while he gathered a heap of dried leaves and moss to rest on. Lying down first he eased her towards him. He was nauseous and dizzy.

The air was noisy with birds. Branches shifted and leaves ran against one another. Trees were dark and the wind foraged between them.

'Thanks for that. Maybe we'd best spend the night here and make our way down in good light,' she said.

'Wouldn't it be freezing?'

'I don't think so.' She put an arm around him and warmth came from her.

He had abandoned Pauley to the depths of the night's dark blue sky, the wisp of a moon. But he'd see him the next day or, if not then, in the days after. He'd always see him around and when he did he would explain.

In the husky dark, the tiny lights of houses showed like the lit windows he used to see from the flat in London. He shifted to get comfortable. The trees, tall as street lights, were slim bodies wrapped around with dark ivy leaves, as she sat solidly beside him with the night breathing.

5

He sat on the low wall outside Delia's while a song sailed out, *'the swan in the evening moves over the lake...'* His mum had sung this when the mood was on her or she had been drinking, but this time the words were clear. He pulled his jacket close. He hadn't wanted to come to the house but it had been Caitlin's idea to meet there. The ragged bush in the front garden bloomed a light pink rose, upright and elegant against black bags of rubbish. The skip for the house opposite had sheets of plywood, skirting boards and broken cupboards upended. She might have come the back way and slipped into the house. He tugged at his cuff, pulling a stray thread until it snapped. He rose and knocked on the front door. It was only the old woman he had to face.

'Who in the name of God is it?' Delia called.

She appeared in the doorway, a dark skirt, its folds deep as waves, falling to the floor. Gold earrings hung low against her neck. Determined as a soldier, with cool blue eyes, she was the oldest woman Torin had seen, with skin leathery and tanned. A scarf, dark red with white stars and moons, covered her head and pressed in her grey-flecked curls.

'I'm meeting Caitlin. Is she here?'

'Who's wanting her?' Grimy hands with curling nails held open the door.

'Torin.'

'Tony?'

'Torin,' he raised his voice. 'A friend of hers. I thought she'd be here.'

'Don't be shouting. I heard you good enough.' The weight of the old woman's arms was folded across her chest and her teeth were chipped and yellow. 'Caitlin's not home. But if you want her, you may come in and wait.'

He stepped into a pool of shadow in the hall and the warmth of the kitchen. The windows were smeared with steam, and a smell of cabbage and dead spuds lingered. A plastic tub was piled with washing.

'I don't know where the girl is.' She switched off a radio perched on a battered dresser. The lower doors were removed, leaving only one shelf on the top section. The counter was cluttered with old newspapers and cups. Leaning on a stick, she shuffled towards two plastic garden chairs. 'Sit and make yourself comfortable. There's no knowing what time she'll come.' An electric fire in the fireplace glared its three bars of orange and the air was stifling. 'Will you have a drop of something?' She held up a bottle of brandy.

He shook his head.

'Will you take a cup of tea, for you might be waiting long enough for that one?'

'Thanks.'

It was when she rose for the tea-pot that he noticed the wooden leg, its dull stamp on the floor.

'It won't be long till it's boiling. It's true. Tea's better than drink. And you can see the future in it afterwards.'

Her silky blue eyes trapped him. He strained with longing to ask when Caitlin usually came in.

'I don't know what's holding her, but will you make the tea for yourself?'

She set a battered kettle upon a gas cooker until it sang and steamed. He poured the water into a worn brown tea-pot. He took down two delicate china cups with gold rims.

'Not them ones.' She grabbed. Light was visible through the milky china, thin as paper. 'Bone china. The finest. I wouldn't want to use those.' She tipped out the tea into another cup.

'I keep them special. For medicines and the like.' She sat and nursed it in her lap.

'This one, then?' He pulled out a mug from the back of the dresser.

'Yes. I was in the yard putting out my washing while the good weather's in it, but I've no longer the strength to be getting everything I want.'

'D'you want any help?'

'You're a good fella, for the devil a one does help me. Wait and have your tea and we'll tackle it both.'

He picked up the plastic basket of washing and followed her out to a rough squabble of grass. Dandelions poking in corners, and the pin-pricks of daisies. She jabbed with her stick at the damp clothes when he set the basket down. A thin strip of plastic line stretched from the house to a rusty pole.

'Many a person'd have flung out these but I take no notice of what style I put on, for who the devil is watching? And I keep hold of them towels I got in Dunnes half price.'

She hung up blouses and skirts along with towels and vests. When she finished, she leaned towards him, her stale breath heavy.

'You're a good lad.' She took his face in her hands, her fingers going around his chin, pulling him into her eyes.

Her hold was tight. Large pores spread her reddened nose and her cheeks had the tracking of tiny red veins. The frizz of her hair sniping from under the scarf made her fierce. He fidgeted, wanting to be out of the place.

'We'll go in and wait till herself comes.' She released her hold. In the kitchen she sat near the dresser. 'I've a terrible thirst.' She pulled out a silver flask from a pocket in the folds of her skirt. After cleaning the neck with the end of her cardigan, she offered it. 'You won't take a nip?'

'No, thanks.'

'As you wish, son. But the brandy has five stars on it. As bright as the lads in the sky. And warm and deep like the fire we used make in the backwoods.'

He shook his head.

'Fair do's to you but you've been a great help. I usually only have this little fella.' She held up the flask. 'No other man'd do.' She gurgled a laugh, wiping her mouth with her cuff. 'This makes me feel good. No, not good, better than good. I'll put on this bit of a meal, for Caitlin'll be dyin' of hunger when she gets in. When she's back, I'm glad for the company. Before we landed here, we travelled all over. Only meself and her. To help pass the time I played her music. Got out me old squeezebox. My father'd taught me. *And straight I will repair to the Curragh of Kildare,*' she sang in a low, gravelly voice. 'Have you any songs?'

He shook his head.

'A pity. A song is a great thing. My husband Tomeen had plenty. It was what I liked. And we fared out well, despite all the ructions from his side. I was sorely grieved when he went before me, though he was twenty years older, but at least I'd herself and I wasn't so lonely.'

'D'you think Caitlin'll be along soon?'

'She will. No doubt but she's held up in the bar. I don't like it, for I've no way of knowing what she gets up to or what kind of person goes in. And I'm telling her to be careful, for it's time she was looking about and settling. Finding a fella from a good family.' She slurped her lips greedily around the mouth of the flask. 'The time does not be long passing. I heard from the father of a boy a couple of months back. It could be all fixed and she'd be set up. She needs to be thinking on it.'

He shifted, wishing the old lady would stop. Leaning on her stick, she rose and pulled the lid from a biscuit tin. She took out two scones and placed them on a plate.

'Take one. I'd the recipe from my mother and she from hers and manys the one had it before them. And it'll not be long till I'm following after. The only road left. But you know, I do hardly leave the house, for I like to be in my own bed, under the blankets, nestled like an egg in a cup. I say my prayers to all the saints and the Virgin above, for there's strength in numbers, to look after my stump of a leg so it won't pain. The last time I was out, was to the Blessed Virgin in Castleallen. She was in the shrine with the real tears and all, beautiful with her white gown. I waited all day to get her picture. D'you see it?'

On the wall above the table, Our Lady wore a big crown. She had a quietness, with flowing white robes, pink lips and delicately arched brows. She was among an array of worn, tinged, unframed colour photographs, held on with yellowed Sellotape, while bits of dry wallpaper flaked.

'Is this Caitlin?' he asked. A small photograph showed a little girl with dark skin standing in front of a fence.

'Indeed it is.'

Caitlin stood awkwardly, with a serious expression, her arms tucked behind her. She was plump and wore a short dress with a cardigan. Her hair was a shock of black curls around a face that looked more familiar the longer he stared at it.

'She looks different.'

'She is, certainly. Different from what she was: a wee one with hands like shells, eyes the brightness of pearl buttons and a flock of curls. She was mad for the music when she first came to me, and many's the time she fell asleep and Tomeen playing. We'd great fun when the mood was on her. She'd be playing at kings and queens, shopkeepers and sailors, or a traveller on a white horse flying through the air. Nowadays I've enough minding myself.' She took a swig from the flask.

'Who's this?' He pointed to a black-and-white photograph of a young woman standing by the steps of a trailer, the old kind he had seen in pictures. A horse strayed in the distance and the woman wore a wide flowery skirt. She looked out strong and serious, like a teacher when he had been sent for detention.

'Her mother, Eva. Before she ran away from all belonging to her, the way we were living at the backside of the world.'

The words dropped, colliding in a devilish dance as he tried to catch her meaning.

'But the road took Eva off and she was ever in a hurry away.'

'Caitlin's mother?'

'It is indeed.'

'Eva? How?'

'Amn't I telling you so? Easy as ever it was to conceive the child. And soon as she'd left Caitlin with her mother she was off again.'

His mum, trapped in the picture, looked out at him looking at her. Fear beaded his neck.

'But. She's mine'

'Is she indeed? Your mother? So she'd you over? You? There's no knowing what a person'd be up to, but cities drew her.'

Delia's words ran inside him. His head jangled and crashed. His eyes were blurring. He weakened and gripped the edge of the table.

The shapes of chairs and the dresser were changing. He was disappearing into her words. He was smothered in a tight box of words. He wanted to lash out at something. Anyone. Her. Or not her, but all she had said which slammed into the open space of his heart.

'What are you saying? Where are you going? Don't run. You'll fall and hurt yourself. Oh, my lovely cup and saucer shattered. I'd it all the way over from Derby or was it another town? There are so many places in England, you'd get lost going from one to the other... but what are you saying? Come back!'

He ran off the estate until he could go no further, and gasping leant against the wall of a garage along the main road. His mum had not told him. The length of his life, she had said nothing. He was empty of all that mattered but he got his breath back and ran on, torn and raging. Ran not knowing where he was going. He ran past the fields, the warehouses and supermarkets on the outskirts of town. He ran until he picked up a track leading down to the sea.

The shore below the old house, in the depths of the evening, with the wind sweeping and the sea snarling for night, was the only place.

She had not told him. Not told him. The world rattled its bones.

He sat on a boulder, trying to hammer Delia's words into sense. He closed his eyes. Caitlin could not have known. A small shift of nausea rose, as if he might spew out. His head reeled. He was not sure of anything and the big noise of waves filled his ears.

He walked along the sand, going up the coast, around rocks and towards the low cliff. All he could do was walk. Walk himself out of the place. On the ground, labels fell off the side of bottles. Wisps of torn rope and cord strayed from the broken-down netting of lobster pots. Silvery slashes of cloud were blades. His mum had been alarmed when she heard about Harjit. She had asked about his parents and three sisters. But she had not told him about Caitlin. He had been buried alive. Bandages were stripped from his eyes. Either Caitlin meant so much and his mum could not bring herself to talk of her, or she meant nothing. As though his mum had been asleep for years.

He kicked a dried crab, put down his foot and smashed it. He scraped off barnacles from a rock, squeezed the shell and pushed down on them with his foot. He stamped and pounded until flesh squirted out, a watery slime with black. He squashed them to mulch. He would leave them dead. Stinking. He flung a fistful of pebbles and they hit the rocks like gunfire. He kicked a beer can, sending it in a spin.

He smashed an empty beer bottle against the side of a red boat. With the rough glass edge, he ran it along the side, gouging with a cold wrath. He wrote his anger. Scarred it. A cutting energy drove him. A feather of wood stuck out from the outer layer. He pulled, ripping, to the golden-white naked lengths. The wood curled off in wisps. He would finish this. Damage. Kill it. Make sure nothing else hurt him. A splintering rage streamed so fast, it was numbing. He tugged the strips, breaking the bones of the boat. Crush the life. Fix it so the boat would never again be the boat it was. He fell to his knees. His hands were mucky with a ridge of dirt under his nails. Sand ran on his fingers. A strange pleasure filled him.

At the old house, no one was around. A pack of beer was stashed in the corner by Pauley's sleeping bag. He pulled out three cans, drank them one after another and slid to his own bedding. He wanted to slam his eyes shut, cut out the light. Deaden the inside of himself.

6

Laughter rose from trailers on the site and three scragglymaned horses rambled in the field. One belonged to the sprawling family of kids who played outside into the late evening. He wanted to yell at their door, 'shut the fuck up'. Two women sat on small fabric garden chairs talking, while a group of kids nearby kicked a ball. It sprang into the air, landing at his feet. He kicked it. Kick her. Get her to tell him the truth. The ball shot towards a toddler with straggly blonde hair. He tottered, falling in a heap, and cried.

'You devil. Look at the child. What you've done.' A large woman with spiky short black hair rose out of her chair, 'You could've hurt him.' She waddled to the boy, bending to his tears.

Torin hurried on and, when he looked over his shoulder, the child was in his mother's arms, his face nestled into her neck. Torin didn't care. He had seen the boy around but he didn't care about him. A gangly lad leaned against the door of a trailer, the peak of his cap down in his eyes as he played a harmonica. Strange whiney notes grazed out. The boy's uncle, an old man with a grey goatee, rocked to and fro in his chair as if enjoying the music. Torin wanted to hit the boy, to trap and stop the notes. Nothing deserved to live and have expression. Not if he couldn't.

He searched under the old tyre by the van for the spare key. Stabbing it in the lock, he kicked open the door. He hadn't eaten but he was not hungry. Edgy, unable to sit, he made tea. Had to do something. Keep busy. She was never around when he wanted her. He lay on the sofa bed. A fug of stale bread and old sprouts. Before he spent time at the old house, she made big slurpy stews which lasted days. He pushed against the trailer walls. Hammered them. He didn't know if he was angry with himself for not knowing, or with her. He wanted to fight. To fight himself. Or her. To squash something in him. In her.

The place reeked. Bacon. The stink of days-old cabbage. Her perfume of stinky roses. Her blouses hung from the handle of a cupboard. He stretched for a magazine and brushed against a flimsy green dress hanging on the back of a door. It slipped off. He squashed the soft nylon into a ball. He jabbed, making it smaller and released the material so it unloosed itself. Lined with creases, it lay on the sofa. He found scissors in a drawer by the sink. Ripped it, streaking down with the blade. Jagged strands of green flared. Streamers. Ribbons. He drew down slits. He pulled open the wardrobe. He struck through the lengths of dresses. All her favourites. Threads loosened, flew like strands of hair. Ribboned, the skirts were shredded. He lay back on the sofa, tatters and rags of material on the floor.

Footsteps. Hers. Closing in. His mouth was dry. He swiped a glass under the tap for a drink.

'You're there. If I'd known. I'd have got you to help with this load.' She came in, settling on the sofa, a hump of shopping bags at her feet.

He was leaden with exhaustion. But he had her. She would have to drag out everything into the light.

'What've you done?' Her thinned, pale face stared. 'My lovely things.' Her hands passed through them. She wept, brushing aside her hair. 'What've you done?'

He had hurt her. He was exultant.

'You should've told me,' he said.

'What?'

'Her. Caitlin.' He forced his voice low. Might as well have hit her in the face. The stamp of the past.

She lay back. Done in. Good. He'd smash this silence. Smash her into some kind of truth.

'Why didn't you tell me?' He pushed on, even if his own voice alarmed him.

He would stalk her. His animal. He stood over her lying against cushions on the sofa. She pulled a tissue from her sleeve and blew her nose. She would not escape. She had brought him to a strange place. She had done him in. His hopes had tumbled down. He had only the complete rage of knowing he knew nothing at all. She had left him stranded.

'I don't know.' She flinched. Her eyes were small and tight with fear and strain written across her face.

'You cheated me out of my life.' He tried to keep a hold on his voice but the buzzing in his head tightened. Knotted. Tension like a gathering of birds.

'I meant to say something. It was in my head to every day.' She wiped her hands across her eyes, smearing her cheeks with mascara and eyeliner. Her face was red. 'I was afraid of what you'd say. But there wasn't a day I didn't think of her. You don't know how hard it was.' She stretched towards him. Pulling. Digging in her hands.

'Don't touch me. She, Caitlin, spent years with Delia when I could have known her. We could have grown up together.' He pushed her off.

'I couldn't manage. I was afraid the Social Services'd be after me. I left her one time with a neighbour and didn't her father, Kaybe, come and report me. I was afraid I'd lose her completely. He'd an awful temper. I thought he might snatch her. All I could think was, the one person who'd keep her safe was my mother. I always meant to come back and get her. But then I had you, and after she died I didn't know what to do so I asked Delia. She'd no children of her own, d'you see, so it was company and a good turn I was doing in a way. And the loss hurt less for me as they were on the road. Travelling all over the country and I'd know I wouldn't come across her. Of course, it was different after Tomeen passed on and she came back to parts she knew.

But I only gave her over for it to be temporary. I wasn't meaning it to last.'

'Nice to know you cared,' he spat out. 'When did you bring her over?'

She blew her nose and sniffed.

'Caitlin was over her first year. Getting big and had a lovely coat on I'd got from a lady I cleaned for. I saved so I could get the train to the boat and not the bother of a coach. I met my mother soon as I came off the boat, for they were on their way north. It was hard leaving her. I can see Caitlin to this day in the blue dress and a blue cardigan and little red shoes with black bows. It was awful hard. I was crying for weeks after.'

'Why was it me wanted and not her? I don't get it.'

'I left her intending to go back. But you came along and how could I? I couldn't search up and down the country to whatever place she might be in. And what'd people think, with the two of you and me not married? I was caught. But I wasn't meant to be.'

He stared out the window. Her words came at him solid as bricks. He wanted to know more. Everything. And yet he didn't.

'I never forgot her. Not at all. She'd lovely springy hair like her dad, and his eyes. Kaybe wasn't a bad man. Not at the start. He'd talk for hours, telling me how we both came from small places. But he left me on my own and I'd to work and London's a big place. A person can get lost in it. But I'll make things up. I will. The three of us'll have a good time together.'

Loss rose through his thighs and guts; through every muscle and bone. A loss tearing. What he might have had. All the flats he had lived in across England, the miles they had travelled from one room to another, one small town to the next. And the last few in London, the one over the barbers, the school caretaker's house where they had two rooms and the use of his kitchen. Evenings when his mum was out cleaning and he was alone. Empty days when she was at the pub and his company was a pile of sandwiches and the television.

'And what about my dad? You haven't told me much about him.'

'Taylor'd come round an odd time but I never knew when. He was good till it all went wrong. A tall fella with a lovely smile and a rich Scottish accent that a person'd roll in. He was in London on the buildings and lived in West Ham. We used go to a pie and mash shop. Black and white tiles on the floor and crystal lights glittering on a Friday night. I would've walked on coals, pulled stars out of the sky for him. But he walked out on me. He was selfish. Always his own man.'

This was the most he'd have. A few facts twisted. Strangled. Knowing them made little difference. Fists of grief rose in his chest. The rug near the table was stained with a splodge of fat merging with breadcrumbs and broken crisps. Love was like this. Changing. Merging into something he could not work out. Against a purple background, gold and orange flowers coiled and meshed.

'I promise—' she began.

'I don't need promises.' He sank to the bed. Tired of his voice. Tired of her.

On the table, slices of a white loaf tumbled out. A tin his grandad must have opened spewed out spaghetti. Neon drips of tomato sauce.

'I'll make it better. Whatever you want.' Her eyes were pinched and thin. 'We'll go into town, the three of us. Buy nice bits. Jewellery, shoes, dresses, ribbons. Clips for her hair with diamonds, bright as stars.' She opened her arms, rising towards him, daring to draw close.

'We can what? What the hell can we do?'

'Please...' Her hands rose to grasp him but he flinched.

He was a tight coil, ready to spring, to get the hell away. She fell against the table and the milk carton shook. Drops bled out. Her hands were on his shoulders, stroking his hair.

'Look at the grand pile of fruit I have.' His grandad came in, carrying a box of green apples, bananas and plums. 'I got the load off a fella who was driving a truck load, was in an accident. Didn't the boxes fall off and they were no good to anyone.' His face glowed with pleasure.

'I've an awful ache. Where's my medicine?' Eva rubbed her stomach, her face in spasm.

She pulled down the small bottles from the shelf where the television stood; she unscrewed the tops but the tablets toppled, pink and brilliant green, across the floor.

Torin stepped away, towards the door.

'Don't be angry,' she called. 'I didn't mean any harm.'

'Don't tell me what to feel.'

'What's the matter? What've I done?' his grandad asked.

'I never meant to hurt you. Where are you going?'

He pushed past his granddad and a plum fell and smashed on the floor. Juices ran and slipped. She could wait. His grandad could wait. His grandad stepped to one side as a squashed tangerine slurred across the floor. Mucked in with dirt and spills from milk on the floor.

'Don't rush, lad.' His grandad grabbed the edge of the table and sank to a chair.

Out the door, Torin ran past the big trailers, dead bikes, empty crates and forlorn buggies.

As he reached the fence, his phone rang. Caitlin. He could explain. Make it all right. He could make her understand.

'Torin?' It was Marcus.

'Oh.'

'You sound awful.'

'No, I'm okay.'

'Good.'

'What's going on, then?'

'Harjit died.'

'What?' he stuttered. His legs weakening, he slumped to the ground.

'It was in the news. Complications.'

'What's that mean?'

'His blood. It went all funny. Infected or something. It did him in.'

Was that good or bad? What did complications mean? What could it ever mean except it was his fault.

'I wish he hadn't. It's all gone wrong,' he wailed, unable to rein his voice in.

'Mate, it wasn't your fault. Not all of it. Him being ill wasn't. It just happened.'

'He didn't deserve it,' Torin gulped, heaving to steady his voice.

'Don't take it rough. It's not your fault.'

'I know,' his voice wavered. He knew nothing except one thing and the knowledge sliced through him. He wanted to run into the furthest distance. Lose himself. Lose whatever it was he had brought with him.

'I gotta go. The match is starting. I'll call again. Let you know what's up.'

Torin walked to the furthest part of the site, to the fields at the far end and bedded down. His jacket was a pillow. The horses in the distance did not bother him. They looked across and lay down, easily elegant. Like models, long-limbed girls on the front of the shiny mags his mum liked. Horses. People. Horses were easier.

He could not sleep at first for the rip of a siren. A low hum of traffic on distant roads, roads weaving through small fields and farms. The Gards might sneak around. They would have found the truth. He dreamt of Caitlin riding in an open top low sports car. He called after her, his voice gliding with a siren, but she could not hear.

California Row

1

Music thumped like blood. A bass wrapped around Caitlin and sapphire lit her hair. She was dizzy with flecks of emerald and lavender. A man with cropped hair bought her a cocktail, golden orange swirling while turquoise lights played over her cheeks.

'Thanks,' she said, leaning on the counter.

'You're welcome.' His smile glistened.

She drank vodka, a slippery silver fish rising, to block out the days, the nights. The man spoke to a younger man at the bar. In the shadowy light, filtering reds and oranges, it could only be Torin. She pressed back against the women behind her. She should leave. Or demand answers. The young man turned, sliding his hands into his trouser pockets. The same light brown hair. The same shaped face. But the nose and eyes were different. She needed to sit. He would never look the same again.

She had stayed late at Breen's checking the stock. Torin had been and left Delia by the time she arrived. The old woman was full of him. How good he was at helping. How he was content to sit and talk and wait. Have tea. Admire old photos. And Eva. How she had come and gone years ago leaving Caitlin behind.

She had shouted. Yelled at Delia for some sense. For something to help her understand, until there was little the old woman could tell her that she did not already know. And what she knew, she did not want to know.

'What harm was in it? Your mother only tried to do what she thought was the best for you. For her.'

Too raw and scared of seeing anyone, Caitlin wanted to be alone. Free of him. Of her. Delia. Eva. All as bad as each other. She would wash off the past. Her skin. Run away from all of them. If she drank and stayed out all hours, she would forget. Kill the memory.

'You all right?' Lola sat beside her

'I was when I came out.'

'Sit here.' Lola pulled out a chair from a table. Caitlin leant her head on her arms The dead beat of garage music prowled the walls. 'Where's Annie?'

'By the DJ last time I saw her.'

'I'll get her. Then let's leave. I've got no more money. You can't have either. Come on.'

'Now?' Caitlin asked.

'It's almost three. I've had enough. You have too.' Lola grasped her arm and tugged her along.

They slipped through the press and pull of girls, stilettos and sequin jackets, pushed up against bangles and bare waists. A fury of music in a barrage of glittery lights. Shadows bubbled, sheets of turquoise tones. At least here she was not different. The last couple of weeks she had seen black people. Some of the men had great jobs in finance or were studying. A few girls were Asian and she had met an accountant from Delhi. It was easier, yet she missed the expanse of land from her window. The pulse of the sea. Wandering where she wanted. Salty air on her skin. Don't be stupid, she told herself. You've had a bellyful. You don't need more air. Sea air or city, what's the difference? It's all around.

A taxi dropped them at the top of the road from the site.

'No point putting off those drivers,' Annie said, leading her along to the battered gate and crushed metal fence.

Annie had been on the site with her family for five years and told Caitlin she slept with a knife under her pillow. Had warned of a tall fella ranging around. He was not from California Row but another part of the city, and Annie had sworn she had seen him once at the back of one of the trailers talking to a bunch of kids.

Nights chill as winter crept towards them. How quickly time passed when no old lady pondered over a fire complaining of rheumatism. But soon it would be the dead heart of winter with no big fires like Delia's. People were less friendly, more hurried, talked of the difficulty of getting dole, how they had to queue everywhere. The cold was getting colder. She pulled her coat close, which did not help because she was heavy and sluggish. Her skin itched, a red, hazy rash crawling on the inside of her arm, the way it used to be when she was nervous and too many things were happening.

Their heels flitted through the site to the trailer where they locked themselves tightly in. In bed, Caitlin pulled a duvet around her shoulders. She was hungry for the city and what it gave, could fill herself with it. Music, clubs and the sheer press of other people blocking out the night.

Lola and Caitlin trawled department stores. They passed through the large plate glass doors of Browns, which opened like arms and made Caitlin want to stay for hours. They hung around cosmetic counters, tried perfumes, asked for samples of cream they would never touch but stash away.

Lying in bed, mid-afternoon, with Annie and Lola up and gone, one for a job, the other to kick around the city, a knock hardened against the door.

'Caitlin, you there?' Shane called.

His dark brown eyes were loyal, watchful. He made her laugh, was always handing over money for drinks. He knew the best place to buy cheap bread and milk. His square-shaped hands had grasped hers a month back when he had come into the bar and said, 'You need to get out of here. I need to get out of here.' She had told him she wanted to leave but did not know how. She had kept back her fears. The knot of confusion of knowing and not knowing which lay at the back of her heart. He had told her he could get the loan of a car and she had thought little of his suggestion until he came to the bar when she was on during the morning. He said they should go and go now.

The battered dark blue Beetle, which a German couple had dumped after a holiday, took them off and they drove along the coast, through midland towns and to Galway She had wanted to go further north but he said their money would run out and they should head for where he had connections and try Dublin.

When they first arrived on the site, she had pushed back the duvet to let him in. She had raised herself, wanting him deeply. To shield her from what she knew of herself. He could make her someone else. Someone new. She beat her fingers on his back, urging him. He could block out what had gone on.

She would fight off the memory. Bury him. But Torin's face came to her. Sailing on the cusp of a breeze as she and Shane surveyed a ridge of headland in Moher or as they crawled in heavy traffic of a market day in a small town. His eyes. A boy as tall as him waiting at a bus stop. The tilt of his head. His hair.

'You all right?' Shane asked, his hands on the steering wheel

'Yes. I'm fine.' She was as right as she ever could be. He leaned over, patted her knee gently. They sped past and when she looked over her shoulder, the boy had gone.

Shane took her into a whirl of speed so the air was hard round her ears. But she wanted to drive further, go to other cities. The length of the country. Even America. It was big enough to hide in. They could travel without being noticed. She could fall into the landscape, be anyone. Be who she wanted to be. Her mother had dumped her, but coming here would make sure she put everything between them. She would cut her off. Have no link. She would not be afraid of who she might see or who was around the next corner. Shane drove fast but kept his eye on the speedometer as though they were the only ones. A frisson of air shot through her, an intake of breath as she slipped to the side of the seat.

They drove as far as the Wicklow hills where he parked and they spent the day roaming. She smelt air sweeter than she had known for a long time. She wondered where Torin was, and as soon as she had, wished she hadn't. Did he think of her? Or was he fighting like her, to forget? She shivered, longing to know. And yet not to.

The girls were out, so Shane had room to lie down on the bed beside her. His hair was long and he had a week's beard. He wore the same denim jacket he had worn when they arrived at the site.

'Good news. We can make some money. Mehall says we can go out with him for a drive.'

'Collecting the scrap?'

'I know it's not what you want to do. Not what I want much, but he'll give us a split of what he makes.'

It was money at least and meant she could go on at this distance. Life without Delia was bound to be tough, she told herself. She grabbed a jacket and folded up the bed. A couple of years since she had lived in a trailer, but the way to manage was coming back. You had to fold and pack away clothes neatly, along with the bed. Anyone at the stove had to move first, and if anything was to be kept safe it had to be mostly stashed high up on a shelf above your head. She did not mind. All she had to do was to keep doing things. Going out at night. In the day wandering into the centre. She threw a cup of tea down. Outside the bright red caravan opposite, an older woman glared, her hands on hips.

'What's wrong with you girls, drawing attention to us with them paintings?'

The moon and stars Lola had painted on the side of their trailer were a shimmer of gold and silver. The woman smoked on as Caitlin and Shane passed and he told Caitlin to ignore the woman, as painting was in their blood. He walked on with his easy pace, a slight swing from side to side as though he was pleased with himself or the hum of a tune was going through him. His own man. Could take her wherever she wanted. With him, she could forget. Be whoever she wanted.

'We'll all fit in,' Mehall said as they squeezed alongside each other in the front.

Mehall, a flat cap at an angle, was quick and nifty. No sooner had he a lorry piled but it was sold to the scrap-yard. One of the women on the site said he must be a millionaire. Caitlin did not care. She reckoned if he was, he worked hard. He was on the lookout for a caravan for the two of them. A good bloke. He never bothered them. He let Shane look after her. They drove following the motorway around the city, passing slip roads and burger bars, past the estates and mega stores for carpets and tiles, heading for smaller roads.

'I'll be going around the good parts. Blackrock, Greystones. You two jump down when I stop and call to the doors. Ask if there's any spare scrap metal. I'll come along after you and help sling it in.' He jerked a look over his shoulder at the scrabble of iron pipes, fridges and gates slung on the back.

The lorry dragged and was surly as it climbed a hill. He drove along wide suburban streets with trees leading to neat roads with tall old houses painted in soft tones like the layers of a wedding cake. They worked through the streets, driving slowly and stopping, the scrap mounting slowly in the back of the truck. With each new road a few more bits were added: the back of a fire, walls of an oven, the pick of an axe, shoe caps, metal hangers and a steel framed chair. Mehall loaded them on with great cheer.

'You've done a grand job. I might have news about a caravan soon. A man who owes me a favour told me he had one.'

It would be good to be out of the cramped way of Shane's cousins, in their own place. Mehall gained speed. They passed onto the main road with rows of shops and the hard work was over. She returned to the trailer to find the girls were out. She lay on the bed with Shane, grateful for the familiarity of him even if by the morning he had retreated to his uncle's place.

She needed a job. The girls asked around, but no one would take her on. Annie worked in the market and Lola, with long dark hair and deep olive eyes, was a dresser in the theatre. She returned with tales of actors' tantrums and drinking sessions, how one was so tipsy he was unable to wear the full costume, going on stage with only a shirt and trousers, the waistcoat hanging from the dressing room door. Once she brought back a sequined jacket which was going to be thrown out and they took turns in wearing it. Annie was good at selling. With her blonde hair and long nails, anyone would want to buy from her. She sold clothes straight out of the warehouses, even if they were loose and not well cut, with beads on the outside of trouser legs or on the lapels of jackets. They tried on dresses and jackets and experimented with free samples of make-up. Annie applied luminous red lipstick and eyeliner. She cut Caitlin's hair close to the scalp and coloured it blonde. With it steely and short, she was like a boy. Tougher. Stronger. No one could break her. Tell the difference, she thought. Watch me disappear.

'What about it, then?' Annie asked. 'You said you could tell the future.' She offered her palm.

Caitlin held it. A broken life-line ran, a winding love line, the moons of Venus and Mars soft and lumpy in the grubby palm.

'Everything will come. But be watchful of too much ease.'

This was clear for other people to understand and they loved it. She wished she could do it for herself.

'Can you see anybody?' Annie persisted.

'I can't see people. I see paths people make and those they might follow.'

'Is there anybody coming up mine?' Annie laughed.

'There is someone.' She held Annie's palm.

'Is he good-looking?' Annie's eyes were dark with longing.

'I can't rightly see. But yes. Leastways, decent looking.'

'D'you reckon I'll go any place? America?'

'There's someone holding a pen or something aloft.'

'It could be the flame herself has. The Statue of Liberty.'

It was good to be wanted. To have something others needed. To be wanted for who she was. Delia had said reading palms came with time and if she looked intently, she would catch a sense of what was to happen. She had to concentrate. It was in the air and in the sounds. Or it wasn't. You were not to let on. People believed seeing into the future was like looking for something on a shelf, or the way you would turn a tap on and let the water flow. Delia had said, feel your way with the telling, the way an animal does in the night, sniffing into corners, letting the smell lead. Foxes or badgers deep in the dark know their way. People dream. They need to, so let them. Don't break it. Dreams are as delicate as the bones of a thrush and if you grind them down, like the poor bird, there will be no flight. Delia led her to believe everyone creates their own future. She had said that every day we get out of bed, we are on our way to it. It was the one thing the old woman gave: how there is only the everyday, the slow tracking forward. Tell people what they need. Tell them more and they'll buckle you for it, push you under.

She would have liked a sister. Someone to grow up with. Help her be herself. It could have been Torin. When she looked at how it was, for both of them, they both had a rough deal. Both had been deceived. But which the greater? Had this been what Eva had wanted? She turned around the facts to make them fit and a swell of sickness rose.

'What's wrong?' Annie asked as Caitlin tore to the toilet.

She vomited, her body heaving. She wiped her mouth, taking a glass of water. She wanted to tell the girls but was scared. In the evening, wrapped in a big coat, pulling the collar up, she headed to the city on the bus with them. They went to Lockets Club, in the north, working their way to The Kitchen, where anyone looking good or unusual, or both, got in. The girls smiled at the bouncers who winked and stood aside as they entered.

A thin boy with slicked back hair looked like a business man, someone who could afford the evening, so she let him buy her a couple of drinks but sought the girls at their table. The days with Delia fell away. She was renewed. Against the glow of the walls and shattering lights, mauve going to blue back to lavender, she and the girls danced, drank, danced more. The incessant beat pulled. She returned to the table flushed and warm with sweat. Her head spun with the reel of music, firing and deadening her, drawing out a needle of pain. The dark and its tones blocked out the day, the light. Torin was clearing out of her system. The longer she stayed in the city, the more she came to bars and met people. Other people, anybody, the more he was washed out. Sluiced. The way a farmer might clear down the yard of shit, she thought, or the way the men with horses cleared out the boxes after them. She was letting in new life. It would be all hers and she would go wherever she wanted.

At two, she left with the girls, tripping down the steps onto the street for a cab. It was so late, it was quiet and early. She could not sleep. Music zoomed through her. The face of the man at the bar coursed through. She dreamt of Delia in washes of shadows. Her wrinkled face peering. Sharp eyes. A swish of her skirt about the rooms. The thud of her step.

'This'll settle you.' Annie offered a mug of hot milk with brandy.

Caitlin wanted more than settling. She wanted deep, cavernous sleep, walls of protection, wind-breaks against disturbance. She slept until the next afternoon, rising with fistfuls of energy.

For days and nights, she knew what to take to keep her awake and what would make her sleep. The girls were out one afternoon when, fired with a need for order, she tidied up, clearing the mess of bread and biscuits, opened tins of soup and beans left out. She swept up crumbs littering the floor. Washing up was dried and put away. She cleared the bins. She was better. Alive. Alert. She rummaged in her bag for a mirror. Her skin was greasy, pores enlarged, and her cheeks had a run of tiny red veins. Her hair was matted and lank. Roots from the blonde dye showed and the crop was growing wildly, over her ears, down the back of her neck. A golden sun shone in the way she had seen on walks to the sea; she opened the door for a better view of the distant trees, which were tall and lavished with bare branches. But turning to close the door, she slipped.

Bleary eyed and headachy, she lay on the bed.

'What happened?' Lola asked, arriving back. She tumbled shopping on the side of the sink and leant over Caitlin to feel her forehead. 'You gotta look after yourself. What did you take?'

'I'm not sure which. I thought the ones to keep me going.'

'Hon, I told you to watch it.' Lola sat on the bed and stroked Caitlin's hand.

'I don't know what's wrong.' Caitlin blew her nose.

'Don't cry. It'll mess your mascara and look awful. And hey, you're slipping away. Thin arms. You're not eating proper. We'll skip going out tonight and I'll get us a take-away.'

The door clicked shut as Lola left and Caitlin lay back against cushions. She closed her eyes against what was missed, what was lost.

2

For four days his mum lay in bed, ashen and drifting between hours. The little table held phials of tablets. A nurse had called twice, stepping over old newspapers and tutting. She had been swift and efficient, opening and closing her bag as she brought out thermometers and blood pressure gauges, seeing to his mum. The nurse had left, tip-toeing down the steps as if they might eat her. His grandad said Eva was tired, but this was a tiredness Torin had not seen before. It flooded every part of her. When he offered her a cup of tea one morning, she fluttered open her eyes and smiled. He held her hand with a weight of questions. How had she left Caitlin with Delia? What was his father like?

'Thanks,' she murmured, raising a trembling hand.

He propped another pillow behind her. The skin on her temples was thin, revealing a network of veins. As if he might see right through her.

He offered a cup. She grasped it, bringing it close. Her nails were purplish-blue, indented with ridges. Her thumb nails were cracked.

'Have more.'

She sipped but grimaced with distaste. He put it down to try again, but it was not drunk two hours later. He tended to his mother, keeping close, the only thing he could do to help her, to urge her out of this darkness, while all the time hoping Caitlin might appear. Surely she would. To find him. To talk. But her absence grew, a load upon his shoulders that he could not shake off until he brushed the notion away in the long nights of his mother's short breaths.

'What did they do at the hospital?' he asked his grandad.

'She'd treatment with the radiography business. You know the kind, whatever it is, she was always weak after.'

Torin stood at the side of the bed. He might wake her, disturb her into some kind of life.

His grandad muttered, 'She's ill beyond hope.'

What did he know? He wasn't a doctor. Torin had seen her this way before, at Christmas and after parties. She would lie down for hours, the day after. Sleep till the afternoon, turning away offers of food until she woke ravenous and would do a fry-up in a celebratory mood. She always recovered. She might look as if she was falling apart but she recovered.

The days drained, stretched hours, until they merged into one long watch by the side of his mum as she weakened. She refused toast and fish fingers, turning down scrambled egg. He was frightened by the wrinkles around her eyes and mouth. He wanted to shatter the silence, hear her talk and talk to her, but it was late. Her face, thin and glazed with lost nights in hospital, looked up but gave no answers. Why had she left Caitlin? Why had she never told him? If she recovered, he would not be angry. He wasn't angry with her. He wasn't. It was the shock. He would listen.

The night after she had been quiet all day, his grandad said he would stay up and watch over her. She lay like a child. Torin lay down to sleep but could not. The night was too alive with her.

In the dark, she turned, shadowed as if the night was breathing. All his years with her. He knew so little. So much. His grandad dozed and woke with a judder.

'I only closed my eyes a while,' he said.

They sat up watching, as if all the watching might help.

'Why did she leave you for England?' Torin asked.

His grandad's face crumpled, his eyes moist.

'She was forever wandering. Eager for new places. We couldn't please her. She was keen to be off. I never knew was it because we had wandered so much ourselves, or she was wanting one place to stay in.' His face was grey and weary.

He was cutting into the heart of his grandad. The real questions would have to wait. Later, when she was up and better, they would sit around and he would get the answers he wanted, find out all there was to find out.

Next morning, she slept on. Torin bent close as her eyelids flickered. She offered so little, yet it overwhelmed him. Could she not open her eyes? He raised a small glass, cupped her head in his hand. Drops of water touched her lips. But she raised no hands to grasp or draw him close. He feared what he knew. She did not fully know who he was. Or where she was. His hands were big and clumsy next to hers, worn-out and bony, slivers of veins tracing grey and blue. Although scared he might knock against her frail skin, he ran his fingers across her cheeks. Cold. Her brows were light without the strokes of the pencil, and her lips were pinched and naked. Her hair was robbed of colour. Otherwise, he might believe she had come in from enjoying the night and the company of men at the pub and was only recovering. In the late mornings, when they had lived in the high flat in Sherlock Close, mechanics from the garage opposite had stood around catching her to chat to, while music came from the workshop. Old stuff. Very old stuff. But what she liked. Sinatra. Marvin Gaye. He set down the glass and went outside. One man, fat as a bear, the other a stick of a man, as his mum would say, sat on the steps of the trailer next door, drinking from cans. They gave Torin one and opened packs of crisps. The men talked and joked in competition with Clint Eastwood, on a laptop propped on a chair, the aerial sticking up behind. Barely listening, and wanting but not daring to tell them about his mum, he drank until a terrible wail rose. He went hot and cold, stumping his drink to the ground. He pushed back his chair and rushed in.

It was over. She had gone, taking herself and part of him. Numb and calm, he kicked a chair. She had let him down. Had slipped away. The way she would nip out for a drink or meet a man in the night. Her skin used to be dewed with rain when she might have slipped out to Shepherd's Bush market on an evening, but she lay waxen, her eyes sealed closed. He half expected her to rise and ask what on earth he wanted and not to leave his dirty clothes lying around. She was there and yet was not, in a coldness beyond the depth of temperatures.

His grandad had filled him with bits of history but his history was her. And she was all there was for him, for a long time. She had been his link to anything that mattered. Given him a sense of belonging. Yet, history was all he had of her. And what she had said. Scraps. Bits of song and story that his grandad had retold. Ragged bits of what his grandad valued. Without his mum, he had a new freedom which was frightening in its enormity. He was lost and going nowhere. Could go where he pleased. Except. He'd straighten things out with Caitlin. Seek her out. He'd seen nothing of her since he'd been to Delia's. She'd be afraid of what she must know, as he was. But he had to see her. Make things plain and good. Afterwards he'd leave. Get out of her life altogether. He realised what he had not seen before: in her crazy, cack-handed way his mum had tried to protect him. She had not intended any harm. She had not expected it. In a strange innocence she had believed what she had done was right.

Men from trailers nearby came in; older women he had not seen before streamed through the trailer all the next day to see her lying in the coffin, across the table. In twos or threes, wearing dark clothes, they filed by. He and his grandad sat through the outpouring of prayer upon prayer. His grandad talked or cried or both, babbling into a wet handkerchief. The slightest cause and he was off. His grandad was crazy, and himself nearly so.

A crowd turned up. Trailers and caravans parked on every verge. Horses stood while vans and cars nudged one another. He wondered if he might see Delia, if she had even heard the news. But if she had, without neighbours or a car to bring her, she would have been unable to get there. The day was overtaken by ceremony. He watched from the side, as his mother was carried away. Everyone followed the big black car through the town to the packed church.

In the cemetery, his grandad stood over the coffin and threw down soil into the gaping hole. So much to know. He wondered about her time alone in London before she had children. How had she lived? No one with her. And later with him. A toddler. He pulled his jacket collar up against a light breeze. Turves of grass were piled on the side. The priest said prayers. Two men hung around with shovels and when the mourners left, they started digging her in.

The rotten bit inside her would be hidden underground; guts mangled, stained like nicotined fingers, going off with mould. He had seen samples in a school in Leeds: lab shelves of jars with animals and insects, a sheep's brain and its eye. The boys who had made fun of his accent said the brain was pickled. The big jar with a goats brain had a gory lump, thick and plasticky. One woman said, it was the way with cancer. You never know where you are, one day a person is fine, the next, they're eaten up with it.

'There was a good few more years left in her,' a voice said, from a clutch of women.

They looked as old as his mum. Even older, with worn dragged faces and cardigans, and he wondered why it was they were there.

'We'd never a cross word between us. She should have lived, been able to enjoy her time,' his grandad said, looking thinner.

Joe walked with them towards the gates.

'A pity I didn't know her sooner,' he said.

His jacket was worn at the elbows yet it was the smartest Torin had seen on him. He wore a dark tie. Grief had scrubbed him of years. He looked younger. If Torin didn't know, he would have assumed he was off to a wedding. Even his shoes were blackly shining.

'What'll you do?' Torin asked.

'I've no call to be staying. I'll head north. There might be more work. Most places have a call for mechanics.' He was a good bloke. The only decent man in a long time. Torin would miss him. 'It's not the dying that's hard. It's the ones left who have it difficult,' he said. His dog lay placid, making no scratches on the ground with her feet, or running in the hope of a stick.

Surely she had only popped out to the shops. Any minute she'd come back, a loaf of bread and pint of milk in her hand.

His grandad cried in the night, shuffled and spat, coughing his lungs out. He lay on his bed, blankets around his chest. Fat tears rolled down his rough cheeks and his frail body shivered.

Torin woke before light and turned to check if his mum was awake. The unused bed was stark and cold. But nothing was real, only the dark outside with fragile glitters of light in the window; a wood without the sound of birds. He could do anything, yet freedom was a burden. She had brought him here but had buggered off, leaving him with his grandad hollering like a baby, like a cat crying out to the moon.

His grandad said they had to clear the caravan. Empty it.

'But why?'

'We've to burn it, for it'll do us no good with only a bad spirit in it.'

'Where'll we live?'

'Another caravan, big enough for the two of us. I've the price of one, even though I'd to give back the money we got for poor Feather. I'll see we're all right with a roof over our heads.'

Torin threw all the cutlery, cups, clothes and washing things he could find into plastic bags.

His mum had bought double eggcups, sets of mats and coasters of British birds, a wooden toast rack, a lampshade with a map, statues of women in full skirts with little dogs, sailors, baskets of flowers, two donkeys and dainty, pale-faced figurines.

'Chuck 'em. I don't want to be looking at their faces,' his grandad's voice weakened. 'What good will those crocks be? I've enough to remember her by.'

Torin had to go along with him and get clean out of the place when they finished. He delved into dresses hanging on the door, taking a green one and lying it limply on the bed, in the way his mum might rest to get her breath. Under the seats, he found dried carnations, hat pins, tortoiseshell hair combs and a clutch of shells. They had a pocked, scarred outside but when he picked them up, the film of dust shaken, they were creamy white.

While his grandad was out, Torin sorted through his mum's stuff. At the far end under the sofa bed, his hand caught the edge of a Peak Frean tin. The lid slipped off. Photographs burst out. 'Brighton Belles' had two young women with rouged cheeks. They peeped from under the fringe of a large Victorian bonnet, and next to them, the face of his mum. She held up her dress, showing thick white legs, bloomers and a blue garter.

Mass cards for people he had never heard of and old birthday cards fell from a worn envelope. A rosary dripped through his fingers like a bunch of grapes, as he tried to work out what to do with it. He sorted through papers. From the belly of the envelope, he pulled a scrap: 'the time came but she was smal I asked my mother to take her so she is no truble at all so you dont have to wory love Eva.'

He turned it over, nursing it for the words might reveal themselves. Tell him what to do. Offer a glimpse of who she was and who she used to be. He read and re-read. The words held him. Caitlin. The note was about Caitlin. He could throw it out with the other stuff. Or keep it. But it was her. A side of her he didn't know. He threw it down with the pile of papers to burn. It was no use.

He sifted through photographs. One showed three young men in front of a gate to a field. From a yellowed envelope, he pulled out one of a man with a flourish of oily black hair. He moved his hand over, gazing into the eyes. The man kept staring out of the picture, an open face and small eyes under a hedge of eyebrows. He scoured the man's face and the way his jacket fell open. 'John,' was scrawled on the back. His father. The most he might ever have. John Taylor, who had left the west of Scotland on a journey southwards to find work and come across his mum, who in her own way was travelling to him. But John moved on. Had visited a few times when he was small and was supposed to have brought him a toy train. Torin pushed the picture in his trouser pocket. For later.

A plastic bag was stuffed under the sofa bed. He pulled it out. Small clothes fell; in yellows and pinks, the soft fabrics were the shapes of babies. A pale lemon jumpsuit, the sort spacemen wore, had 'Today's Angel' on the front. A matching hat fitted his fist. Stuff his mum had nicked. Wasted. She could have made money selling it, or at least given it away. He shoved the garments back in the bag.

As he left to chuck out her old perfumes in the toilets, rain began. Heavy splodges chucked down. He grabbed a man's jacket from the back of a chair. His mum had said it had been given to her by a fella who was an actor. Sleekly black, it was cut with shiny lapels of midnight blue. He pulled it on and put up the collar. When he had worn it before like this, his mum had laughed and said he looked like a curate. In the wash-house, he poured the few remaining drops of perfume down the toilet and they swam like urine, squirling down, drained to the sea.

The men from other trailers helped his grandad take the caravan to the far end of the site. It was stripped, abandoned. Ready. Joe and one of the fellas poured a can of petrol inside; splashes going on easy as water, lapping the sides of shelves. Joe bent forward and lit. Flames whirled, whelped higher and higher. A flare. Glows of flame waved and swirled, drowning the small trailer. Windows shuddered and curtains fell, little shelves where his mum had kept Marmite, jam, HP sauce and pickles, collapsed.

Metal cried and plastic which had been the base of the beds and chairs, shrieked and curled. The place she had lived in was blackened metal, last gusts of smoke like breath, wound up. The bed she had slept in was grazed and gnawed. Wooden drawers for underwear fell apart, jittered in the shock. Flames jived and jumped the sides, the front door creaking till it fell on itself, banging the step. Window frames thrilled with snakes of fire. In a puff and squander of smoke, Torin's eyes stung. Flares turned on themselves and lay down. His life was lit. Torched. Gone in an instant.

His grandad had word of an empty caravan he could buy. It was old, with scuffed metal and a scarred door. The curtains, once a thick brocade, were rags. Torin couldn't bear the sight but it was either this or be kicked onto the road. His grandad said years back he had lived under a tent of ash with waterproofing stretched over it, and how he did not so much wish to be done with all the old ways after all.

'I wonder what'll become of us, bunched in like this? I wish it was like it used to be when I was in the seat along with the others and only the lurch of the caravan over stones and the puddles to bother us. Instead, we live among rubbish mounting and never collected 'til summer when the corporation starts to notice. We're dross. If the tap on the site doesn't work, they won't bother to see to it 'til families are ill and the doctor has to be put out of his way to come.'

How would they go on, knocking against each other, lost to themselves? He'd never wanted his mum around much and now she wasn't. He'd got his wish. It was stark and all around and he didn't want it like this. This emptiness.

His grandad opened the door to the trailer and they stepped into a smell of damp. Rust on the cooker. The sink blocked.

'Is this what we were born for, when once we were the noblest people on the road? The years have climbed into the clouds and we're not wanted.' He sat on a seat under the window. Cushions were worn at the edges and foam stuck out. Torin opened the wardrobe. Dust piled in little heaps along the edges and corners. He walked outside, his nostrils full of dust and the stale air. Dark was coming down. He wanted to be anywhere but there, stone cold with fears, his fingertips frozen and the wind whistling through.

His phone shivered and his phone rang.

'Hi mate. How you doin'?' Marcus voice shook Torin into another place and time.

'Okay. How are you? What's going on'

'Big Ian got prison.'

The words thudded, barely registered until they did.

'Prison? For what? Harjit?'

'No. Not him. A job he did on a boy from South London. He had found him wandering around Vanbrugh Tower and jumped him.'

'Just that? For no reason?'

'The boy was only twelve. Come over to see a mate. Ends up with his face smashed in and his arms broken. So Big Ian's sorted. Ten years. Last week.'

'For real?'

'You don't think I'd mess,' Marcus laughed.

'But the knife? Didn't the police find it?'

'I chucked it in the canal. Had to think quick. Didn't want more aggravation.'

Torin slunk by the side of the fence. The knife gone. Sunk in the depths of water. They used to hang around under the bridges. Good place to smoke. To kip out on a warm night.

'But the cameras. Didn't they see anything? Didn't the police check them?'

'Cameras? In that poke of an alley? It's so crap there ain't none. On the High Road maybe, with the shops, but not there. The police ain't been around for ages. Got too much to do in other parts. I mean, bad stuff. Really bad stuff. Rapes and such.

Like this old lady got mugged in Chiswick. That's a nice place isn't it? She was on her way to the shops and they took her bag. She only had three pound fifty. Old ladies can't do nothing these days. They can't defend themselves. So you coming back or what?'

'Yes. I will. Nothing to stay for.'

'Let us know, then. See you.'

His body expanded. He was free. Didn't have to stay, or do anything he didn't want. No one to be bothered about him. His grandad was past it. The long night ended. The evening they had met Harjit. Harjit with his hands in his pockets. Torin lay back, wanting to put his arm around Marcus and say, 'Great news mate. Great,' steering off to a pub or a snooker hall. Blasting out on beers.

3

He made his way to the old house, along the tracks and the small road near the sea. It had grown as familiar as old clothes. When his mum arrived in London, she must have been only a bit older than he was now, and it could not have been many years after that she met his dad. Tall and a former fisherman, she had told him, he had been working on the buildings. What was his father like and what was it she had liked about him? Over the years with her, he had learnt not to ask. He kicked a stone. Damn it. He should have made her tell him.

At the door, he pulled back the stone holding up the crumpled, wretched piece of wood. He untied the knot of rope holding for a lock and pushed in. The drear call of wind rattled the roof and whistled through gaps in loose window frames. He had half expected a shifting of the stars and planets to have swept the house out to sea, but everything was as before: bundles of stale towels piled in the corner, jeans sprawling on the only chair, old bits of bread, cans, bottles, sweet papers and a tin of biscuits on the floor.

He lay on the mattress. Through the ragged doorway, waves clattered. He had not had a good sleep for nights and he half expected Caitlin to come through the door.

'You're back,' Pauley said, coming in. Torin raised himself on his elbows while Pauley sat. 'You look terrible.'

'My mum died.'

'Oh. That's bad. When?'

'Ten days ago,' Torin said, though the days had blurred into one.

It was like an age away. Or a minute. Skin close. Yet so remote it was hardly possible. They stared through the open door to the ocean. He didn't want to talk about her. It was over. She had gone. Pauley fiddled with a blade of grass, his eyes watery and blue.

'I never had anyone go and die on me. I'm sorry,' he said.

Silence lay inside him; a thick fug he could not break out of. Pauley threw tiny pebbles out the door, their sharp spitting cutting the air. Torin slung out a pebble, some kind of an acknowledgement of Pauley's words which came like the sea's heartbeat. Flies circled a half-chewed doughnut from which a sickly smell arose. Crusts of bread were thrown along with empty cans. The silence was easier to bear than trying to fill it. Torin let it hang between them.

'I got these. Want some?' Pauley leaned towards a plastic bag, removing a can of baked beans. He pulled back the ring on top and dug in his fingers. Beans fell on the ground and glistened. Torin shook his head. 'You should eat. You'll feel better.'

'I know, but I don't want those.' He stretched out. 'Shane around?'

'Haven't seen him. Not for a while, so you're okay. He might've gone away.'

'Where?'

'He's got cousins. Different places.' Pauley shrugged.

Torin rolled over.

'What's wrong?' Pauley sucked on the blade of grass. It made a sound like a bird.

'Wish I could go away.'

'Where?'

'Back where I came from.' Torin laughed. 'Not much for me here.'

'I heard of a party tonight. What d'you say?'

Torin sat up and fiddled with the lace on his trainers.

'I don't fancy it.'

'You used to like parties.' Pauley spooned out the beans and ate them.

'I did. Once.'

'How many do we hear of?' Pauley took off the baggy trousers and pulled on a new pair. 'You'll feel better. You might meet someone you know.' He picked up a handful of tiny pebbles, letting them fall.

He may as well go. And after, he would go back. Back where he belonged.

'If Caitlin's there, she won't want to see me.' He bent to avoid Pauley's eyes.

'I know things haven't worked out. I suppose the question is, can you go through the rest of the world without her?' Pauley bit into a biscuit which had been in the house for weeks. 'If you can't, go and get her.'

'Find her? I'm not sure she'd want me to. She's not answering calls or messages.'

'Don't you think you should find out? One way or the other?'

'How?' Torin sat back.

'Go to Breen's. Ask there. If you want something, go and get it. What've you got to lose?'

'Nothing. I've got nothing.' Torin picked up his jacket and followed Pauley out of the house.

A wind swept through the narrow streets and roads until they reached the centre of town. Pauley led the way up an alley to a flat above a hairdresser's; a woman with long black hair let them in. Men lined the hallway. A girl sat on the floor blocking the way to the living room. Pauley pointed towards the kitchen for a drink so they edged through a crowd.

They shifted and weaved past men in denim jackets and leather coats, a girl with a thin top showing her ribs, a tall man with a blonde pony-tail. Torin followed up a flight of stairs to a lounge. A couple were talking animatedly in the corner and two blokes stood by a table, drinking.

He and Pauley sat on a large squashy sofa. A depth of luscious, textured red cushions took their weight. He spread out and drank from a can. A fat girl approached, plonking in between them. Her rich black hair flopped, a deep fringe falling over a pale face with lashings of dark eye make-up. A streak of red lipstick made her mouth.

'Hi there.' She gave a little wave.

'Hello,' Pauley said.

Her skirt rode up, revealing plump thighs as she sat.

'How you doing? You're not from round here?'

'London,' he said.

'A bit of a way to travel for a party.' She gave a skittish laugh. 'I'm Natasha from Belfast. Would you like some crisps?'

She rose and waddled to a table nearby.

'She's got nothing on,' Torin whispered.

'It's a skirt.'

'It barely covers her arse.'

The dark was smoky. Every other kind of girl was there. He strained to find Caitlin. Holding a bowl of peanuts and two sausage rolls balanced on top, the girl plopped back on the sofa. She thrust the bowl under his nose. He shook his head.

'My boyfriend couldn't come but he knows this crowd. I kept telling him...'

Pauley stifled a laugh.

'You wanna dance?' She leant over Torin, smothering.

'No, thanks.' He shied back.

'He's hurt his leg,' Pauley said.

'Has he?'

'Real bad.' Pauley nodded vigorously.

'Shame. How'd it happen? Football?' she asked, thinly arched brows rising from the plum depths of her eye make-up.

'Eh... yes.'

'No,' Torin said.

From a small, glittery bag propped on her knees, she pulled out a mirror. Tubes and little jars clustered, the tops gunged with spills. Balancing the mirror on her knees, she applied mascara while music thudded in from the other room, a deep bass in the background.

'That's better. How do I look?'

'Fine,' Torin said.

'Like a clown,' Pauley whispered. 'Let's get out of here.' He dug Torin in the ribs. 'We gotta go.'

'But I like talking to you.' She pulled at his tee-shirt.

Torin grasped his right leg in imitation of a hurt footballer and followed Pauley downstairs. Other people pressed against them. Pauley was talking to a girl in hot pants and high heels who was opening a bottle of beer.

'Natasha's supposed to be helping serve.' The girl spread her arms out indicating a long table of food, bottles and glasses. 'I can't manage on my own. I have to find her.'

Pauley talked to the man with the pony-tail. Torin strained to listen. Poetry. He had done it at school. A poem about a bird savagely eating the skin of a sheep. He had liked it but afterwards they had to read ones about flowers and snakes and he had stopped listening. He had another drink. Pauley could be right. If he kept looking, he might find Caitlin. She might be at the party anyway. Amongst the faces, the tanned men in sleeveless vests, girls in short skirts.

An older woman floated across the room in a long yellow skirt, her face lit up. She wore a loose blouse with a flourish of necklaces and approached pony-tail man, offering a small bowl.

Pony-tail and Pauley shook their heads.

'What about you?' Her eyes glittered on Torin.

'What are they?' He sat up.

'You'll get a kick. Feel good inside.' She leant towards him and taking hold of a bottle of vodka from a table, poured a glass and sprinkled in the tablets. 'Makes your head spin. I promise,' she smiled, giving him the glass and moving on to a blonde girl in the corner.

He sat in the armchair, leaning back. This was easy. Sleek. He was like this with Caitlin in her small room, in a bed which had been unsteady, with one leg missing so the corner was held up by a piece of wood. To the side of the cabinet, through the window, a sea of pin-pricks of light. His spine fizzed. He was alive. It was not late and she might come. Might be in the house already, in the kitchen or hall, helping herself to a drink. His body flowed out of him but his head was a realm of birds fluttering. He could not get his breath but staggered to the bathroom in time to sit down as the room turned.

The innermost of his bones were empty and his head ached as he sank to the floor against the legs of a chair with a cushion pushed up to it. Sweet aromas from flowers filled his nostrils, working their way through the paths of his skull. A different kind of aliveness climbed in his veins. His skin opened. He was not in his own body.

Night drove on. Harsh notes fractured the hours. He was being cut into tiny pieces. A dark face emerged but it changed and as the focus came and went, it was Caitlin. His head was heavy. Eyes stared. He raised his hand. Her head bent with intent towards him. He called but she turned away. He crossed to a table and picked up a half-used can and drank.

'Hey, there'll be full ones down in the kitchen.'

'But if those girls are around?'

Pauley turned to leftovers, the few crisps and nuts remaining, and scoffed them. Torin picked up a can shoved in the corner and drank, the lager going down clean and fast. He was an idiot to think she would be there. He slugged another half-drunk can abandoned on a coffee table. The beer, clean and refreshing, cut against the roof of his mouth. He slumped to a chair. He could enjoy this. He could stay watching.

Natasha appeared in the doorway and made a path towards them. Pauley tugged on Torin's sleeve.

'We can crash out here,' Torin said, sick in the pit of his stomach.

'We can't. Come on.' Pauley dragged him through the room and downstairs.

Natasha leant against the banister in the hall.

'Hi, there,' she said, but they made for the front door where two men and a woman crowded the entrance. 'I'd say the leg made a miraculous recovery,' she shouted as they pushed into the chill night.

Lone stalks of telegraph poles injected the dark sky. A glossy moon threw down light onto the solitary window at the top of a battened-up house. Scaffolding jutted from the side and bricks were stacked in a block. A skip overflowed with ragged bits of carpet, plywood and kitchen cabinets. Torin picked up a brick and, easily as he might let go a ball, powered it towards the gleam of light on the lone window. The glass smashed. Spilt smithereens shook down like stars. Drawn by the shimmering beauty of the glass falling, he was in a trance.

'What d'you do that for?' Pauley pulled his arm.

'It was so perfect. I wanted to kill it.'

'You're sky-high.'

'There's nothing wrong,' Torin slurred and hung on to a lamp post. He wiped his mouth with his hand. 'We can kip here.' He sneezed and shook, thinned out by the cold.

'We bloody can't. Come on.'

Pauley held him and they walked, reaching an industrial estate at gone three. A grey monochrome of warehouses spread. His head was clearer. He was an idiot. Anyone from the houses nearby might have called the police. They could be onto him already. But they could hide. Crash out. Bring down the blinding sky over him and block out the light. Fold into the dark. There was nothing he could do to make things better.

Pauley gripped his waist so they walked in step. If he was not with Pauley, he did not know where he would be. Lying pissed out on the edge of the road. Rain fell as they passed a scrubby field bordered by a wire fence. A bedraggled tortoiseshell cat slunk along and a cluster of kittens watched dartingly from a bush.

'This looks all right,' Pauley said.

They scanned the walls of the biggest shed until Pauley found a door. He pulled on the bolt, sliding it open. If a security man caught them it could lead straight to the police. His head rang with worry but he followed Pauley. Pauley knew what he was doing.

'Thanks, mate,' he said.

'We've all come this road some time or another.' Pauley's eyes were hard and bright.

They entered the space as though owning it. Torin walked the length of the walls. Big enough to hide in. Lose yourself. Plastic crates were stacked in a corner at the far end, the dark lozenge of a laptop on the floor beside them. He bent to open the lid and pressed the switch but the screen was dead. The keys were battered and the middle ones were missing. Useless.

Calmly and without looking back, Pauley jumped on plastic crates the height of himself. Stacked against the far wall, they shifted slightly but stayed in place as he sprang up, grasping edges, finding hand holds. He balanced. Moved with the quickness of a fly. Stiff with fear, Torin held his breath. Pauley climbed higher, hands leading the way, feet nipping after, his legs taking the strain of him. He lay his arms against the bare walls, driving on. He skimmed the walls, as if barely clinging. He scaled the wall, climbing the air, leaping from crate to crate. Like an insect, alert with tension to each hold, he made his way.

'This is good,' he shouted. 'But not as good as the sea in winter. You ever swum in it naked? A chill up your backside to get the blood racing. Then you're really alive. The whole of the world tingles through your veins.'

In a sleek jump from the height of four packing cases, Pauley dipped into the space beneath with a quick scissor collapse of his legs. Torin blinked and shivered, hating the way Pauley scared him. Climbing. Diving. Pauley slipped into other places Torin could not hope to arrive at.

'Where'd you learn that stuff?' he asked.

Pauley laughed.

'I was eight. Used to climb out the bedroom window after me dad'd lock me in.' He straightened, brushing his face with his hands. He walked around the shed, inspecting it. 'Look. Covering.' He lifted a large sheet of canvas. 'We can make a bed for the night.' He dragged out a couple of sheets from the corner. 'They don't smell either.' He lay them on the floor and fell down on top.

Torin lay and pulled a sheet over and stretched out. It was good to float into his own thoughts.

'You still awake?' Pauley folded back a corner of his sheeting.

'Yes. But my head's banging all over.' He should have taken more stuff to block out the night. He turned to one side. Distant traffic hummed in the thick dark.

'This is good,' Pauley whispered, close.

Torin shut his eyes. He and Caitlin had rolled into one another, skins enveloping, defining lines collapsing.

'What's the matter?' Pauley asked.

'Nothing.'

'Something is.'

'Not much.' Torin wished he could hide his eyes.

'Your mum?'

Torin shook his head.

'The old man?'

'No.' He threw down the word. 'I'll head off soon.' His eyes stung. He closed them and tried to sleep. Pauley's hand on his shoulder, cupped the bone. Warmth spread through the thin fabric of his tee-shirt.

'Everyone feels lonely some time.' Pauley's mouth flexed into a thin smile as he leant over. He had looked deep into his heart and seen the well of emptiness. 'When I was young,' he said in a lower voice, 'My dad'd come in late from the pub. That was why my mum left. He spent all their money and when he didn't, he was out of his head causing fights and rows. I used to go to bed to get away. Home from school. Tea, a bit on the computer, then upstairs. Mum might be out at a friend's, I used to try and sleep but would hear him come in from the pub. A slip of his footsteps on the stairs. I'd pretend to sleep. He'd sneak into my room. The shiver of his jacket in the dark. He'd get into bed beside me. He smelt awful. He'd do things. I was taken over by him. Like there was nothing left. Or I was nothing. Or only something he trampled. He scared the shit out of me. One time he broke the wheel of my bike. Hit it against a wall. It was so bloody cheap it fell apart.' He rolled back, his arms wrapped around himself.

In the echoey silence, Torin heard his own breath and his bones were cold.

'But it's good with you. I'll go along with you when you go back to London.'

'You mightn't like it. It's a big, mad place.'

'Not a problem for me then?' Pauley gave a little laugh and Torin turned away. 'But you don't want the bother of me.' Pauley's voice was pale and serious.

'It's not that. It's...' Bringing someone else was complicated. Torin didn't know where he fitted in or where he'd stay, let alone anyone else. 'You'd be lost.'

'I'm lost here. In London, I could earn money. Do something. Be someone,' Pauley said.

'It might not work out.'

'With you, I'd be all right. You know, I like you,' Pauley said, with a slow, forlorn insistence. He stretched over Torin's shoulders, putting his hands against his chest, moving upwards until he grasped Torin's shoulders.

Torin's spine tickled, as a finger traced a path to his shoulder blades. The tracery of a leaf's veins in the dazzle of the sun, an intense yellow, beyond green. Pauley's fingers were going over the bones of his back. A whisper of pressure stroking, urging.

He sensed the river of absence between them but it was no good. He could not be what Pauley wanted. Pauley had to be lonely, really lonely, to be coming on to him.

'I like you too but...' Torin withdrew, pulled up his legs.

'But what?' Pauley asked.

Torin pulled the stiff, dark cover over him. His legs ached and a dullness surged in his head.

'Not like that.' He pulled the sheeting up closer, 'Sorry. I need to sleep.'

'Okay. I can deal with that.' Pauley withdrew and breathed deeply behind him, into the night.

Torin turned away. His legs and upper body were stiff. Ridges in the roof were clear. Behind him, the continual rise and fall of breath, Pauley's words creeping like an old prayer. In the grip of the dark, the cold held. The inside of his bones strained. Rain clattered on the metal roof like hooves and he saw Caitlin riding across a field. A thunder of gallops. He saw her riding away. Everything going. Losing.

Next morning, the doors rolled like thunder as Pauley opened them. Torin blinked towards the shaft of light. Pauley was the same as he had always been: optimistic, wanting so much. Torin rose, pushing the cover behind. He put his arm over Pauley's shoulder and in the new day, was exposed, raw.

4

Stark trees slipped out of view and merged into the horizon. The HGV drew to a halt and the driver declared, 'Blackrock.' Early morning rain turned to a glimmer of sun. It would have been good to know exactly where he was, but the edge of Dublin would have to do.

'Everything okay? You've gone awful quiet the last half hour,' the driver said, a baseball cap reversed on his head, so he looked about twelve. 'Know where you are?'

'Yes, thanks,' Torin lied, opened the truck door and jumped down. The man leant down from his little window. 'Thanks.'

The door slammed shut on the sweaty cabin. All he knew was, after getting on outside Longford, he had ended up on the outskirts of Dublin and the distance was grey with rows of houses. He pulled his jacket close and started walking. His grandad was probably still on the site or stumbling along a road from the pub. He should phone, but his granddad had never bothered much with them. Torin had left a note and saw the choke of pain on his grandad's face as he read it. Leaving had been cruel. He'd dealt his grandad a blow but he couldn't help it. Besides, most of his grandad's life had been without them. What was different? But he'd grown to like him. Enjoyed his bits of songs. Snatches of an old life Torin would never know, stories of those who had lived in tents of willow with old coats and tarpaulins flung on the top, the most protection out of the rain. He would not hear again of the harvest jobs on farms in the midlands or slabs of thick ham in a sandwich from women in the big houses. He'd been good company. Especially at the end. But company was not enough.

The beginning of December crept into his bones. Discount stores, garages, supermarkets. In cracks between pavement flagstones, weeds fought for life. Nothing else but strands of dry grass. Even if he found Caitlin, he did not know what he would say. Words he might try echoed around his head. He was empty of what he could offer. He was coming with only himself.

The centre flowed with cars and trucks passing while the railings of a hospital lined the road. No one was walking. It was all traffic. He turned into an empty street. Rows of neat houses stretching. He could have been in London. Except it was different. More space. An airiness or perhaps, because he was on the brink of going back, the two places overlapped. For the first time in a long while he missed the run of fields. He had not realised how they had got to him but soon all this would be over and he would be gone. Clean out of the place. Soon as he found her. He would say what he had to say and go. She would be glad to see the back of him.

At a junction a café was open, with thickset men bulked around tables. He was thirsty and it was somewhere to sit. A large woman with an apron and heavy make-up, approached.

'What can I do for you, dear?'

He ordered a fry and sat near the window. If she passed. If he saw her face, he could run out. But he knew she would not. The woman set a big plate of egg, bacon and sausage before him. While he ate, she sat, telling him about her husband who had died two years previously. She had a daughter abroad and one at the Mater Hospital, a nurse.

'I go nowhere,' she said. 'But I love my garden in the spring and I'm waiting for it to come. When I'm not in here or cooking out the back, it's there you'll find me, for the pears'll be out again next year, whatever happens.'

The winter sun was on his neck and he ate, while half expecting his mum, laden with shopping, to come through the door. A smell of bacon and fried bread rose from the kitchen. He was hungrier than he had thought. When he finished, the woman directed him towards the centre, said it was as easy to walk as to catch a bus.

The streets burst with men and women, slicker and better dressed than he had seen for a long time. They looked at him and away quickly. He was a stranger but he would be out of the country soon. It had claimed his mum but it would not take him. A woman with a red and gold turban crossed in front. On a bridge sweeping over the river, he was lost in the crowd. A little boy walked along, holding the hand of a grey-haired man. The child tugged and danced, nagged the older man, said he wanted sweets.

A trail of lorries shot past. The wind echoed. Leaves swirling against bleak grey-stone terraces. He kept walking and realised he might have to bed down in a station, park bench or doorway of a shop. Sleeping outside would not be as easy as lying in a field.

Near the millennium bridge a young boy busked, strains of a guitar lashing against the traffic and the rattle of people going by. Torin spent the afternoon in St. Stephen's Green watching the pigeons and tiny birds hip-hopping to scatterings of crumbs. It seemed too far to even think of finding her. It was too much to do more than find a bed for the night.

In a pub wide as a barn, an old geezer with a solitary slick of black hair coiled over his bald head ordered a shandy and told the barman he had been to the races.

'I won 100 euros in Galway and, in the summer, 350 in Dublin. Isn't this the way to live?' the old geezer hiccupped.

A young man wearing a cap and a denim jacket joined them. They chatted about music and venues until the guy left. Torin went to the gents. It was only when coming out he noticed that the wodge of notes, a tight fist of euros which had been in his back pocket, was missing. It must have been taken while he was talking, when the young fella came in. He pulled out all his pockets. He swept through the bar, remains of beer in his glass. He walked by the river, glazed and alight with tall buildings. He did not know where to go, and the city with its lights lowered unnerved him.

He stopped at a tiny bar north of the centre, and ordered only a Coke. A man with a red scarf and heavy rimmed glasses came in and chatted to the barman. They talked about the city, how so many flats and houses were empty.

'I'm looking for somewhere for the night,' Torin said, rising out of his seat to join them.

'There's a couple of hostels at the back of the station,' one man said.

'I don't have much money.'

'You could try a place north of here. A big old place. Was run by nuns. Home for kids,' the red-scarf man said.

'Nuns? I don't want that.'

'No, they're long gone. Kind of squat with all sorts in it.'

'Could I get there from here?'

'Course you could. Take a bus. Or walk, if you want. On the way to the airport. Adelaide Street. Rough on the outside but you can't miss it with the statue. Saint or someone, Joseph or one of them in the front garden. Ask for Maeve. If she's still in it.'

Not until he was on the bus heading south did he realise he was going the opposite direction for the squat. He jumped off at the traffic lights. Two old ladies tried to explain the correct direction but the one in a maroon hat did not understand him and he had to shout. The other pointed up the road, where she said her sister lived. Fearing he was going to hear her life history, he hurried on.

The street full of neat red-brick houses was the most unlikely place to have a squat, but out of tiredness and curiosity, he kept walking. A world of gardens and curtains. He searched for an old house needing repair, arriving at a plain grey-stone face of a building with leaking pipes running down. In the garden the worn stone face of a man with a flower pressed close. The front door fell open at his touch and led into a hall with bags stashed against the wall, as if someone was moving out. A faint line of rock music drifted between rooms. A willowy blonde girl approached, her jeans slashed so the flesh of her thighs gaped.

'I heard there might be a room going?'

'For who? You?'

'Yes. Someone in a bar suggested I ask.'

'Alex, was it? What was he wearing?'

'A scarf. Red with a diamond pattern.'

'Tell me the bar, then I'll know.'

'Daly's. He told me to ask for Maeve.'

'He's a smart one. Telling others about us and I haven't seen a bit of him in a while. There's a spare room upstairs at the back. No one's been in it for ages. Five euros for the key if you want it.'

She led him upstairs and along a corridor.

'You working in town?'

'No. Hoping to meet up with someone.' He thought he'd have to scour and sift and it might take days to find her. He would be out of there soon. Starting to live again.

'It's draughty but empty. The curtains keep falling down but you can use safety pins. There's a mattress. It isn't much but...' she shrugged, 'it's not meant to be a hotel.'

She turned the key in a padlock, releasing them in. He let down his bag and his shoulders eased. Dingy light soaked through old nets on the windows while worn red plush curtains hung on either side.

'How long you staying?'

'It could be a couple of days. A week. I don't know. Two weeks.'

'Okay. That's short term. Fine. All right for you?' She opened her arm wide.

'Sure. Definitely.'

'Don't lose the padlock. That's the most we've got.'

'The others here, they staying long?'

'Some, yes. Kind of taken up residence. But that's good. Continuity. A couple of artists and designers using the place to work in. We don't know when it'll be knocked. Could be anytime. They've made a start on houses further up. But no wild parties or bringing back loads of people.' He paid and she smiled. 'I'm in the basement so let me know when you're leaving for good.' She smiled more easily and walked back up the corridor, her curtain of blonde hair swinging.

The mattress on the floor was grimy but dry. The springs were okay. He lay down. The emptiness of the room, big as the trailer, enveloped him. A dirty chest of drawers held a long mirror with chipped edges. Dust flew up from the floor. Ghosts. But he didn't believe in them. Fifty-one days since his mum died. Fifty-two since she last spoke, her face turning in a whisper as she raised her hands, attempting to hold a cup. He had seen her in the faces of older women, dawdling over cups of tea and thin slices of toast in cafés as he had travelled across the country. He had seen her in women with worn-out eyes and thin cheeks. Sometimes, late at night, he saw her as she used to be, before they arrived here, before anything that had happened, had happened and life was simple; dozing in the heat and rush of a day before, walking along the High Road into the shops and pubs, to cleaning jobs. She came to him like mist around a mountain. She was probably waiting in heaven, crossing a field in the sky or sitting in the bus station in Dublin.

He had spent days the previous week asking about Caitlin, only getting a lead at Breen's when a man came in who had heard she had slid off to Dublin. His mum would have been little older than Caitlin when she left for London. Where had she gone first? And how, in all her wanderings, had she met his father? He was angry, for she had taken away all the information. But maybe she had not understood its meaning or how much he wanted it. She had to keep silent, he supposed, as some kind of protection. For both of them. From the past and the future. If only he could reach back and tell her it didn't matter. If he could look in her eyes. Say it was all right. He had not understood her completely, but he saw something of what she had wanted for him.

The belly of the dark came down and he slept, even though the moon leaked in through grubby net curtains.

The next morning, he ate a roll from a café at the corner and walked into the city. A man with a ginger beard told him of a site.

'California Row opened a year ago. They made a big splash, for there are facilities or whatever it is them people want. I'm thinking they have it better than the rest of us.'

He caught a bus north to looming blocks of flats, scourging the sky. The site, bigger than Caulnamore, was bordered by a wall of planks around a sprawl of trailers. They were rough. One stripped of paint left a silvery underlay. Another's door was half boarded and a smaller blue trailer had a stack of crates where the door should be. A silver trailer had a triumphant yellow moon painted on the side. He knocked and a grey-haired woman answered. She said a couple of trailers in the far corner were classrooms and to ask there.

He walked past huge trailers with awnings and chrome decoration, canopies opening over the front doors. Caitlin might have attended for lessons or even to help. Two wiry dogs, their ribs visible, scampered. On a concreted area, a man with his sleeves rolled up revealing tanned forearms was shoeing a black horse. Beyond was barely a field but two horses strolled as far as they could, on the end of ropes, twitching up their heads as he neared.

Lost to the trailers and caravans, small white ones, others painted red or the colours of the flag, he almost missed the wall of breeze blocks poking out, protecting a statue of a woman with a pale face and tiny eyes. Her hands were gathered together while bits of cloth tied to twigs flapped in the wind like lost flags. She was cool and calm, the way a girl he fancied would be, looking and waiting, while he knew he had to say something or the chance would be gone. The woman's gown floated over painted cement, like gales of white sheets spreading. Her long blue dress swelled above bare feet whose nails were painted pink. She stood on half a football decorated with a crested moon and stars made from shiny paper. Dark plastic flowers and a cluster of stale milk bottles, burger cartons and sweet wrappers, cluttered the base. A note stuck into the ball, said two boys aged four and six had died a year ago. They had been run over by a car. That was how it was. Or how it could be. He saw them under the pressure of tyres. Nothing made sense. The woman's sharp blue eyes deepened. Cars and vans had passed that night with Harjit, their lights burning into the dark, as he stood with the others on the pavement until slipping to the back of the crowd. The last he saw of him. His eyes closed, jacket fallen open, a trail of blood caught in the zipper.

He wandered between caravans, trailers, wrecked cars and vans. The best trailer had a plastic table and lots of chairs outside. Small toys littered the ground like a school. At his knock, a gangly man with stubble and stringy hair appeared.

'Hi. You all right, there?'

'I'm looking for a girl.'

'We only work with families if there are youngsters,' the man said. He was young with the start of a goatee beard and a pale face. Torin saw him leaning over books, having the kind of inside life he had never had, knowing facts he never could know. 'What age is this person?'

'About my age.' Torin shrugged.

The man rubbed his chin and looked to the end of the site.

'There are a few trailers up by those cars, with girls in.'

It was pointless chasing with no hope of finding her. And if he did, what would she say? But he would press on. See her and leave. Get the hell out.

At a cluster of crazily coloured caravans, a gang of small kids rode a plastic trike and another had a toy tractor he kept getting in and out of. Torin knocked at the first. A long silence followed. He tried one with brightly painted flowers. Footsteps, and a woman with curlers stood in the doorway.

'Is there a Caitlin here?' He managed to make a sentence out of the words stoked inside him.

'Who?' the girl drawled.

'Caitlin. I wondered...'

The woman looked over her shoulder. She was here. He had found her. He expanded inside. All the searching was over. They would talk and things would be better.

'No one that name. Only my Ma and sisters.'

'But have you seen anyone? I mean, someone you didn't know?'

'I've enough to do watching over the ones of me own. What would I be doing looking for people I didn't know?' She stood defiantly, arms crossed over her chest. 'Try them over there and a couple of trailers further up has girls in.' She closed the door.

He shifted off. At the smallest caravan, there was no answer. He tried one decorated like the night sky. The door opened and a girl with long blonde hair and a bare midriff stared at him. A ring hung in her belly button and she sucked strands of hair.

'Anyone here called Caitlin?'

'Who's wanting her?'

'Torin.'

'Torin.' She twirled a necklace round her neck. 'That's a nice name. Haven't seen you around here before?' He wished she would shut up and stop wasting his time. 'There's a Caitlin here. It doesn't mean she'd be the one you'd be looking for.' Her pouty face challenged.

'Can I see her?'

'If she were here, maybe. She's out.' The girl's bare arms hung loose, lightly tanned, as if she belonged to another season.

'Where?'

'Shops. That's where she usually is.'

'Can I call back later?'

'S'pose so. Tomorrow, maybe. Early.' She shrugged.

The door shut. She was bound to tell. Next time he called Caitlin would have cleared off, so all he had to do was find out about the ferries, get a ticket or sneak on board.

Maeve told him about a party she was having in one of the downstairs rooms, the largest in the house. 'You're welcome,' she said, knocking on his door that evening.

At the opportunity of food, he slunk down late, when he hoped most of the people had arrived. The room was packed. Maeve was draped over a man. Torin looked for Alex but could not see him. He got talking to a Chinese girl who wore a short, tight dress and he drank more than he should. The girl sat on his knees and stroked his hair. The night tore on until he did not recall leaving and making his way back to his room.

When he woke next day, at midday, his head split and he was tired. But he had to make it to the site. He stumbled out of his room at nearly one and caught a bus.

'She's out.' The blonde girl stood at the door of her trailer in large gold earrings and smiling a lipsticky smile. She was enjoying messing around with excuses. 'But she might be back in half an hour.' She chewed gum, her lips going lazily up and down.

He wandered around caravans and trailers. Three boys clambered on two abandoned fridges. A washing machine lay on its side. He sat on an upturned crate watching two little boys in wellingtons jump over a puddle. Caitlin might pass and he would catch her attention, without having the bother of others knowing more than they had to. He would go somewhere quiet. They would talk. He would be calm and explain. She would listen and whatever had gone on between them would be done and over.

He hated having to make his way back but giving up was pointless. She could not so easily strike him out of her life. Beyond the trailers, a hill of sand and cement stood. Skirts and tee-shirts draped from small washing lines. Two men stood near an outside tap, talking, with hard, serious faces. One pulled on a fag. They would know he was a stranger. Might even know why he was calling. Of course. The blonde girl would have spread the word.

He waited at the steps, his neck hot, his hands clammy. Running off would be easier. He knocked and in less than a breath, the door opened. Caitlin. In a jumper and skirt with heavy black make-up around her eyes making them larger, though her lips were bare. A wave hit his stomach. She was different. Her hair was electric. Blonde, almost white, cut close to her head, accentuating her cheekbones.

'You,' she said.

She knew everything there was to know. About him. And her. She stood, idling against the door frame. Her. And yet not her. He stared weak with relief, fearing she might disappear into the depths of the trailer where a radio sang and a red-haired girl looked up from doing her nails. That girl most likely knew about them. Every detail which had split them.

'Who's that?' The girl peered.

'No one,' Caitlin called.

The sooner he got out, the better.

'You okay?' the girl called.

'I'm fine.' Caitlin pulled close the door, but stayed on the step.

Once he had kissed her fingers, turning them in his mouth, loving and sucking them and she had laughed. His heart shrank to a tiny bouldering weight. He thought, she will calm down. And I will... what? What could he do?

'My mum.'

'Why didn't you tell me?'

'I didn't know.' Caitlin was in front of him, but there were miles between them. He was in a strange, dark cavern. 'Did you know about me?'

'How would I? Delia knew nothing. Only living in a world of holy pictures and statues.' She slunk down, her shoulders rounded, flicking at a ridge of old paint.

He would see this out. Talk and keep talking. Make her understand the little he knew about her. About them.

'I used to wonder what my mother was like. I'd imagine her face, the kind of lipstick she'd have and then the thought would leave and I'd never think of her until months later and it would start all over again.' She stared at the ground. 'She screwed up my life.'

The words bruised and the day was bottomless.

'Don't say that.'

'Why not? It's true.' She beat his chest and he took it until he caught her arms but she twisted and hit on, her small rage rising.

'She didn't mean any harm.'

'How d'you know?' Her voice was hard in a way he had not heard before. 'I was shunted away. Delia wouldn't've told me the price of a pound of butter, if it didn't suit her.' Her voice grated as though she had been up too many nights. Or plain did not want to see him. 'But what are you doing here?'

'You could've said you were leaving,' he said but with a flick of her head she went back up the step. 'You didn't see her, Eva, then?' He wanted to bang on the side of the caravan. To split the walls.

'I'll see her next time.'

'There won't be a next time. The cancer got her.'

His soul was sand. There was no point hanging around. He crossed into a cemetery on the other side of the site. It was darkened with trees heavy with overarching branches, where even the headstones could not stand straight. A couple had corners knocked off, others were so old that dark moss crusted the face. One angel had hair curled about her shoulders and was in bare feet. They opened their arms holding books or lilies or nothing, waiting to be given something: a drink, a sandwich. Rosaries draped and eyeballs were rounded, and the lips so full he would think they were alive. Headstones were sunk into the ground. In a far part where trees were thick and clustered with leaves, a couple sat on a gravestone in the long grass. Even though it was freezing, and the days were stumbling towards Christmas, trees at the back were a lavish green, growing thickly against each other. A stone figure held a bunch of flowers to its chest. He could not decide whether it was a boy or a girl. He rubbed his eyes at the trick of the light, working out how long it would be until he got back to streets he was used to.

5

When he called to the trailer the next day, a girl he had not seen before answered. She stood in the door with slick dark hair and a black leather skirt barely covering her thighs. White lettering on her black tee-shirt said, 'If you think I'm a bitch, meet my sisters.' She said Caitlin was not there. Of course not. She was lazing on her bed, fiddling with nails or hair, listening to him. Him at the door performing for her. If that was the way she wanted it, he should leave for good.

'She's at work.' The girl slouched.

'Where's that? I didn't know she had a job.'

'Give her a break. She's not interested,' the girl said in a tauntingly sing-song voice, and she shut the door.

Battered and worn, it stared back. A woman jabbered on the radio inside.

He roamed the streets like a lost dog. He sat in doorways. He sat on the wall of the cemetery. He would not let this go. It trapped him but he would fight a way out. Fight to see her and go. Get out of her life, the way she wanted him to.

He picked up an old newspaper left by the side of the wall. From weeks past, the front page had a photograph of a space-probe. Slim as a lighter, it hung suspended in the galaxy. He read of probes searching for grooves in rock, signs of water. While it was up there, out of the way of things, he'd had his first days on earth without his mother. The craft had gone in a far place. A platform had extended, supporting a telescope with a huge lens. Angular as an insect, it had wheeled over the dry surface, tracking rock formations and changes, rummaging and digging the planet's surface, outside time.

In late afternoon, he watched the entrance. A gaggle of older kids moped in doorways, waiting for something to happen. A lanky boy kicked a ball against the flimsy wooden fence as a girl passed. Caitlin. Walking between trailers. Dodging between vans, he shouted her name. But she quickened her pace, steps smacking the air. Even as she made distance, he ran, calling her. The back of her blonde head. He would know the shape and fall of her shoulders anywhere. He wanted to put his hands on her, feel her shoulders, stroke her. In the greying light, she was hurrying, not quite running but walking fast.

'Do what you want but don't drive me away. Not yet,' he called. But she broke into a run. 'Give me some time and I'll go. You won't see me again.' She stopped and faced him. Her eyes were darkly ringed and heavy lidded. Worse than yesterday, her skin was blotchy and unwashed. He should not have come. Should have shifted back to London, where he fitted in. 'You're all I've got. Aren't we anything to each other?' Our mother... he wanted to say. The words would not come. But words were all he had. This was it. She would slam shut the past on them.

'She's brought all this down on top of me, on us. I thought you were different. Ha!' Her words strangled out in a cackle. 'It took her long enough to come back. To see what the baby had grown into. It only took all my life. While you had her all the time, and she you.'

'Can't we talk?' He grasped her arm.

'I'm done with talking.' She twisted out of his hold.

She was right. There was nothing between them. It was easy for her. Easy to make him think he didn't matter. Quick and clever. She always had the edge of him.

'One more time and I'll clear off. You won't hear from me again.'

'If you say so. One more time can't hurt.'

'Is there somewhere we can go?'

'The café at the end of the street, if you like?' She led the way and he fell into step beside her. After so long it was unreal, and he kept looking to check she was beside him. 'I'm starving. The girls spent what we had on wine and crisps,' she said and sneezed as they entered.

She pulled off the cardigan and sat opposite him, her eyes watery and red rimmed. She had been crying or had a cold. Her slender fingers with bright nails spread on the table as she leant forward to unfurl a silky scarf from her neck. The stark rise of her breasts startled him and he had an impulse to touch her. But no. It was over. They were not lovers. There could be no playing at what they could not be, only a strange distance through which he tried to see her differently, as when he was a kid looking through a kaleidoscope to shatterings of gold or red or blue, sprinkling from a central point to the edges, making up a star in the middle before disintegrating again.

'I could do with a load of chips with tons of vinegar,' she said.

'But you don't like vinegar.'

'I do now. I've got an awful taste for it.' She gave an odd half-laugh, chucking back her head, but her eyes were sharp with a malicious brightness he had not seen before.

'I wondered if I'd see you again.'

'Well, you have. I've appeared.' Her voice was a mocking sing-song.

He fidgeted. He wanted to grasp her hand, say it was all right, they could work out this stuff together, but she had a mad sprightliness which unsettled him. In this place she had the advantage and was showing it off. But it would all end soon, he thought. Soon. And he would scarper.

'You been here a while?'

'A few weeks.' She licked butter off the toast and it melted on her fingers.

'You know people?'

'Shane does,' she said.

'Shane?'

'We came here. We'd hung around the coast. Stayed in a caravan for a bit until he said we may as well come and stay with his cousins. They're round about.'

He sank in his chair. The café was hot with the smell of bacon and chips. She pulled off a jumper, stretching her arms in an arch over her head, a necklace falling around her neck, a stump of grey and brown fur hanging.

'What's this?'

'He gave it to me.' She ran her fingers over the fur. 'Rabbit's foot. He said he shot it.' She fiddled with the tab and pressed it against her chest, stroking down the fur.

'So he knows? About us?'

She shook her head, avoiding his gaze.

'Not the whole business, if that's what you mean.' She kicked out the words and folded the fried egg into the toast; the yolk dripped out along with the grease.

'I've been all over, looking for you.'

'That was how it was meant to be. But how'd you know to come here?'

'I called to Breen's.'

'They were supposed to say nothing.' She fiddled with the salt and pepper, clutching and releasing the plastic containers. 'We had to get out. Shane was upset. Pauley... You didn't hear about him?'

The folds around her eyes had shadows. He shook his head.

'He had an accident.' She pushed around the crust of bread on her plate.

'What?'

'He was at his dad's. They'd had a row. He went up to his room. Fell from a top window. It might've been an accident but we don't know.'

Her face was a blur coming and going out of focus. Tiny lines around her eyes were pronounced. What she said did not make sense. He had seen Pauley. He loved swimming and climbing. He had an alertness, a verve, a kind of bravery not even his mates at home had. Nor anyone. Who was she talking about? Someone else.

'He'd taken a load of his old man's tablets. His dad had so much stuff, Pauley used to say it was like a bloody pharmacy.'

He should have let Pauley come. They would have gone to London. He was weighted, unable to arrange the facts which broke. Facts which she was in charge of, while the small part of the world he lived in fell apart.

'He was trying to fly. He was so out of it. He got like that sometimes. You'd never know what mood he'd be in.'

Torin pulled himself upright.

'It started around the time some man who owned one of the boats accused him of damage. But he was always on the shore, wasn't he?' she continued.

The shore was Pauley's place. He belonged there more than anywhere else. But it was useless. It was all useless. Even hearing her talk, having found her, was useless.

'He was cut badly and bleeding after. Shane couldn't handle seeing him.'

Her words, far off, coiled in his head. He shifted, to stretch his legs. Part of him had left, shadowed out. Gone elsewhere. He saw the shine of Pauley's gold cross, catching the sun as he dived. Going down. Taken into the earth. What was worse, losing a mother? Losing your life? The choice twirled and spun.

'You all right?' She leant towards him.

Her eyes were soft and saw deep inside, to the cool heart of him, to the day when he had dragged the bottle across the breast of the boat. He caught the side of her face. Their glances touched.

The table surface was dark blue Formica with tiny gold stars shaken up by crescent moons. The answer might be within the galaxy under his hands.

'You have all the advantages.' She sat back. He did not know what she was she talking about. 'You knew your mum. So you know who you are.' She took two huge teaspoons of sugar and stirred them into a mug of tea.

'I'm not sure I do.' Beyond the café window, a light fall of snow dusted the pavement, smeared the glass. The cold had come to something. He dragged a tissue from his pocket, felt the edges of the photo and lay it on the table.

'Who's this?' Caitlin asked.

'Mum dancing.'

She was thinner, the folds of a dress flapped, the camera capturing a tantalising gaze. She was in flight, in time with the music. Her own rhythm. Those eyes and lips. Her hair long because she had not bothered to go to a hairdresser. It straggled and ran, tearing away.

'You don't look like her. I mean you do, but different.' Caitlin lifted the photo and put it up against him, turning it side to side. She squinted and placed the photo on the table. He picked it up and held it near her.

'You're like her too.' Her skin was warmer, a luscious brown, and her lips were rounder. Her eyes were more almond shaped and widely placed; they were heavy lidded with thin brows, but they both had a round chin. There she was. His mother in front of him. 'I thought she could fight but the cancer got her.' His hands were awkward and he did not know what to do with them.

'There's something else.' She raised her eyes to his. 'I'm pregnant.'

The nerve endings in his fingers went cold.

'What? What are you going to do?' His voice was hoarse, out of control, not making the words he wanted, like 'this is all a mistake. I did not mean this.'

'The girls say I'd be mad to keep it. How'd I cope? They say I should get hold of a doctor. Get sorted.' She frowned. 'Funny. The only place I planned to go was America.'

'We... I...' He was stiff with fear at all this going on without him. Because of him.

'It's not yours.' She laid her hands on the table, like cards from a pack. 'It's Shane's.'

'Does he know, then?'

'Not yet. I'm not sure if he'll need to. The girls say there are places in England.'

'Places? Oh.'

'Except I don't really know what to do. I don't want it ripped out of me.' She fiddled with the sugar shaker.

The mound of her belly rose under her jumper. A baby was growing inside her. She had changed. Grown beyond him. He could not keep up. No matter what was going on, he was always behind.

'Hey, it's not going to jump out,' she announced with a small laugh and rubbed her hand over the mound, flattening crinkles of her top. 'I suppose though, I can't make a worse job than was made with me.' Her voice sank, her eyes glassy with tears. 'What will happen to us?'

'Nothing will happen.'

'I mean, how we are?'

'We'll still be ourselves. To each other. It doesn't matter what went on. What happens ahead is all that matters.'

'What's behind seems long ago. But you know you can get to the sea from here,' she said.

'I thought it was far.'

'Not if you follow on this way. You want to go along there?'

They finished up and walked down the street, steps matching in the drawing light of evening. She led through narrow, cramped streets where washing lines hung across yards. The air was cold when he opened his mouth, freezing breath charging into him. They stopped at a small supermarket, bought crisps and sausage rolls.

At the harbour, cranes were loading containers, sailing like dragonflies against the sky. He could steal away on a boat. Leave quickly, quick as his mother who lay in the cemetery under the wings of a flyover. She had been all he had for years. All he had belonged to. She had been misguided. Daft. Crazy. But in her own way she had loved him, he saw, because she had brought him back.

At the sea, Caitlin walked close to the water. She shivered and sneezed.

'Here. Put this on.' He pulled off his jacket, draping it over her shoulders.

'I'm all right.'

'Take it. You don't want to get cold.'

She slipped easily into the sleeves while the body of the jacket flapped around.

'This is nice. A bit big, but nice.' She pulled on the sleeves.

'It was hers.'

'I like the collar.' She sleeked her fingers along the satin. Light and shadow caught on it. 'They wear this kind of thing to operas.'

'She kept a lot of junk. Even if she didn't want it, she kept it.'

She drew out a scrap of yellowed paper from the chest pocket.

'What's this?' She gave it to him.

'Mrs Finch. 11. Mrs Simpson. 2.00. Present for T. One week pay- my sore foot. Wax for Number 36.'

'Might be the people she worked for? And that might be you.' She pointed to the letter 'T'.

The scrap was torn from a notebook with a thin red line down the side like a margin. The edges curled. It was hard to know what to believe.

'Can I keep this?' She patted down the collar of the jacket.

'If you want.'

She could have the jacket for all he cared. Further down, two teenage boys sat throwing pebbles uselessly at the waves. He walked to them, leaving her sitting on a boulder. Thin, crispy curls of shells crushed under his feet. He picked up a dry scrag of seaweed. Empty shells strayed by stones. All these dead things. It wasn't the way he had hoped. The tide fluttered at his feet. If he kept walking, he would be all right. If he kept walking.

He slipped off his trainers and went near the edge. The water tipped his toes. Swimming in winter. Pauley could, but Torin was not brave enough. He let the waves, chill as glass, rise up his shins. It lashed in little weals. Scrawls of shiny dark strands of seaweed ran on scratchy grey stones. Minute particles of sand were suspended in the water. The air was salty and sharp, driving. Gulls screeched and the edges of his trousers seeped.

The waves crept faster. The foam rode high. His legs were uncertain and knocked against each other. Words of his mother echoed. Her voice called inside him. He could forgive her, easy as water flowing over stone. If he didn't, he would carry it with him. What was the point? But how easy it would be to let go, to lie down, sleep and let loose the bird in the cage fluttering wildly in his head.

If he went in deeper, the weight of water would pull him down and his arms, freed, might float away, lifted up. The whole of him taken and gone beyond gravity. He walked out, back up the shore. He wanted to ask what Caitlin thought of their mother but it hardly seemed worth it.

'You want to keep it? I mean, the kid?'

'I didn't know I did. But I do now.' She walked on the sand, purposefully, with force.

'I'll help. If you want, I'll help you,' he said.

She probably did not believe him, or care about what he said, so he kept walking because it was something to do.

'You would?' She slowed.

'Why not?'

Waves rolled and leapt in the distance.

He walked beside her and a train hurtled by, breaking the far sigh of traffic.

'I'll bring the child to the sea. We'll walk on the beach and the sand'll tickle its toes. I'll dress it in lovely clothes.' She rolled up her sleeves, bending to the water.

The underside of her arms had the fish skeleton of scars. She stepped back, shaking her arms dry. He had something to hold onto. Someone. No more than that. His grandad as well. All his mum had led him to.

When he had been on the shore with her in Yarmouth, she'd said the sea was where they came from. He had been about ten and tried to work out how they could have descended from fish, not knowing what she meant. He had not realised either, how she had travelled along the coast, going between men in London and other cities, men who brought her promises, who had taken the range of her feelings or her time and left. Maybe this was all there was, travelling from one place to another, finding and losing and finding. And finding out, after all the years of cramped rooms, as Caitlin walked ahead by the scrawl of waves, there was room enough for all of them.

Acknowledgements

Thank you, thank you Kevin Duffy and all at Bluemoose Books for having faith in me. Thanks to Lin Webb for navigating a way through my own writing. And many thanks to Tim Pears for his support.

In the course of completing this novel I was fortunate to have valuable input from Bernadine Evaristo and encouragement from Joanna Briscoe. A reading of an early draft by Rodge Glass was very helpful, as was the publication of an excerpt on WritersHub from Birkbeck, University of London, directed by Julia Bell.

Thank you Samuel for being around. For everything and more, thank you Jonathan Barker.